TALK OF THE TOWN

TALK OF THE TOWN
BOOK 1

RACHAEL OGLE

AUTHOR'S NOTE

Eighteen months ago, when I originally wrote the manuscript for *Talk of the Town*, I wasn't sure it would actually ever be something I would publish. The majority of the books I've written—many of which will probably never see the light of day —contain much heavier themes.

Truthfully, my writing has helped me work through a tremendous amount of my trauma and most days, I will freely admit that writing has saved my life.

But, as is often the case for most of my characters, they keep demanding their place in the sun. Gemma and Brewster were no exception. Theirs is a major departure from the angsty and sometimes heartbreaking stories I'm used to telling.

I'm not mad about it.

After the mental and emotional toll editing and publishing *Crash into Me* (Knox County book 4) took on me (IYKYK), I was in dire need of a palette cleanser. Gemma and Brewster were exactly the breath of fresh air I needed to bring me back to an even keel.

Honestly, from a marketing standpoint, releasing one book

while you're in the middle of entirely different series probably isn't wise. As I often tell y'all, though, mental health comes first. My mental health *needed* Gemma and Brewster and their swoony, fluffy tale.

No angst. No heartbreak. No third-act breakup. Just two people finally realizing what was there all along (and having fan-fucking-tastic sex in the process).

I truly hope you love this dynamic duo.

And if you just can't live without angst and trauma, don't worry. Book two will be right up your alley.

All that being said, *Talk of the Town* does contain **accidental drug use** and a scene involving a conversation regarding the **death of a child** (off-page, historical, and not belonging to either MC).

As always, protect your mental health.

Much love,

Rach

CONTENTS

CHAPTER ONE

GEMMA

Pain. Searing, aching, throbbing pain. Everywhere. There isn't an inch of my body that doesn't feel like it's been hit by a train. Especially my brain. It feels the worst of all. I try to roll over, but nausea threatens to bring up every bit of the copious amounts of alcohol I consumed last night. And it must've been tons, because I remember nothing. Every single moment after Brew and I left the restaurant and started playing craps at that casino is a total blank.

I shift my hips and I'm greeted with a wholly different kind of pain. Not an unpleasant pain in the least, but the familiar ache of vigorous sex. I try to remember if I had sex, but I draw a blank. Attempting to clear away some of the brain fog, I drag my hand down my face and something snags on my nose ring.

Something metal.

I dare to squint, praying it's not as bright as I suspect it will be when I open my eyes. I examine my left hand through barely parted lids and see something glint on my finger. My *ring* finger. And despite my blinding headache and roiling guts from my apparent hangover—or hell, maybe I'm still a little drunk—I open my eyes wide and focus on my hand.

Why the fuck is there a gold band on my finger?

I'm awake now. More awake than I've ever been in my life. I still can't sit up, because I know I'll puke. I try to rack my brain for any explanation other than the fantastical scenario I'm working up in my mind as to why I'd be wearing what looks like a wedding band.

And that's when I hear it. Snoring. Next to me in the bed. My heart pounds and I will my brain to tell me what is going on. I'm praying to all that is holy that I'm hallucinating because Brew and I made a spontaneous trip out to the desert and we're tripping on shrooms and I'm having some sort of extremely detailed fever dream.

But then, my bedmate moves and the mattress squeaks and I know I'm not alone and it's not all a dream. And having the confirmation that I'm not alone sends sharp pangs of fear to my stomach and it knots up, threatening to puke for a completely different reason than the lingering alcohol in my system.

Just get it over with, Gemma. Find out who you slept with. You can totally laugh about it when you're sober. You and Brew can share horror stories about this weekend when you get home and you can tell all your listeners about your wild, drunken night at the radio broadcasters convention.

I blow out a steadying breath and try to roll over without moving my head; which is exactly as difficult as you think it would be. It seems to take hours to get my pounding brain to cooperate with my aching limbs—seriously, that must have been some *really* excellent sex.

By the time I'm facing my unknown bed companion, I see the back of a head with long, light brown hair. For a split-second, I think I might've slept with a woman, but then I see the outline of a dark bearded jaw and realize that it is, indeed, a man. Then my eyes catch on a very familiar tattoo against pale skin that I've seen almost every day for as long as he's had it.

The tattoo of that fucking goose that I've never stopped giving him shit for but secretly love. It's only then that my brain catches up with my body and my heart stops.

Brew is in bed with me.

What. The. Fuck.

Even though I already know what I'm going to find, I lift the blankets and yep, I'm totally naked. And by the looks of it, sporting some really impressive hickeys and bite marks. I sit up as quickly as I dare and try with every functioning brain cell that remains after last night to piece together the events of the previous evening.

Out of sheer curiosity, I lift the blankets to glance over at Brew to confirm what I already suspect I'm going to find. Yep, he's naked, too. And damn, he's got a nice ass. Shit, how did I not know that? I drop the covers and scrub my hands over my face. Again, the ring on my finger snags on my piercing and I look at it.

It definitely looks like a wedding band, but surely not. There's no fucking way Brew and I got married. Yeah, we're in Vegas, but still. It didn't happen. But, as if to provide even more proof, Brew rolls over in his sleep and his left hand comes to rest on his chest. He, too, sports a gold band and my heart stops again.

Surely, there has to be some logical explanation. This has to be some crazy stunt Brew cooked up while we were drinking and I was just drunk enough to go along with it. Maybe we decided to do it to show our listeners how easy it is to get married in Vegas?

Think, Gemma.

I make a mental list of things I know for certain, right this minute.

I'm naked in a hotel room.

I'm naked in a hotel room with my co-worker and best friend.

I've had sex. *With Brew?*

Brew and I are both wearing wedding rings.

Brew has a great ass.

I'm hit with the need to satisfy another curiosity now that Brew is on his back. I glance at his face and his mouth is open in obvious sleep. And I know how *not* a morning person he is and that he'll probably sleep until noon if not roused by his seven alarms. He's out cold and I can't not look, so I pick up the blankets and glance at his dick. My mouth falls open in utter shock. Even only half-hard with a morning erection, it's impressive. I quickly drop the blankets as heat travels from my cheeks down to my torso.

No wonder I'm sore. Fuck.

If I were making a list, I'd also have to add that Brew is HUNG.

Attempting to not freak out more than I already am, I try to wrap my mind around what is the most likely scenario of what happened last night. Brew and I went to supper. We were talking about how everyone our age was settling down and getting married and starting families. I joked that I'll probably never get married because no one would want to put up with the fact that I'll always put my job first. Brew said something about how he didn't think that was true and that when I found the right person, my job wouldn't be so important.

We left the restaurant where we'd already had a few drinks, but we weren't drunk in the least. Maybe a little buzzed, but we weren't driving, so it was fine. We went to the casino down the street to play craps, since Brew had always wanted to play. They started bringing us drinks and...

The rest is a blank.

I jump out of bed and immediately regret it when the room starts to spin. I brace my hands on my knees to remain standing and glance around, realizing this isn't even either of our rooms. *We're not even in our hotel?* A peek at the clock on the night-stand reveals that it's after nine. We're supposed to check out today and go home. I look around and attempt to find my clothes, trying to remember what I was even wearing last night before I see my dress. I keep searching and finally come up with my bra, panties, and sandals as well.

I gather up my articles of clothing, step into the bathroom and take the longest pee ever. After I flush the toilet and wash my hands, I glance at my reflection in the mirror. My makeup is smudged around my hazel eyes and my long, dark-brown hair is wild. And yes, my naturally tan skin is covered in bite marks, starting at my breasts down to my inner thighs. I try not to think about those as I hastily pull on my clothes. I grab a washcloth, wet it, and wipe away as much of my makeup as I can. I run my fingers through my hair, attempting to tame some of the tangles. When things are as good as they're going to get, I head back out to the bedroom and try to track down my purse or phone or anything that might indicate that we actually did what I'm fearing we did.

I know I also need to get Brew up, since it's going to take him thirty minutes to come around anyway. I don't think about the fact that we most likely slept together and, by all accounts, I really enjoyed it. I don't think about the fact that Brew and I have known each other for ten years and before last night, hadn't ever even kissed; regardless of the flirtatious banter that is our entire working relationship.

You don't know if you even kissed last night, Gemma.

Trying to focus, I steel myself and walk over to his side of the bed. I plant my hands on Brew's shoulders and try not to react to how firm his delts feel under my hands. *How have I never noticed that before?* I shake him none too gently, because I know how deeply he sleeps. "Brew. Wake up."

He lets out a soft grunt, but doesn't stir. I shake him harder and say his name louder. By the third time, I'm practically screaming.

"Jesus, Gem. What?" His voice is gravelly from sleep, and I don't like how it stirs something in me to hear it.

Nothing has changed, Gemma. You don't even remember shit. Stop it.

"Brew, fucking get up." Even to my own ears, I sound freaked out because I am. He must hear it in my tone and it alerts something in his brain because his eyes pop open and he sits bolt upright.

"What's wrong?" Then his own hangover seems to hit him and he grabs his head with both hands. "What the fuck? Did someone jackhammer my brain? Shit."

"Yeah, apparently we got really drunk," I supply, still panicked.

His eyes are barely open, and he finally seems to realize I'm in the room with him. "Gem, how did you get into my room?"

"We're not in either of our rooms, Brew. We're in a different room. I think it's that casino we went to after supper."

He glances around, his movements hesitant. "What?" He starts to rise from the bed and I shoot my hand out to stop him.

"Also, you're naked, so you might want to wrap a sheet around yourself or something." His brow furrows in confusion and he peeks under the blankets to confirm what I've told him.

"How did you know I was naked?" I open my mouth and nothing comes out, and he gives me a knowing smirk. "Did you sneak a peek at my junk, Gem?" My expression must convey pain or some other equally unpleasant emotion and he blanches. "Well, shit, that's not typically the reaction I get from a woman when they see me naked."

"It—It's not that," I stammer. My next words come out in a rush. "I was naked, too. I think we had sex. And I also think we got married, but I don't remember anything after we started playing craps."

All the color drains from his face and I don't know whether to be pleased or offended. I feel like that must've been what I looked like when he asked if I looked at him naked.

He finally notices the gold ring on his own hand. "What the fuck, Gemma? What did we do?" I open my arms, palms up, as if to say, *no damn clue.* He starts to climb out of bed again and I hold up my hand. Shaking his head, he rolls his eyes. "What, Gem; you've apparently already seen it all. Don't pretend you're a prude. We both know you're not." His tone is flat, as if me seeing him naked in broad daylight is no longer a big deal. Except to me, it is. I turn to face the wall and look up at the ceiling to offer him a bit of privacy. "Jesus, Gemma. We're adults. It's just a dick. Not like you haven't seen plenty before."

"Yeah, but it's *yours*, Brew. I was never supposed to see yours."

He chuckles. "Well, too late now, Pearl." The nickname he gave me years ago suddenly grates on me, because it feels like things have changed between us, even if I don't yet know how. I hear him go into the bathroom and come out a few minutes later. "I'm decent."

Relieved, I turn around to see him pulling his rumpled T-shirt over his head. "Have you seen your phone? Or mine?" I ask.

He shakes his head. "Where's your purse? Surely whatever paperwork we have will be in there, right?"

"Help me find it. We also have to get back to our hotel and check out by eleven. And our flight home is at two."

"We can't fly home until we annul this. *If* we really even

got married. Maybe we just got rings. You know us, we're stupid. Well, I am. It would totally be on brand for me to convince you to go along with some crazy scheme I've worked up. I probably said we should pretend to be married to see if we could get people to buy us drinks and stuff. I mean, obviously, we had a lot of drinks, because I'm trashed." He tosses the pillows onto the floor, trying to find our stuff.

"And hey, maybe we had sex," he says with a shrug. "I don't remember it, and I'm guessing you don't either?" I shake my head. "Okay, so that's like it never happened. It's going to be fine, Gem." He goes back to pulling blankets off the bed in a continued attempt to locate our phones.

"I'm glad you're so calm because I'm freaking the fuck out, Brew." His head snaps in my direction and he must see the panic in my face, because he stops searching and comes to stand in front of me.

He doesn't touch me and I don't know whether to be happy or upset, because it's nothing for him to squeeze my arms in friendly support or even pull me in for a hug. But he doesn't, which makes me feel like things really have changed between us. "Hey, it'll be fine, Pearl. We'll get it figured out, okay?" His voice is soft, and he gives me a smile that normally would put me at ease, but now, just makes me burst into tears.

And honestly, I'm not even sure why, except that I possibly married and slept with my best friend and everything's weird now. Brew pulls me into his arms. "It's okay, Gemma. Don't cry. Like I said, we'll sort all this out and when we get back to work, we'll laugh about it." He rubs my back, even as I continue to sob. My face is in his chest and as his scent enters my nose, I have a flash of something from what I can only assume is last night.

Me, pulling Brew's shirt off over his head and kissing my

way down his chest and falling to my knees as I pushed him down to sit on the bed. And he's not wearing pants.

I step back from him suddenly. "Sorry." I flush from the memory and hurriedly wipe my eyes. "I'm fine. Just overwhelmed."

He's about to say something when both our phones ring at almost the exact same time, snapping us back to reality. Brew drops to all fours next to the bed and pulls my purse out from underneath it. He opens it to find both of our phones. He hands mine over and takes his.

The screen says it's my mother. My very religious and proper mother, who doesn't believe in things like sex outside of marriage or divorce or swearing. I debate letting it roll to voicemail, but I know she'll just call me right back, so I steel myself to answer. "Mom, hey." I hope I sound as carefree as I'm pretending to be.

"Gemma Hopkins, what is the meaning of all this?"

Something niggles in my mind, as if I should know why my mother is calling, but I have no clue. "All what, Mom?"

"You get married and you don't even have the decency to let your father walk you down the aisle? We never even thought you'd ever get married and you take this away from us?"

My stomach drops all the way to my feet and my heart lurches. "What?"

"What do you mean, what? You sent us the video of you and Brewster getting married while you're out in Las Vegas. Now, I always knew y'all were close, but I never knew you were dating or serious or anything. And as much as we love Brewster, your father and I are still hurt that you'd leave us out. And y'all aren't even dressed in proper wedding attire. It's a bit tacky, if you ask me. When you all get home, you'll do us the courtesy of at least letting us throw you a decent reception."

I can barely process what my mother is saying and I need to get out of this conversation. "Mom, I'm sorry. I have to go."

"Wait, I just want you to know that even though I'm not thrilled you eloped, I'm really happy for you. Truly, honey. You and Brewster will come for Sunday dinner, right? And where are y'all going to be living? Everyone will want to get you wedding gifts. I shared your wedding video with the ladies' group at church and they can't wait to spoil you."

I must have died and gone to a special place in hell. There is no other explanation. "Mom, we'll have to see. I'll talk to you later, okay?" I don't wait for her to respond and disconnect the call.

Apprehension floods Brew's gaze. "Do I want to know what your mom said?"

I close my eyes, blow out a breath, and tap the corner of my phone against my forehead, as if the movement will magically make me remember last night. "Um, apparently, I sent her a video and she sent it to her ladies' group and they want to throw us a shower. My parents want to give us a reception and also, we're expected to show up at Sunday dinner next week." I start to hyperventilate and Brew guides me to sit on the edge of the bed and forces my head between my knees.

"It's okay, Pearl. We'll explain it to your parents. They'll have a good laugh."

My head pops up. "Bullshit. You know how crazy they are. This is liable to get me disowned. Like, properly. They had enough of a shit fit when I pierced my nose. *This* is a whole other level of insanity you've never seen before, Brew."

He chuckles. "Gemma, you're not a kid. You're thirty years old. Your parents will survive this and so will we." He seems to consider something. "There's a video?"

CHAPTER TWO

BREWSTER

Gemma's face tells me she doesn't want to think about my question. The fact that there might be video footage of us getting married and the fact that neither of us remembers anything from last night boggles my mind. She starts to panic again and I put my hand on her shoulder and push her head back between her knees.

I sit next to her and rub her back. It won't do for both of us to fall apart right now. And if Gemma—who for the past ten years, has almost always been the calmer one of the two of us—needs to choose today to be the one to freak out, I can try to quell my own rising panic.

I glance down at her and see an impressive purple bite mark on her shoulder. "Jesus, did I do that?"

She looks back up at me. "Do what?"

I brush my thumb over the bruise. "This. This bite."

Gemma tries to see it, but can't. She stands to go over to the mirror and pulls her coffee-colored hair over her other shoulder to get a better look. She sighs. "Yeah. I guess. That's not the only one."

I give her an apologetic smile. "Sorry."

She shrugs and comes back over to sit on the bed and grabs her purse. After she digs through it for a minute, she looks back up at me as she pulls her hair into a messy bun with a hair tie she pulls from a pocket in her bag. "There aren't any papers in here."

"What, no license or anything?"

She shakes her head and I stand to check my pockets and come up empty. Then I remember I was wearing a flannel that Gemma had given me shit for wearing in Nevada in March. I look around for it and finally locate it on the other side of the dresser, next to the door.

Guess that was the first thing to go when we got in here.

I look through the chest pockets and finally come up with a folded sheet of paper. I return to sit next to Gemma on the bed and unfold it. Sure enough, it's a marriage license. I should be shocked or dismayed or feel something akin to regret, but it's just a piece of paper. And it's Gem, not some stranger, so at least that makes this easier.

"Well, it's all legal and shit." I run my fingers through my hair to dislodge some of the bigger tangles before pulling it back and securing it with a rubber band.

My words make Gemma lose it again and I pull her into my side as she cries. I rest my chin on the top of her head. "You know, I could take offense to you crying so much after what was obviously a wonderful sexual encounter for you."

Normally, a smart-ass comment like that would earn me a playful punch to the gut. I brace impact, but it never comes. It's only then that I know Gemma is legitimately upset and not simply being dramatic. Not that she's typically a dramatic person. If anything, she's pragmatic and levelheaded, nearly to a fault, and so much of a realist she refuses to even discuss fantastical hypotheticals, except on the show.

"Come on, Gem, it'll be okay." I feel like I've said this about a hundred times already, but honestly, it's all I've got. I have no clue what to do, except get it annulled. I know Gemma's upset because she told her parents and they think this is all real and I know her relationship with her parents is complicated. So I honestly don't know what to think about her sending a video to them. Except that maybe "blackout drunk Gemma" is a conniving bitch who wants to hurt "sober Gemma."

I try to think rationally, like Gemma normally would.

Step one: Calm Gem down.

Step two: Watch the video.

Gemma is still snuffling softly against my side, and I rub her back swiftly. "Alright, Pearl. Let's go."

"Go where?" Her words come out between hiccups, and I try not to smile at how adorable she sounds.

"You need coffee. Everything always looks better after coffee. I know you've got to be jonesing." I stand and tug her up off the bed before going into the bathroom to wet a washcloth and bring it back to her. "Wipe your face." She does as I tell her and then hands the rag back to me. I toss it back into the bathroom, not even bothering to aim.

"Brew, why are you so calm? We got married. This is such a mess."

I shrug. "We can't both fall apart and I figure you're due. This is what we do. We take care of each other during our freak outs. Yeah, this is a mess, but like I said, we'll figure it out. And on the bright side, at least we didn't marry strangers."

She nods slowly and grabs her purse. She looks around, her panic seeming to rise again. "Why aren't there any condom wrappers?"

"What?" I'm so thrown, it takes a minute for her words to register.

"If we had sex, why are there no used condoms or wrappers or anything?"

I shrug. "Maybe we didn't really have sex."

She glances at me, her face coloring. "No, we did. Pretty enthusiastically, if my whole body soreness is to be believed. And the bite marks. They're...everywhere."

I try not to smile since I know she's still in panic mode. "Well, you still have your IUD, right?" She nods. "Okay, then we're good. I'm clean. I haven't been with anyone since Alyssa, and I got tested after I found out she cheated, so it's fine."

Gemma's face registers confusion. "Alyssa? That was months ago. You haven't slept with anyone in six months?"

I shake my head. "No."

"How can that be?"

I sigh. "I don't know, Gem; I just haven't. Are you clean? I assume you are, right?"

She nods. "Yeah. I got tested after I broke up with Kyle."

The thought of her ex-boyfriend, Kyle Smith, always makes rage settle into my chest, but I keep my expression neutral. "Okay, then it's fine. Let's go get some coffee." I look around the room one last time to make sure we've got everything, but apparently, we only showed up here with the clothes on our backs. I tug her out of the room and down the hall toward the elevator.

Gemma's quiet, but at least she's not crying anymore, so there's that. When we get down to the lobby and the elevator doors open, my head pounds as the tinny sounds of slot machines, the ticking of the roulette wheel, and the smooth jazz from the overhead speakers all bombard my ears. I glance at Gemma—who's looking around, trying to piece together bits of memories from last night—as she finally speaks. "Do you remember coming here?"

I try to think back, even as we make our way toward the exit. "Not much. I know we played craps for a while, but I don't remember how we ended or anything." I have the fleeting thought that I might've cleaned out my bank account as we played, and I put my hand on her arm to stop her from leaving the building.

She looks at me, confused. "What?"

"Check your bank account. Right now. Make sure we didn't blow through all our money while we were drunk."

The color drains from her face as she pulls her phone out of her purse and we both take a minute to access our accounts. When I get logged into my bank, my heart lurches. The last time I checked my account a few days ago, I had just over fifteen hundred in my checking. Today, I have twenty-six thousand dollars.

I refresh the page, thinking there must be some mistake, but no, it's there. I check the transaction log and see a wire transfer from the casino. Gemma gasps next to me but I don't bother looking up from my phone. "You have money, too?"

"Brew, why is there a deposit for twenty-five grand into my account?" Her voice comes out barely above a whisper.

"I don't know, Gem; I have one, too."

She looks at me, eyes wide and face even more pale. "What did we do last night?"

I let out a heavy sigh and drag my hand down my face. "I don't know, but we'll get some coffee and work backwards, okay?" Her nod doesn't look at all as though she's agreeing with me, but what else can we do?

We start walking toward the exit again and a short, thin older man with deeply bronzed skin dressed in a suit steps in front of us. "Mr. and Mrs. Lincoln. How was your stay last night? I hope you found your accommodations to your liking?"

Gemma's got that look like she's going to panic again and I grab her hand and give it a tight squeeze. I look at the guy, who obviously knows who Gemma and I are, even if we don't have a clue who he is. I give him a tight smile. "Sorry, we've not had our coffee yet. Last night's a little hazy."

He grins. "Yes, you did seem to be enjoying those tequila shots. I understand. I won't keep you; I just wanted to ensure your room was acceptable."

"It was fine. Thank you."

"It was our pleasure. We hope you two lovebirds will join us again in the future."

I'm struck with a thought. "You'll have to forgive me, but I'm really hungover, and I'm drawing a blank on your name."

"Edward," he supplies, his tone friendly.

"Right. Edward. Sorry. Would you happen to have video footage of us at the craps table? I'd like to put together a video montage for our friends and family to show them our weekend."

He seems unsure, so I lean in and give him a conspiratorial grin. "I've been telling Gemma that she must've done a fantastic job blowing my dice for us to have done so well." I quirk a brow and Edward's cheeks turn pink. Gemma squeezes my hand, pain shooting through my fingers, and I try not to wince.

Edward doesn't notice and seems to consider. "Your request is a bit unorthodox, but I think I might be able to pull some strings. Would it be possible that I email the footage to you? I need to clear things with security."

I nod, as if this is something I do all the time. As if getting married in Vegas while I'm blackout drunk and winning fifty grand playing craps is a normal, everyday occurrence for me. "Of course. Let me get you my card." I fish my wallet out of my back pocket to pull out one of my business cards and hand it over to him. "Thank you, Edward."

"My pleasure, Mr. Lincoln. I hope you and Mrs. Lincoln have a wonderful remainder of your stay in Las Vegas."

I nod and tug Gemma out the front door before any other casino employees can accost us. When we clear the automatic sliding glass doors, the dry desert heat greets us. I look around, trying to get my bearings and see a coffee shop a couple of blocks away. I pull Gemma with me down the sidewalk in that direction.

"*Blow your dice*, Brew? Did you really say that to him?"

"Yeah, well, I thought if we could get the video footage of us at the casino, it could help us work through our night."

She pinches the bridge of her nose. "How are you even able to think? I can barely remember my name, let alone formulate coherent plans."

"Not my first hangover, Pearl. Or yours. You should be used to this." A few minutes later, we enter the coffee shop and I deposit Gemma into a chair at a table and she lays her head on her folded arms. "Lightweight," I say with a grin. She doesn't look up at me, just flips me off as I go to order our coffees. I order Gem's standard vanilla latte with extra foam and add two shots and get my regular caramel macchiato and also add extra shots. At the last second, I throw in a couple of muffins for good measure.

When our order comes up, I walk back over to the table and place Gemma's breakfast in front of her. She slowly raises her head off her arms and pulls her coffee toward her. Her expression is still so tense and upset, I can't help but feel a pang of sadness. Because I know this has to be my fault. I'm the impulsive one. I'm the one who throws out crazy suggestions when we're planning at work. There's no way I didn't suggest this.

I feel my jaw clench the longer Gemma goes without making eye contact with me. Even if neither of us remembers anything from last night, things are different between us now. And even if we can't remember that we had sex, we definitely did, according to Gemma, and that makes me feel even worse because I don't remember it.

I'd be lying if I said I hadn't thought about what that might be like over the years. More in the recent past since I broke up with Alyssa, but even so, I don't know that I ever would've acted on my feelings, even if I wanted to. Any guy would look at Gemma and want her. She's fucking gorgeous and the best person I know and my favorite human on the planet. But I never would've done it if I was in my right mind. I care about our friendship too much.

She nibbles her muffin. "Who called you earlier, when Mom called?"

"Oh, it was Curtis. I was getting ready to answer when I heard it was your mom calling, so I let him go to voicemail." I dig my phone out and click on the play button on our production manager's voicemail.

"Brewster, what is this video I just got? You know we sent you and Gemma to Vegas to rub elbows with the syndication bigwigs, not get married. Call me."

My mouth falls open and Gemma's brow furrows. "What?"

"Apparently, I sent the wedding video to Curtis."

The color drains from her face. "Fuck, Brew. He's going to kill us."

I nod. "Yeah. He's pissed. I should call him, right? Tell him the truth?"

She shrugs. "What choice do we have? Although, we should probably watch the video before you do, right? Since my parents and our boss have seen it and we have no memory of it?"

"Yeah, definitely." I go to the videos on my phone and sure enough, there it is. I click it and angle my phone so we can both see it. And for fifteen minutes, neither of us says anything as we watch us—an us that we can't remember—go through vows.

We stand facing one another, in front of Elvis, because, of course, it would have to be Elvis. And somehow, we both look like we're sober and not swaying in the least. Our words come out clear and not slurred and quite possibly the thing I notice most of all is my face. I have this huge grin on my face that I don't even recognize, but it looks genuine as we slide gold bands on one another's fingers.

And then something flashes in my mind just before I see it happen on my phone screen. The memory of Elvis saying, "You may now kiss the bride". And then I do. And it's like I'm watching someone else's life; even though I know it's us. I watch myself grip Gemma's face in my hands and kiss her and it's a tender kiss, as if she's precious, and something in my chest tightens. But then I remember something else and my heart stops.

I'm just thankful you can't hear it on the screen, because I don't know how I'd explain my words. I remember kissing her and my mouth moving to her ear. *I'm so happy it's you, Gemma. So fucking happy you're mine forever, Pearl.* And in the video, she doesn't say anything, just pulls my mouth back to hers and kisses me and it's definitely not a tender kiss. It's deep and there's tongue and Elvis eventually nudges us to remind us to keep it PG and the video cuts off.

I glance at Gemma across from me and her face is bright pink. "Well, I wondered if we actually kissed. I guess that answers that."

I huff a laugh, trying to pretend like I don't remember confessing some sort of serious feelings for my best friend. "Yeah, looks like it. So. Now what?"

She taps her phone screen. "We have to get our stuff from the hotel. Call Curtis on the walk back." She rises and tosses her drained coffee cup and food trash into the garbage and I pick up my uneaten muffin and cup of coffee and we head out the door.

CHAPTER THREE

GEMMA

I don't know what to make of Brew's expression as we walk back toward our hotel. It's almost like he's seen a ghost. Maybe the shock of the video and having the fact that we got married confirmed has finally caught up with him? Who can blame him? I'm just as astounded by this bombshell that's been dropped into our lives.

He's trying to juggle his coffee and muffin and use his phone, so I finally just take them from him so he'll have his hands free. I know if he gets to talking, he'll end up dropping them since he can't speak without moving his hands.

He gives me a grateful smile and I watch as he taps our production manager's name on his screen to return his call. He blows out a breath after their hellos and starts to speak, but apparently Curtis says something that gives him pause. "What, Curtis... No, of course not, I know that..." He runs his fingers through his beard and I know whatever Curtis is saying has him on edge since, if his hair was down, he'd be raking his fingers through that instead, but it's not, so he settles for his beard. "Curtis, listen—." Our production manager must cut him off with something else, because all the color drains from Brew's face and his mouth falls open. "You're fucking kidding me... There's no way... No, not happening... Curtis, be serious; we're not going to do that... I don't give a fuck; it's not happening... Hello?"

Brew looks at me, his expression some sort of combined rage and panic and I think that my time to be the one to freak out is done, because he's clearly taking over. "What did he say?"

"Apparently, I didn't just send him the video. I also uploaded it our show's social media accounts. And Curtis said that the fans are loving it. He wants us to livestream some big reception. That lots of local companies have come forward wanting to sponsor the event."

My mouth falls open, very much mirroring his earlier expression. "Why didn't you tell him we were drunk and don't remember anything?"

"I tried, Gem. You know Curtis, he doesn't let you get a word in. He said that he knew we were probably drunk or something, but this was too good to let lie. He said our ratings have gone through the roof and several syndication offers have come in since the video went viral. Curtis said it has over a million views.

My breath catches. "You're joking." He shakes his head and opens his mouth to say something, but his phone rings and he hangs his head when he sees who it is. "Curtis again?"

He nods and answers. "Yeah, Curtis... What? You're kidding... Why... This is fucking insane, Curtis. Surely you see that... We're not even prepared for something like that. I don't even have to ask her; I already know the answer. Don't—." He pulls the phone away from his ear. "Fuck! He hung up on me again. That bastard."

"What did he say that time?"

"They want us to go on a honeymoon and do a promo spot from a cabana or some shit."

My eyes go wide in shock. "A *honeymoon*? Where?"

"A travel agency is sponsoring us for an all-inclusive stay at some beach resort in Florida."

"We can't go to Florida; we have to work."

He laughs, but there's no humor in it. "Yeah, that's why we can't go. Because of work. Never mind that we're *married*, Gem. And our boss is trying to exploit it. And your mom is probably planning on just how to make my death look like an accident since your dad didn't get to walk you down the aisle."

I frown in confusion. "How'd you know they were pissed about that? I didn't tell you anything she said, did I? Other than the reception stuff, right?"

His expression softens. "Gem, you're their only daughter. Your parents bring up you getting married anytime you're around them. Of course they brought it up."

We finally arrive at our hotel and once we step onto the elevator, I slump against the wall. "Okay, so what do we do about this Florida thing? And an annulment. Fuck, how am I going to explain this to my parents, Brew? And now, *everyone* knows. Not just my parents and Curtis. At least a *million* people."

"We'll figure it out."

"You keep saying that, but I don't know how we get out of this without a lot of damage. Why the fuck would we send those videos out? And why can't I remember anything? At all. We don't even look drunk in the video. Anyone who saw it would say that we were stone sober. What the hell, Brew?"

The tears start again and he pulls me back into his arms. "It's okay, Gem. Please don't cry." And again, the smell of him triggers some sort of sense memory and this time, it's my face buried in his hair as his lips close over my nipple. His tongue flicks over it, and fuck, it feels good. My pulse instantly ratchets up and I have to step back from him again. His expression looks puzzled, but I ignore it and he speaks again. "Curtis wants us in Florida tomorrow. He's extended our stay here by another night, but our plane leaves at ten in the morning. We're there for a week. He's emailing me the plane tickets and said for us to expense any clothes or whatever else we need. We do the promo on Tuesday, but other than that, he said we could just treat it like a vacation."

"So, we're just supposed to go to Florida? Because Curtis said so?"

I don't even notice that we're at my hotel room until Brew stops in front of my door. He blows out a breath. "How about this; we both get some sleep? I'm still hungover as shit and need a shower. This evening, we'll get together for supper and we'll talk through our options."

"Brew, seriously; how are you so calm?"

He shrugs. "Like I said, it won't do for both of us to fall apart. I'm sure I'll have a moment sometime, but right at this second, there's nothing we can do. Go get some rest. Give me my breakfast and I'll see you at six and we'll go find some supper, okay?"

I can only nod as I hand over his coffee and muffin before digging in my purse for my key. I unlock my door and step into my room and when it closes, I lean against it and try to breathe. For a good five minutes, I don't move, but then my phone dings in my purse and I pull it out. After I read the text on the screen, I nearly want to throw my phone across the room. It's an unfamiliar number, but by the words, I know exactly who sent it.

Unknown: I always knew you were a lying
cunt. Telling me all those years that there was
nothing going on with you and Lincoln. Quite
the coincidence that not even six weeks after
we break up, you marry him, wouldn't
you say?

I don't bother responding to Kyle's text or his accusation, simply because I don't have the energy and I don't owe him an explanation. So I just plug my phone up and set an alarm for four so I'll have time to shower before Brew and I meet for supper. I fall into bed, not even bothering to undress.

It's not my alarm that wakes me, but a pounding at the door. I feel like death and it takes me a few minutes to register that someone's knocking, and it's not just my hangover still banging around in my brain. I check my phone and see that not even an hour has passed since I laid down, but I climb out of the bed and drag myself to the door. After looking out the peephole and seeing Brew on the other side, I hurriedly open the door. "What?" I notice he has his bags and his expression is near murder and I'm instantly on alert. "What's wrong?"

"That fucker. He cancelled my room. When I got to my room, my key wouldn't work, so I went down to the front desk and they told me that Curtis had only extended *your* room. Housekeeping had to escort me to my room like some kind of criminal to gather my things. I'm going to kill him, Gem."

I take a deep breath and open the door wider for him to enter. I'm not even surprised, honestly. And I could rail and scream like Brew's now doing, but what good would it do? Especially when all I want to do is crawl back into bed.

"How come he cancelled your room instead of mine?"

Brew chuckles. "If I was to guess, because my room was a double and probably more expensive. Yours is a single. He's fine spending money from the sponsors, but when the station has to foot the bill, he cheaps out, you know that."

I nod. "Okay, whatever. I'm going back to bed." I crawl back under the covers and close my eyes.

"Toss me a pillow."

My eyes pop open again. "Why?"

"So I can lie down on the floor."

I scoff. "Brew, get in the bed."

"It's weird." His tone sounds hesitant and I sit back up.

"Why? We've apparently done a lot more than just sleep, remember? This should be a piece of cake. We're both exhausted and hungover. Get in the fucking bed, Brewster."

He seems to have some sort of internal debate with himself before finally crawling into bed next to me after pulling off his shoes and shirt. "Did you set an alarm?" he asks and I can tell he's rolled away from me, just by the way his voice sounds.

"Yeah, for four."

"Okay."

When I wake up again, it's with my cheek against Brew's chest. Somehow, in our sleep, we both turned toward one another and his arm is around me and my leg is thrown over his. I try not to examine the fact that this feels way more natural than it should.

I try not to breathe him in, for fear that another flash from last night will hit me, but it's kind of difficult *not* to smell him. Especially when he smells fantastic. He's never worn cologne or anything, but I know whatever body wash or soap he uses is the same one he's always used and it just smells like *him*.

His chest is surprisingly solid and I try to think if I've ever seen him without a shirt on in the past ten years and I can't say that I have. Despite the innumerable times we've hung out, even outside of work during the past decade, we don't regularly see one another sans any article of clothing. We've never even been swimming together.

I raise up a little and see that his pecs are dusted with coarse hairs and he has a very defined line of dark hair trailing down from his navel into the top of his jeans. His chest and abs aren't chiseled like he's cut from stone or something, but he's plenty solid. He's just *Brew*. He's stocky and likes pizza and beer and gives the best hugs.

My eye snags on the ring still on my left hand and I'm struck by the fact that Brew and I are married. Legally married. Had I not seen the video, I might not believe it, but here we are. And apparently, we were real proud since we just had to send it out to everyone we knew. And yeah, Brew's right; at least we didn't marry strangers, but this is *Brew*. And I keep getting these flashes of us in bed and it's starting to be weird.

And the way I kissed him in the video? Good lord. It looked like I practically attacked him. And that was after the really sweet kiss he gave me that I don't know what to think about or the smile on his face as we were saying our vows.

I try to extricate myself from his embrace and not wake him, but then again, I remember, this is Brew and he can sleep through just about anything, so I just get up. I check my phone and because it's a little after three, I go ahead and turn off my alarm. Seeing that I also have two texts and a missed call from my older brother, I don't even bother to read them or listen to his voicemail, knowing it will be some variation on what Mom already said.

I go over to my suitcase and pull out a change of clothes and head into the bathroom to take a shower. Once the water's hot, I strip down and step under the spray and quickly go through the routine of shampooing and conditioning, washing and shaving. Again, my eyes scan the bite marks that are scattered all down my torso and upper thighs. I touch a rather prominent one on my hip and something flashes in my memory.

"Fuck, Gem, I could eat you up. You taste so good."

If I recall, the words were muffled because Brew's mouth was barely hovering above my pussy, so close that I could feel his breath on my overheated skin. And that's when he bit me and I gasped and pulled his face to mine and I tasted myself on his lips.

I shake my head, trying to drive away the memory. Because I don't need to be thinking about Brew like that. Even if I seemingly enjoyed our night together. A lot. Even if the smell of him alone is now enough to send my pulse racing.

The bathroom door opens with a soft groan and I freeze. "Brew?"

"Yeah, Gem?"

"You realize I'm naked in here, right?"

He chuckles. "Yeah, but I have to piss. Just stay in there if you don't want me to see anything." I heave a sigh and rest my head against the wall of the shower and close my eyes. I hear Brew urinating and then he groans, and another flash hits me.

This time, he's moving above me and his hips are pounding against me in a brutal rhythm that fully explains my soreness today. Brew groaned, *"So fucking good, Pearl. Jesus. Come for me, Gem."* And then I had. Hard. And even the memory of it is enough to make my nipples tighten to hard points and my breathing grow shallow.

Brew flushes the toilet and the water runs in the sink as he washes his hands. "Leave some hot water for me, okay?"

"Yeah, okay." My voice comes out strained and I crank the shower to cold to cool my suddenly heated skin before turning it off and reaching for my towel.

CHAPTER FOUR

BREWSTER

I try not to think about Gemma in the shower. And if I hadn't had to pee so badly, my eyeballs were floating, I definitely would've waited for her to come out. But I couldn't. I made it as quick as I could and definitely didn't picture where else she might have bite marks besides the one on her shoulder. She said there were more and I find myself wanting to know where they are, even if I definitely shouldn't.

The shower cuts off and I start to gather my own supplies to get cleaned up. Gem's phone dings and I glance at the screen to see a text from an unknown number.

> Unknown: What? Nothing to say for yourself, bitch? We were together for three years, Gemma. You wouldn't marry me, but you'll marry him? I always knew you were a whore, but I didn't know you'd whore yourself out just to gain a professional edge.

I know the text must be from Kyle, and I immediately want to throat punch him. He's always been such a douchebag. But then my eyes scan back over the text again. *You wouldn't marry me, but you'll marry him.* Kyle wanted to marry Gemma? Did he actually propose to her? And she said no? *What the hell?*

The doorknob to the bathroom door jiggles, and I drop her phone back to the nightstand. Gem comes out of the bathroom dressed in a pair of shorts and a tank top, her hair in a towel. My heart lurches when I see a purple mark on her thigh peeking out from under the hem of her shorts. Fuck, why can't I remember last night? I mean, at least more than what I said at the wedding.

"Bathroom's free," Gemma says, her posture stiff. And I've noticed that ever since this morning, it seems like she's super aware of both of our bodies and she won't even let me hug her. Anytime I've tried, she pulls away almost immediately and I hate it. We've always hugged and now it's like we're strangers.

Heaving a sigh, I rise from the bed with my own clothes and toiletries and pass her to go into the bathroom. I quickly shower and after I dry off and begin to get dressed, I realize I've forgotten underwear. Because of course I did. I wrap my towel around my waist and walk out of the bathroom and over to my bag to grab a pair of boxers and return to the bathroom without looking at Gemma, but I hear her quick intake of breath and I'm not sure what to think about it.

I dress and towel dry my hair and leave it down to dry, knowing when we head out, I'll pull it back. When I come out of the bathroom, Gemma has her hair in a thick braid over one shoulder and has put on a little makeup, but her face looks like she's on the verge of tears. I cross the room to sit next to her on the bed. "What's wrong, Gem?"

She shakes her head. "Nothing. I'm fine. Still just tired, I guess."

"Are you sure?" I wonder if her expression has anything to do with the text Kyle sent her, but I don't want to pry.

She nods. "Oh, Curtis called you while you were in the

shower. I didn't answer, so you might want to call him back. I don't know why he hasn't called me."

I shrug. "He probably feels like he can't talk to you the same way he does me. He likes you, so he's hesitant to tear you a new asshole. But me, not so much. Probably because I'm the resident fuckup and he knows this is probably all my fault, so of course he's going to take it out on me."

"Why do you think it's your fault?"

I chuckle. "Because, Gem. It's pretty on-brand for me. I don't plan things, I just do them. You, on the other hand, like to have every moment organized and scheduled. It's why we work so well together. You ground me and I nudge you out of your comfort zone."

She shrugs and hands me my phone and I see Curtis has left me another voicemail. I sigh and listen to it. *"Oh, by the way, Brewster, there's something I meant to tell you earlier. If you even think about getting this marriage annulled, you and Gemma can both kiss your jobs goodbye. It would be too detrimental to the ratings and the station after all the sponsorships that have come in since you released the wedding video. People are eating it up and expect y'all to live happily ever after."* The message ends and my stomach clenches.

"What did he say, Brew?" I hold up a finger and call Curtis, my rage barely contained. He answers on the second ring.

"Oh, I see you got my voicemail. I hope you and that new *wife* of yours are nice and cozy in your room."

"Listen to me, Curtis," I grit out, my voice comes out almost shaky from my anger.

"No, Lincoln, you listen to me. I don't really give a fuck why you and Gemma got married. I don't care if you were drunk or high or tripping balls on acid. You're the one who shared that video on our social media accounts. And because of that, everyone assumes it's real. Especially with the on-air chemistry y'all have always had. We'll be spinning this as a beautiful love story. You and Gemma will get on board. You will go to Florida and do the promo spot. You will livestream a lavish reception and cut the fucking cake and Gemma will wear a designer dress and you will wear a tux and y'all will dance and paste smiles on your fucking faces and go along, because we're getting hundreds of thousands of dollars in sponsorship deals.

"You did this to yourself; you're going to live with the consequences. After the publicity dies down in a few months and we have all the syndication deals inked and set in stone, you two can quietly dissolve this thing if that's what you want. But until then, you will look like the happiest fucking couple that ever walked the face of the earth. You'll allow yourself to be photographed canoodling or whatever the fuck people call it these days. Y'all wanted the big time, you've got it.

"If y'all ruin this, neither of you will work in this business ever again. You will be blackballed from any form of entertainment. You won't even be able to get a job at your local PBS for their three AM news spot. I'm going to assume that because you're not answering, you agree. Your plane tickets are in your email, along with the script for your spot on Tuesday. Don't fuck this up, Brewster." The line goes dead and for a solid minute, I can't breathe.

"Brew, what happened? Your face is all white; what did Curtis say?" I'm nearly shaking with suppressed rage and I feel my hands curl into fists. I'm staring straight ahead and my breathing is shallow. Gemma lays a soft hand on my arm and my face snaps to hers. "What did Curtis say, Brewster?"

Her eyes look almost frightened, but I don't know if it's because she's scared to know what he said or because of my reaction to what he said. But seeing any kind of fear in her eyes makes something tighten in my chest and I take some deep breaths so I can calm down.

I relay what Curtis said and color rises to her cheeks and her own hands curl into fists on her lap. "So, we just go along with it?" she asks.

I shrug. "I don't think we have a choice, Pearl. If we don't, we kill every single thing we've been working toward for ten years. It's only a few months, and it's not like we hate each other, right?" I could tell her it's very much the opposite for me, but I don't even know that I can tell myself that right now; even if I remember exactly what I told her at our wedding.

She gives a small shake of her head and her eyes close. "This is so fucked up, Brew. Can they really make us do this?"

"No, but they can make it so that if we don't, our careers are shot to shit. From a publicity standpoint, you have to admit, this is pretty genius." I sigh. "You can move in with me for a few months; I have that second bedroom. It'll just be like we're having an extended hangout. We'll play house and buy groceries and go out for drinks. It's not like we have to make out in public or anything. And it's not like we're celebrities. We're not going to be swarmed with paparazzi. Things will die down in a few months and we'll go back to normal.

"When we get back from Florida, we'll do the reception thing and enjoy the big party. Curtis said you'd get a designer dress out of it and I'm sure some really fancy cake." I nudge her with my elbow. "It's going to be fine, Gem. If I have to survive a few months of marriage, at least it's to my best friend."

She bites her lip and nods. "There's that, at least." After a beat, she stands. "I shouldn't want to, but I need a drink. This is insane."

I nod. "Okay, let's get a drink. But can we please stay away from the craps table?"

She huffs a laugh. "Yes, please. No casino tonight. Looks

like we also need to go shopping. I have nothing to wear in Florida."

"Alright, so let's go. Shopping first, or drinks?"

Gemma considers. "Shopping, I guess. You need some shorts."

"I don't wear shorts."

"You can't not wear shorts if we're going to the beach. You'll wear shorts, Brew."

"Jesus, we're not even married a day and you're already nagging me."

She laughs and I'm happy to hear it. She's been so serious and freaked out since we got up this morning, I don't like it when she's stressed like this. "Whatever. You'll still wear shorts. Did Curtis give us a spending limit?"

I smirk. "Nope. So, let's take advantage. He wants us to bow down; we can at least make him pay for it."

"Alright, let's go."

Two hours and well over a thousand dollars later, Gemma and I both have practically brand new wardrobes and suitcases to take with us on our "honeymoon". We take our bags back to the room before heading down to the hotel restaurant for drinks and dinner.

We take seats at the bar and I order a beer and Gemma orders a glass of wine, along with some burgers and fries. I nurse my two beers over the hour we spend eating, but Gemma keeps going. And by her fourth glass, I notice her eyes are hazy and she seems to sway a little in her seat.

We've gone out for drinks plenty after work, but I've never seen her order more than a second glass of wine. Part of me worries that she's trying to drown her sorrows and I could almost understand it; she doesn't want to be married to me. Apparently, though, I wanted to be married to her, if my memory is any indication, and so her getting drunk does sting a little, not gonna lie.

I pay the tab and hoist her off her stool once she drains the last of her wine. "I'm not done; I want another drink." She's unsteady on her feet and I practically have to carry her out of the restaurant.

"Come on, Pearl, I think you need to go to bed more." I finally get her to the elevator and press the button for our floor.

Gemma leans into me, and when she speaks, her voice is slurred. "Do you remember anything about last night?"

I'm not about to tell her what I remember, so I lie. "No, why?"

"Because I do."

I can't hide my surprise. "You do? What do you remember?"

Does she remember the wedding and what I said? And if she's getting drunk after she remembers that, does that mean the thought of me having feelings for her makes her want to drink?

"The sex. Parts of it."

My heart stutters for a beat and I'm nearly at a loss for words, and all I can muster is, "Oh."

She nods against me, her arms slung around my waist. "Your dick is huge."

I huff a surprised laugh. "Thanks, Gem."

"No, thank you, Brew. Kyle never fucked me like that."

I know she's drunk and I shouldn't be hearing anything she says, but part of me can't help but feel smug. A moment later, the elevator doors open on our floor and Gemma seems to be struggling even more to walk. "Where's your room key, Gem?"

"Purse. Outside pocket."

I dig in the pocket she's indicated and come up with the

room key. And because I'm tired of dragging her, I finally just stoop down and pull her over my shoulder in a fireman's carry. Gemma's not a large woman, but she's not rail thin, either. Actually, she's pretty perfect, but dead weight is dead weight and by the time I get her to the room and onto the bed, I'm breathing heavy.

"Gem, you want your pajamas on?" She waves me off and just strips out of the shorts she wears and I try not to look at her —I really do—but her in a simple tank top and panties? And a thong at that? Jesus. Not to mention, the bite marks on her thighs. My cock immediately swells at the sight of her. But when she starts to strip off her shirt, my brain kicks into gear and I yank it down. "Gemma. You don't want to get naked with me here."

She nods sleepily, and I lay her down on her side and cover her with a blanket. I go into the bathroom and pull my hair back and splash cold water on my face and try to breathe. Fuck, Gemma's sexy. And not that I didn't know that; I've always known that. I mean, look at her. All that tan skin and dark hair, her wide hips, round ass, and tits I would imagine would perfectly fill my hands. There's also her warm brown eyes and full lips. But the thing is, I've never let myself dwell on her considerable physical attributes.

Yeah, right. You've thought a lot about her attributes *since you and Alyssa broke up.*

Up to this point, I managed to not think about Gemma when I fantasize. I'm pretty proud of myself for my ability to separate how objectively attractive I find Gemma and who I imagine when I masturbate. But I've never seen her in her underwear and she's never told me that sex with me is good. And even if I don't remember it, I'm glad to hear that she enjoyed it. And I'm guessing by the marks I left on her, I enjoyed it, too. I just hate that I have no memory of it. Because, God, what must it have been like?

I have the briefest inclination to take care of the ache that's settled into my balls, but I fear I'd think about Gemma and it would make things even more weird between us, so I don't. But I also can't go to bed like this and possibly roll toward her and her feel it, so I sigh and take down my jeans and boxers and brace one hand on the sink as I take myself in hand with the other.

And despite my best efforts to not picture Gemma, the image of her ass in that lacy thong and all those bite marks is all I can see. And her voice, husky and a bit slurred from the wine, telling me she remembers the sex we had, is all I can hear.

Kyle never fucked me like that.

Within just a couple of minutes, I'm spilling into my hand, my breaths coming in ragged, quiet gasps. Although I know that I've technically done nothing wrong, it still feels as if I've crossed some sort of line and I can't look at myself in the mirror as I clean up.

I quickly brush my teeth and go back into the bedroom. I dig my phone charger out of my laptop bag and plug it in on my side of the bed. Knowing our flight leaves at ten, I set my alarm for seven, since Gem and I will both still have to pack. I strip down to my boxers and climb into bed and notice that Gemma's already snoring.

I just lie there for what seems like hours. And all I can think about is the fact that I'm married. To my best friend. And it was probably my terrible idea and then I fucking *uploaded it*? What the hell? Why would I do that? And now things are different between Gem and me and I don't like it.

Not that I haven't always harbored some level of romantic feelings for her; I'd be lying if I said that. No man can be friends with a woman and not at least wonder what it would be like to take them to bed. But I've never considered acting on anything because she's my best friend and I've always valued that over everything else.

I'm struck by the thought that until six weeks ago, Gemma and I have never been single at the same time. I feel like that has to have something to do with this. We've come to this conference for the past five years and have never done anything remotely close to this. We've always had good chemistry. Always. But we've never even skirted the lines of friendship and *more*. Because she was always in a relationship, or I was.

For ten years.

I feel the gold band on my finger and roll it around with my thumb. I wasn't lying when I told Gemma I'd rather be married to my best friend than a stranger. At least I know her. And she knows me. Better than anyone. I've always loved her because she's my best friend, but I didn't know I had feelings for her like *that*. But I know from my memory of the wedding that I do. And I don't know what to do about that, either. If I have genuine feelings for Gemma and we're going to be playing house, it's going to be really hard to not fall in love with her. And I don't know if she feels the same way.

I'm almost asleep when Gemma rolls toward me. She snuggles into my side and throws her leg over me. She lays her head on my chest and mumbles something in her sleep, but I can't make it out. And I'm not about to push her away, even though I probably should. But her left hand rests on my hip and I can see the gleam of her own ring in the moonlight filtering through a crack in the curtains.

Gemma is my wife.

So instead, I put my arm around her and pull her closer and breathe in the familiar scent of her shampoo. And then, a few minutes later, I'm out.

CHAPTER FIVE

GEMMA

I'm not on Brew's chest when I wake up this time. Nope, this time we're facing one another and our foreheads are almost touching. Our legs are tangled together and his hand is on my hip. I should be alarmed. I should quickly extricate myself from his embrace, but I don't. And I don't know if it's because I remember—at least partially—what Brew's hands and body can do and I almost wouldn't mind if there was a repeat performance that I could actually remember every bit of.

Brew's phone sounds from the nightstand on his side of the bed and I realize he must've set an alarm. *Right. Florida. Flight at ten.* When he doesn't stir, because, duh, it's Brew, I reach over him to turn it off. When I do, he pulls me against him as I'm on top of him and his hips shift and his dick, half-hard from the morning, grazes my inner thigh. My breath catches, because even only semi-erect, it's still impressive.

"Brew, wake up," I say as I push off of him to get out of bed. He simply grunts and pulls me closer. His face burrows into my neck and his breath is hot on my skin. His hair is down and a bit wild and I can smell him. That clean, woodsy smell that is unique to him and I should pull away, but dammit, his arms are wrapped around me and one of his large hands is skimming under the back of my tank top. His nose runs along the side of my neck and although I should recoil from him touching me like this, I don't because it doesn't feel wrong.

I know he's still sleeping, because Brew is such a hard sleeper, but I didn't know he was so handsy in his sleep if he's not hungover. I'm having trouble forming coherent thoughts with his hands and breath on my skin and his dick inching up my thigh. For the briefest of moments, I almost want to let his hands continue roaming, because I find that I really don't hate his hands and his breath all over my body.

But then sense comes slamming into my brain and I try to rouse him again, thinking that if he was awake, he wouldn't be trying this and he'd be mortified to know he's doing this now. I clear my throat and put my mouth next to his ear. "Brew, wake up." I'm louder this time and he slowly comes to and realizes that he's practically holding me hostage. His hands loosen suddenly and he shifts his hips away.

"Sorry, Gem. God. You should have slugged me. I'm really sorry."

I can't help but chuckle as I push off of him and sit up. "It's fine, Brew. But your alarm went off. We have to pack, right?"

He slowly drags himself up to sitting and scrubs at his face. "Yeah. I didn't mean to be a creepy groper, Pearl. I'm sorry."

"It's fine. I knew you were asleep. You're just too strong for me to be able to get away. I tried." I stand up and it's only then that I realize I don't have my shorts on. And I have hazy recollections of taking them off as soon as we got back to the room. Because of course I did. "Brew, did you see me take my shorts off?"

He glances up at me and then quickly averts his eyes and it's in that moment that I remember I'm also wearing a thong. I yank my tank top past my hips. "Yeah, I asked you if you wanted to put on your pajamas and you just took your shorts off. You started to take off your shirt, too, but I stopped you."

"Thanks for that." I grab my shorts off the floor and pull them back on. "I'm decent now." I step into the bathroom and hurriedly brush my teeth and take my braid down. I run a brush through my hair and grab my toiletries from the shower to pack.

Brew already has his new suitcase laid open on the bed and most of his clothes packed in it. "Wow, you did that quick."

He shrugs. "It's pretty easy when you just roll everything and only have a couple pairs of shoes. We can't all be like you and have to bring twelve pairs."

I scoff. "I brought four pairs. That's not that many."

"For a *weekend* trip. That is that many." But his tone is teasing, and it makes me feel like maybe things aren't quite as weird as I thought they were. Because, after all, it's me and Brew. We're friends. And as strange as all this is, that's still true, right? "Did you hear me, Gem?"

I snap my head toward him, not even realizing I'd zoned out. "I'm sorry, what?"

"I said, I'm going to grab a shower. You think you can be packed by the time I get out? I don't want to have to eat on the plane."

I nod. "Yeah, of course. Did Curtis at least get us nice seats on the plane?"

He walks into the bathroom, but leaves the door cracked. "I'm not sure; check my email. I'm guessing if the station paid, then we'll be stuck near the bathroom. Maybe if that travel agency paid, we might fare better." I grab his phone off the nightstand and click the icon for his email and scroll down until I see the email from Curtis with our tickets. The agency must have paid because the seats are first class. At least there's that, I guess.

I hastily toss items in my bag and wonder why I got so many bikinis when I don't even wear bikinis. And yet, I have three. I also got some really cute sundresses and shorts and tops, so I'll look good sitting on the beach at any rate. Also, I can't remember the last time I went on vacation, so this might not be all that bad. We really only have to do that one spot on Tuesday, which, knowing Brew and me, will take one take to get through. We've gotten so used to memorizing the scripts Curtis gives us, we knock them out quickly.

Somehow, all the things I bought yesterday, as well as everything I'd brought with me to the conference, fit snugly in my new suitcase. I don't bother wearing any makeup, but stick my makeup kit in my purse so I can do it on the plane before we land. With any luck, I'll be able to take a nap on the five-hour flight from Vegas to Miami.

I quickly re-braid my hair and change my shirt since I'm still wearing the tank top I wore to bed last night. I choose one of my new shirts; a flowy red tank top that's comfortable and still cute. But now, I have to change my shoes, so I pick a pair of black sandals. Finally, I slap on some deodorant and call it a day.

Brew's shower cuts off and I try not to think about him naked, despite how nice a sight that is. I briefly wonder if I should feel guilty that I've seen him naked, but he doesn't remember seeing me in the same state, so I don't dwell on it.

He exits the bathroom without a shirt, but has on one of his new pairs of shorts, slung low on his hips. And in spite of the fact I don't think I've ever seen him in shorts, he's got some great calves. He tugs his shirt over his head and pulls his hair back to secure it with a rubber band. I glance at his face and see that he has leftover toothpaste in his beard.

I reach up and he pulls his face back reflexively. "What?"

I keep reaching. "You've got something in your beard." I brush away the fleck of Crest with my thumb.

"Oh. Thanks. Are you ready to go?"

I nod. "Yep. And we're in first class. They've already secured our rental car, too."

"Well, that's something, at least. Let's go, I guess."

After our five-hour flight to Miami and two-hour drive into Key Largo, we finally pull into the resort. It's gorgeous and my mouth falls open. "How much do you think it would cost if we had to pay for this?"

Brew's jaw seems to have gone just as slack as mine. "Fuck if I know; I don't know how to act in a place like this. I feel like this is one of those places that celebrities visit. Shit, this is nice."

"I guess it's a good thing we're not paying for it, huh?"

"Yeah." He parks the car and we pull our bags out of the trunk and roll them into the reception building, where Brew gives our names at the desk.

The clerk, a blonde woman in her early fifties, offers us a warm smile. "Welcome Mr. and Mrs. Lincoln." I'm still not used to being referred to as *Mrs.* anything, let alone Brew's last name, but I try not to react. "We have you booked in one of our waterfront bungalows for your honeymoon." I also try not to react to that word as well, since *honeymoon* brings to mind images of copious amounts of sex and alcohol and never leaving the room. "You also have a credit for a one-hour couple's massage and, of course, all of your meals and drinks are included; you only need to peruse the menu and call to place your order.

"If you'd like to arrange any kind of sightseeing while on

the island, we'd be happy to arrange it for you." The clerk
gestures to our right. "If you give Roman your bags, he'll escort
you to your bungalow. Please let us know if any part of your
stay isn't satisfactory."

We nod, and Roman, the apparent bellhop, dressed in linen
shorts and a floral print shirt, takes our luggage and Brew and I
file behind him. He leads us through a pair of open French
doors and we're greeted by a gorgeous view of the ocean, as well
as the breeze off the water. Brew leans in to whisper in my ear.
"Fifteen grand, easy." My head snaps to him and my eyes
nearly bug out of my head.

"What?" I hiss.

He nods. "Private bungalows with all the food and drinks?
A couple's massage? There's no way it's any less than that."

I'm still trying to catch my breath when the bellhop stops at
a door. "Your room, sir." Brew lays the key against the reader
and opens the door. The bellhop brings our bags in and sets
them at the foot of the lush king-sized bed. Brew reaches for his
wallet and the man smiles and holds up his hand to stop him.
"Not necessary. Gratuity is included in the price of the room."

Brew nods. "Okay. Thank you."

"Our pleasure, Mr. Lincoln. I hope you and your lovely
wife have a wonderful stay. Please let us know if you need
anything at all."

Mrs. Lincoln.

Honeymoon.

Wife.

All these words make something in my chest tighten and I
don't know how I'm supposed to feel. Brew shuts the door after
the bellhop steps out and he comes to stand in front of me and
squeezes the tops of my arms. "Pearl, you okay there? You look
like you're about to have a stroke." His tone is easy, but his
expression is concerned.

I shake my head. "This is just surreal, Brew. Seriously."

He nods. "I know. But just think of it as a company-paid vacation. We'll eat lots of steak and lobster and drink the most expensive wines and make them regret even sending us." I can tell he's trying to make light of things because I'm always so serious and this is what we do. I fret over the little things and Brewster rolls with the punches.

He glances around the room, and when his eyes land on something, I follow his gaze. He walks over to the coffee table in the small sitting area and opens a note that sits next to a bucket of iced champagne and tray of chocolate-covered strawberries. "With our congratulations on your wedding. May your marriage be blessed with many years of happiness. Your friends at C and H Travel." He tosses the note on the table. "Well, I'll give them this; they sure know how to pick a location. Do you want me to open the champagne?"

I can only shrug as my eyes wander over to the large sliding glass doors that overlook the beach. I set my purse down on the bed and walk toward the slider to open it and step out onto our little deck that overlooks the ocean. I'm struck with how beautiful it is; especially as the sun is beginning to set toward the end of the island and everything is awash in that gorgeous pinky-orange that always seems to accompany beach sunsets.

All of this is absurdly laughable. Even if Brew and I had gotten married *for real*, there's no way we could've ever afforded anything like this on our salaries. Especially if his guess about the price of the room is anywhere near accurate.

I hear the cork pop on the champagne bottle and roll my eyes, because Brew knows I love champagne and even though I'd only shrugged when he asked me if I wanted some, he knew full well to open the bottle anyway. He steps up behind me, but I don't turn; even as he puts a glass of champagne in front of my face. I only hesitate for a split second before accepting it. "Thank you."

He's still behind me and leans in close to my ear. His breath is warm on my skin and I try not to allow my breathing to change or let myself lean back against him, or do anything that would signify that he's not just my best friend.

"I know this is weird and I'm sorry. But we can still have a good time. We're still us, Gem." His tone is sincere and I turn around to look at him. In the light of the setting sun, his blue eyes look a bit more green and he gives me a soft smile.

"I know, Brew. I'm sorry I've been a mess. You've been great." I try not to think about all the ways he's been *great* and I take a sip of my champagne. "I'm sorry you didn't get to have a freak out moment. I've hogged them all."

He laughs. "It's alright. I figured I owed you a few. You've been the rational one for so long; it was time I tried it on for size. It's a little overrated if I'm honest, Pearl."

I can't help but laugh. "Yeah, totally." I gesture to the adirondack chairs on the small deck. "Want to sit and watch the sun go down?"

He gives me a small nod and smiles before stepping back into the room to retrieve the champagne bucket and the tray of strawberries. As we sit, it's quiet, but not awkward, since long stretches of silence are fairly normal with Brew and me. We spend so much time talking for work, sometimes, it's nice to just sit in peace. And I can't deny that this is pretty lovely, with the breeze off the water and the sound of the waves crashing as the tide comes in.

I glance over at Brew, who lounges in his chair. His elbows are resting on the arms of the chair and his hands are folded over his stomach as he looks out toward the water. I take the opportunity to simply look at him, and I don't know that I've ever noticed just how handsome he is. Truth be told, I don't know what to think about that. I've always considered Brew good looking in the general sense, but now, it's *different*.

Not a lot of men can pull off the long hair and beard like he can. And although he's not this bodybuilder type with all these bulging muscles, he's tall and broad and solidly built. His hands are calloused from where he helps his brother do construction jobs on the weekends. Relaxed like this, he's exceptionally handsome and unexpected warmth spreads through my middle at the sight of him.

He starts to turn his head, so I quickly look away and out toward the water as I sip my champagne. I try to relax, but I feel his eyes on me and I'm suddenly nervous. I down my drink and grab the bottle to pour myself a refill. When I set it back into the bucket, I pick up a strawberry and take a bite. "Gem?" I look over at Brew, and his eyes drop to my mouth as he simply watches me eat for a beat before continuing. "Why do you think we did it?"

I think for a long moment as I chew and swallow and take another sip of my bubbly. "Honestly, I don't know. What's your theory? You must have one. You're good at coming up with some good ones."

His teeth rake over his bottom lip in contemplation like I've seen him do so many times over the years. Except now, I have a flash of his teeth raking over parts of me, and my cheeks heat.

"I've been trying to rack my brain. The only thing that I can think is that this is the first time in ten years we've both been single at the same time. We were talking about everyone getting married and having kids at supper, and that must've settled somewhere in our brains."

He lets out a breath and drags his fingers through his hair. "I hate that we don't remember. I feel like there has to be a good reason, right? This is not something we'd ever normally do, but we must've decided it was a good idea for one reason or another. I just wish I knew what it was. Are you're sure you don't remember anything? You know, besides what you told me last night."

All the blood drains from my face. I was drunk last night; I know that. Sweet Jesus, what did I tell him? When I speak, my voice comes out a bit strained. "What did I say?"

He gives me a slow smile. "If you don't remember, I'm not going to tell you. I'm just going to assume that drunk you likes to get sober you in trouble."

I cover my face with my hand. "Seriously, Brew, how bad was it?"

He laughs. "Oh, believe me, it wasn't bad. I was flattered, to be sure."

"Well, fuck. Yeah, drunk me is a total bitch. Remind me to shoot her."

He shrugs. "I don't know, Gem. I think I might like drunk you. She likes to tell me things and take her clothes off in front of me." He takes my champagne glass and sets it on the other side of his chair. "But drunk you doesn't remember things. I want you to remember things. Don't get drunk, okay?"

His voice is low and I'm not sure how to feel about his tone. It's playful, but also a bit pleading. His gaze holds mine and then travels down to my mouth and suddenly, even though we're outside, there's not enough air. At least, I can't seem to drag in a deep enough breath.

His eyes come back to mine. "Okay, Pearl?"

I can only nod.

CHAPTER SIX

BREWSTER

I watched Gemma sleep during the flight to Miami. Nearly the whole time, she slept with her head on my shoulder and I liked it way more than I had any right to. She was quiet on the drive from the airport to the resort and I don't know if she knows I saw her have an almost visceral reaction to being called Mrs. Lincoln and my wife.

I could be put off by this, but that's just Gem. This whole thing flies in the face of the planner she is. Type-A to the last, spontaneous elopement in Vegas and honeymoon in the Florida Keys is a lot for her. I know this.

She's shaken. I'm shaken. But there's a growing part of me that's not sorry. If I have to be married to someone, I could do a hell of a lot worse than Gemma. The fact that she enjoyed sex with me is a huge plus, even if I can't remember it. But she doesn't remember the ceremony and part of me is thankful for that because I don't know if I'm ready to talk about that yet— the possibility of genuine feelings. Fun sex I can handle. Temporary (maybe?) marriage to my best friend I can handle.

The existence of anything other than a platonic future between us? I'm *so* not ready to jump into contemplating that.

I also don't know what to think about Kyle's text. It keeps coming back to me and I want to ask Gemma about it, but I can't bring myself to do it because again, that implies there was a possible engagement that she turned down and I don't know that I'm ready for that conversation yet either.

I watched her walk out onto the deck and even though she'd only shrugged when I asked her if she wanted champagne, I knew she'd want some. Gemma loves champagne, so I didn't hesitate to pour some for her. I just looked at her standing on the small porch for a minute, loving the look of her against the backdrop of the ocean. She takes it all in with that quiet way she absorbs things and all I can think is that I hope she's not feeling regret.

Because I'm certainly not.

She thinks I don't know that she was watching me for a long time as we sat while the sun went down, but I always know when her eyes are on me. The same way that when we're in a crowded room, my eyes automatically find her. In a sea of people, I can always pick her out. My gaze never ceases to gravitate to her thick, nearly black hair and those big hazel eyes and that dimple when she smiles. Now, it would seem I also can't stop staring at those full lips that I know I've kissed but can't recall how it felt; only that it was incredibly nice.

I'm jealous of her and the fact that she remembers what our wedding night was like; even if it's only flashes. And so, I have the wild thought that if Gem and I are married, there's no way I'm not going to act like it. I'm not about to sleep with someone else, but I'm not going to be celibate, either. And even if she doesn't have *those kinds* of feelings for me, I know she's attracted to me and we both know—hell, everyone knows—how good our chemistry is.

But what would that do to our friendship? Am I willing to risk that just to get laid?

You have actual feelings for her, dumbass. What if she doesn't feel the same way?

You never know until you try, right? What if it could be really good? What if it could be amazing between us?

You only live once.

I know there was no mistaking what I told her about not getting drunk. I saw the color come to her cheeks and the way breathing suddenly seemed like a chore for her. Secretly, I love having an effect on her. But now, I have to be smart. If I push too soon, it could be weird and we're stuck here for days with nothing but tension. If I don't push her at all, though, she'll keep things exactly as they are. I could think it nearly comical that I know her so well. Know every button to push to get her to talk. Know what to say to calm her when she's spinning out. Know how to make her smile. And for all this, I'm more than grateful. If I'd somehow married almost anyone else, it wouldn't be like this.

Yeah, but if you married anyone else, you would've gotten an annulment as soon as you woke up and gone home and not thought anything about it. You would've laughed with Gemma about it.

My phone dings in my pocket and I pull it out. I nearly groan as I read the text from Curtis.

> Curtis: I expect daily social media posts of the two of you being acceptably adorable. Kissing is highly encouraged. Everyone wants to know you're having a great honeymoon. Make sure to tag and hashtag the travel agency.

Gemma hears my frustrated sigh. "What does Curtis want now?"

I almost want to smile because she knows who, without me even having to say, would cause me to make that sound when I read the texts.

"He said we have to do daily social media posts, and that kissing is highly encouraged."

Gemma pinches the bridge of her nose. "Does it have to be on our personal profiles, or the show's?"

"I'm assuming the show's since he wants us to tag the sponsor." I shoot off a quick text to confirm.

> Brewster: Personal or professional profiles?

> Curtis: Personal and then share to the show's accounts.

> Brewster: We'll do one joint post daily. We'll decide what we post.

> Curtis: It better be convincing. You're supposed to be on your honeymoon. Hell, I'm not even above a leaked sex tape, you know.

> Brewster: Fuck you, Curtis.

> Curtis: Save the sweet talk for your wife, Lincoln.

I curl my fist around my phone and nearly want to toss it into the ocean.

"What did he say?"

"It's not worth repeating, Gem. I hate that guy."

"Oh, that good, huh?" I hand my phone over to her to read the thread and she lets out a disgusted sigh. "He's a pig. Remind me why we work for him?"

"Because he's good at his job," I reply, my tone flat.

And the truth is, Curtis is very good at his job. He's an

opportunistic prick, but he knows how to schmooze and make the station big money. He knows how to take regional DJs and talk show hosts and turn them into nationally-known entities. So him jumping on this and grabbing all the publicity and sponsorships is a good business decision, even if Gem and I might get hurt in our personal lives. But because we're also both good at our jobs, we'll still perform; even if we've got a lot of shit going on. Curtis knows that, too.

"Get a second champagne flute," Gemma says. "And grab my lipstick from my purse."

I don't even question why she wants these items; I just grab them and bring them back out to the deck. Gem swipes on some lipstick and fills both of the glasses and presses her lips perfectly to the rim of one of the glasses. She positions the flutes on the deck with the backdrop of the setting sun.

She pulls out her phone and lays down on the deck on her stomach to get the correct angle. I just watch her with a smile on my face. She's always been good at throwing together social media posts. She checks the several shots she's taken and shows it to me.

"It's supposed to be our first day on our honeymoon. Most people will probably think we're just lying around naked. Maybe tomorrow, we'll do one of us on the beach with our toes in the water. Each day, we can do one that's a bit more personal. It'll almost be like a story; sharing ourselves in pieces."

I nod, impressed. "You're good, Pearl."

She shrugs. "Now that Curtis has his pound of flesh for the day, can we order supper? I'm starving."

"Sure. Let's look at the menu." I bring the tray of strawberries back into the room and Gem grabs the glasses and champagne bucket as she trails behind me.

Following what could be the best stuffed flounder I've ever had, with a salad and a glass of white wine, Gemma and I are sitting on the bed, watching TV. She chooses an old episode of *Hell's Kitchen* and becomes entirely enthralled in it, even though she's seen every episode of the show. She harbors a mild obsession with Gordon Ramsey, so I'm not about to get between the two of them.

My lids grow heavy about twenty minutes into the episode, and I lean back against the headboard. I let my head drift to the side and I'm about to nod off when Gemma says my name.

I open my eyes to give her my attention. "Yeah, Gem?"

"Come on, let's go to bed."

I shake my head. "No, I'm alright. Which team won?"

She huffs a laugh. "You can't even hold your head up; I know you have to be exhausted. Go brush your teeth. You'll be pissed at yourself if you don't."

I stretch and see that she's already changed into an over-sized T-shirt and her face is free of makeup. I must've actually fallen asleep for a few minutes, because I never even heard her get up and move around or anything. I swing my legs over the side of the bed to pick up my suitcase. I open it, pull out my toiletry kit, and take it into the bathroom.

Once I finish brushing my teeth, I come back out to find Gem already under the covers. I set my suitcase back on the floor and strip down to my boxers. I'm surprised to notice that it no longer feels weird to crawl into bed with Gemma. It just feels normal after the past couple of days. As I roll toward Gemma and pull her into my arms, she lets out a little squeak.

"You okay, Pearl?"

"Yeah, just surprised is all."

"Sorry, I can roll the other way. I just figured since we

usually wake up tangled up, it might be nice to choose it for once." She doesn't say anything, but when I begin to pull my arm away, she grabs it and puts it back and I can't help but smile. "Goodnight, Gem."

"Night, Brew."

———

Warm and soft are the first words that come to mind when I wake up. And for once, Gemma is still asleep. Her body is still pressed against mine and my cock is nestled right up against her ass.

Very nice.

And then I realize that my hand is under her nightshirt and is most definitely cupping her breast. And yes, it's soft and warm. At least until I move and inadvertently graze her nipple with my thumb and it pebbles, rising to meet my touch. Fuck, it's perfect, and my cock stirs to fully, painfully erect.

I should let her go. Now that I'm awake, it's a huge violation for me to touch her like this since she's asleep. I slowly bring my hand out and it skims her stomach as I attempt to not wake her. Gemma shifts in her sleep and lets out a soft moan and sweet Jesus, I'm going to die because it's the sexiest sound I've ever heard.

I close my eyes and breathe, but it doesn't help, because my nose is practically buried in her hair. I only smell *her* and that definitely doesn't help either. I'm contemplating the best way to extricate myself from around Gemma without waking her when she rolls toward me and, same as the other day, snuggles into my chest and throws her leg over mine. I'm stuck, but honestly, I can think of much worse ways to spend my time and I can't stop myself from planting a kiss on the top of her head; even as I nod off again.

When I wake for a second time, Gemma is unfortunately not still in bed. I smell coffee and hear the gentle clanging of a spoon in a coffee cup as I sit up, stretch, scrub my eyes with the heels of my hands. I stand up and walk into the bathroom to pee and splash cold water on my face and brush my teeth before coming out to pull on a pair of shorts and a T-shirt. After folding and tucking my dirty clothes back into my bag, I look around, but don't see her.

I glance out the sliding glass doors and see her sitting on the deck with a cup of coffee. She has her hair pulled up into a mass on the top of her head and she's smiling as she talks to someone on the phone. Judging by the smile and a sharp laugh a moment later, it has to be Augusta, her best friend. I also see that she's left the coffee maker on, so I put in a pod and fill up the water reservoir to start a cup for myself. I drag my fingers through my hair, shocked to find it not as tangled as usual.

Once my coffee finishes brewing, I take the mug and I'm about to open the sliding glass door when my phone rings on the nightstand. I almost ignore it, because I'd rather be having coffee with Gem, but I reluctantly walk back over to pick it up. Glancing at Gemma one last time, I sigh and answer my brother's call. "Lawson, hey. What's up?"

"So, you get married and don't even tell your brother? What the hell, Brew?"

"Yeah, sorry. It, uh, definitely wasn't planned."

He sounded pissed before—justifiably so—but he immediately switches into big brother mode. "So, what happened? Are you going to get it annulled?"

"Honestly, we don't remember anything. Like, at all. We remember going to supper and I know we were buzzed when we left the restaurant, but nowhere near anything that would account for total amnesia. We went to a casino and played craps and apparently, did really well, because we woke up the next morning with twenty-five grand in each of our accounts."

"Fuck, Brew."

I huff a soft laugh. "Yeah. I'm hoping this guy at the casino can come through and get us the footage of the craps table when we were there. Otherwise, I don't know that we'll ever know what led to the wedding."

"And you just *had* to get married by Elvis? Seriously? Granted, Grandma would have loved that, but a little on the nose for Vegas, don't you think?"

"Again, Law, we have no memory."

"So, you remember nothing? Gemma remembers nothing?"

I heave a sigh. "Well, not *nothing*. I remember one thing from the ceremony."

"Oh?"

"Yeah. And it freaked me out and now things are weird, because I haven't told Gem what I remember."

"What is it?"

Aside from Gemma, Lawson is the only person I share things with. He's ten years older than me, so I've always valued his input and wisdom. I glance up to make sure Gemma is still on her phone so I know she's not about to walk in. "Okay, so after I kissed her, I'd whispered in her ear and I said, 'So fucking happy you're mine forever.' And I don't know what the hell to think about that."

My brother lets out a breath. "Wow, that's serious. I didn't know you liked Gemma like that. I mean, y'all have always been close and have great chemistry, but you have real feelings for her?"

"I mean, it's Gem. She's amazing, and after Alyssa and I split, I'd been thinking about her more like that, but she was with Kyle. And they *just* broke up, so there's no way I would've acted on it that soon. But Gemma apparently remembers at least parts about the sex, which was supposedly great, but I don't remember anything at all."

"Wow, so you actually slept together, too? Shit, that does complicate things. And now you're in Florida?"

"Yeah, our production manager is running with this whole thing and apparently it's been a huge plus for the station and we now have syndication offers and stuff. And not that that's not great since Gemma and I have been working toward that for years, but Curtis expects us to live together and at least project to the public that this is a real marriage."

"Can he do that?" he asks, his tone concerned.

"Well, if we don't, he can pretty much torpedo our entire careers. And I told Gemma that if I had to be married to someone, at least it's my best friend, but she's freaked out."

"So, what are you going to do?"

"Stay married; for now, at least. Curtis said that once things calm down and the fairytale angle has netted as much as it can, we can get it annulled or whatever. But I don't know. What if, by then, one of us has genuine feelings? I mean, more than I apparently already do. It's liable to get real messy."

"Yeah, it is. Your production manager sounds like a real peach."

"Tell me about it." I glance up to see Gemma rising from her chair. "Gotta go, Law. I'll talk to you later." I don't wait for a response, just disconnect the call and watch my wife walk back into our room.

CHAPTER SEVEN

GEMMA

It was nice to talk to Augusta. In all the chaos of the last few days, I haven't gotten to speak with her, in spite of the several calls and countless texts she sent me following her viewing of the wedding video. But in her very own Augusta way, she was absolutely no help when I was talking through everything. I told her what I'd remembered and her only response was, "Do it again."

"I don't know if I can do that."

She scoffs. "Why not? You know you think he's hot. He's a total sweetheart, and he's got all that great hair. Seriously, it's unfair how amazing his hair is. Please tell me it felt fantastic to put your hands in it."

I shake my head and chuckle. "I don't remember. I told you, I don't remember much at all."

"You remember enough to know that you enjoyed it. And y'all have always had such great chemistry, how can it not be great? Honestly, I'm shocked y'all haven't hooked up before now."

"Brew's theory is that neither of us has been single at the

same time until now. And I could see that, but I don't know why it would make us think about getting married."

"Maybe because y'all were always supposed to get married."

"Augusta, you know I love you and your kooky theories about fate, but I don't think that's how it works."

"Well, you like Brewster, right?"

I roll my eyes. "Yeah, I like him. He's my best friend; he's great."

"Well, solid, lasting marriages have been built on less. Maybe it's a good thing that Curtis is making y'all stick it out; as much as I hate the guy for using this situation to make money."

Sighing, I pinch the bridge of my nose. "It just feels like things are different now. I don't know how to act around him. We used to be able to hug, and he'd squeeze my arms and stuff, but now, it's like everything is just *tense*. He knows I'm freaked out, and he's been amazing."

"Well, sounds like y'all need to jump back into bed even more. Figure out if the sex really was as good as you remember or if it was just the booze. If it's terrible, then you know y'all are just friends and in a few months, you'll go back to just being friends and co-workers. And if the sex is good, well, hey, don't rub it in. Some of us are getting no action at all."

I can't help but laugh as I stare down into my now empty mug. "Alright, girl. Thanks for talking me off the ledge. I need more coffee and I think Brew's awake, so we have to do our spot for work. I'll holler at you when we get back home and maybe we can go out?"

"Sounds perfect. Seriously, sleep with your husband. You're on your honeymoon. Act like it." Augusta disconnects the call and I just sit for a moment.

Husband.

Brew is my husband. And Augusta, with all her hippy-dippy thoughts about serendipity and romantic notions, isn't wrong. I do like Brewster. He's probably my favorite person in existence. He knows me better than anyone. He knows my coffee order and knows that I love supreme pizzas but hate olives, so he orders our pizzas without, even though he loves them. He knows what foods I like when I'm PMSing and has even made tampon runs for me in the past. He went with me when I looked for my first apartment and helped me pick out my first brand new car. He took me to get laser surgery on my eyes and stayed to make sure I wasn't blind. He's my person.

He's kind and sweet and funny and legitimately my best friend. I just wish things weren't weird now. And although I haven't had any more flashes of our wedding night, the ones that I have had keep replaying in my mind. I can't deny that I'm curious to see if it would be as good as my alcohol-hazed memories have convinced me it is.

After last night, I think Brew wants me. His words about wanting me to remember things and asking me not to get drunk anymore could only have been his way of saying that, right? Also, I'm pretty sure his hand was on my boob this morning, and I don't find the idea remotely repulsive. Waking up next to him no longer feels foreign; it just feels like I've always done it. I watched him sleep for a while after I got up and yeah, I still think he's hot.

Do I dare risk our friendship to see if this *marriage* could be real? I mean, it can't get weirder between us, right? Might as well throw the towel all the way in, I guess.

I rise from my chair and walk back into the room to see Brew sitting at the small desk with his laptop open. He glances up at me. "How's Augusta?"

I frown in surprise. "How do you know I was talking to Augusta?"

He chuckles. "Because you have a specific look on your

face when you talk to her. No matter how stressed or tense you are, it falls off you when you hear her voice. It's like you've taken some sort of sedative. You're just relaxed."

Something in my chest tightens hearing his words. As if I needed further proof that Brew *knows* me. Now, I find out he can tell who I'm talking with just by the way I look or sound? I walk over to the coffee maker to make myself another cup. "Is it just Augusta you can tell with, or can you tell when I'm talking to other people, too?"

He leans back in his chair, abandoning whatever he's been working on, and gives me a lopsided grin. "Yeah, I can tell. When it's your parents, and especially when it's your mom, you get this little line between your eyebrows and you tend to break a lot of pencils in half. When it's your brother, you roll your eyes a lot because he likes to think he knows what's best for you even though y'all are nothing alike." He seems to consider his words before continuing, his tone more serious. "And when it was Kyle, your jaw clenched a lot and you hardly ever smiled."

I brew my coffee and try not to think about his words and how transparent I never knew I was around him. I just nod and wait for the liquid to finish dripping into my mug and clear my throat. "What are you working on?"

He gives me a quick nod, knowing I want to change the subject. "Just looking over that script for the spot Curtis wants us to do. It's garbage, but it shouldn't take too long to knock it out."

"How bad is it?"

He scoffs. "Typical Curtis. Full of innuendo and double entendres."

"Nice. Well, do you want to eat before we work, or just knock it out and be done with Curtis for the week?"

"I'm good to wait to eat, if you want. The piece is only about fifteen minutes total, even though there's about thirty minutes of material. I'm pretty sure he wants to be able to use it for multiple segments."

I nod. "Okay then, let's do it. Do we have to do it out on the beach, or can we do it in here?"

"I think he'd prefer to have the beach sounds, but it'll be too much feedback. I can ask Tallie to add in some stock sounds when she does the edits."

"Sounds good. I'm gonna pee and then we can get started."

"Alright, I'll get the mic setup."

An hour later, we've recited the last line of the promo spot Curtis assigned us. In typical Curtis fashion, our script was full of words like *lush* and *succulent* and *wet* and *hard* and *sexy* and *slick*. Although Curtis is an absolute pig, I still find myself feeling more than a little on edge after our performance. I know it's because Brew and I have slept together and I see him differently now. For the past ten years, we've had to do a lot of these same sorts of scripted promos and I've never once felt my skin prickle with the words before. Things are different now and I honestly don't think I hate it.

"Do you want a bloody mary with breakfast? It's almost noon," Brew says as he looks over the room service menu.

"Sure. That's fine. After we eat, do you want to go down to our cabana and we can go ahead and knock out the social media post, too? It's supposed to be overcast until later this afternoon, so the lighting will be better than if we wait."

He nods. "Okay. Sounds good." He calls down to the hotel kitchen to place our food order and when he hangs up, he leans back on the couch and props his feet on the coffee table, sipping his coffee. He looks over at me. "You never did say how Augusta was. Did you have a good talk with her?"

I smile. "Yeah, of course. She gave me shit for getting married without her, but seemed a little too excited when I told her we got really drunk and have no memory of it. She almost sounded proud."

He chuckles. "Well, Augusta's a free spirit. Lawson ragged me about letting Elvis be the one to marry us. 'A little on the nose for Vegas, don't you think?'"

I pull my knees up on the sofa and rest my chin on them, getting comfortable. "He's not wrong. Definitely not how I would've chosen to do it. You know, under normal circumstances."

Brew nods. "Oh, I know. You eloping in Vegas is definitely not something I would've ever expected from you. Or me, for that matter. Not that I've ever really thought about getting married, but still."

I try to think if Brew and I have, in all our years of friendship, ever talked about marriage. While I'm sure, in the course of our show, it would've had to come up at some point, I can't recall if we've ever discussed it when it's just us. I can't help but ask, "You didn't think about marrying Alyssa? Y'all were together for over a year."

He shakes his head. "No. She doesn't want kids, so I knew I was just biding my time with her. Honestly, her cheating was probably a blessing. I was comfortable and I think we would've broken up way before she did what she did if I hadn't been."

"Oh," is all I can say. I always thought he and Alyssa were happy, but now that I think back on it, he wasn't as upset as I would've expected him to be after finding out his girlfriend cheated.

"What about you and Kyle? Did y'all talk about getting married?" I nod and take a sip of my coffee. His eyes register a bit of surprise and he asks, "Like, in passing, or seriously?"

I don't want to tell him how seriously Kyle and I discussed

getting married or the reasons I broke things off with him. Brew and I are finally talking and it doesn't feel weird or stilted. I'm enjoying it too much to bring Kyle into it, so I just keep things vague. "Well, we were together for three years, so yeah, it came up. We practically lived together and I'm pretty sure my mom already had a venue booked for sometime next year, despite what she said about her thinking I'd never get married."

He nods slowly, absorbing my words. "Do you think you would've gone through with it if y'all hadn't broken up?"

"No," I say without hesitation, and even I'm surprised by my quick answer, although I know exactly why I wouldn't have ever married Kyle. But I don't know if I'm ready to get into all that with Brew.

"Really?"

I simply shrug and Brew's about to say something else when there's a knock at the door. I almost want to sigh in relief, because it felt like I might have spilled everything to him if he kept pressing and I'm not prepared for that conversation yet.

A woman dressed in what must be the standard staff uniform of linen shorts and a floral-print button-down shirt pushes a cart laden with covered dishes. She smiles and bids us a good day before backing out of the room. Brew rolls the cart closer to the couch and hands over my bloody mary. I take a sip and wince at the sheer volume of vodka.

"Too strong, Pearl?" he asks with a chuckle.

I cough as the liquor burns the back of my throat. "Just a little. Man, a lot of these types of places water down the drinks, but not this one, I guess. I better get some food on my stomach before this drink hits me. What did you order?"

He removes the metal domes over our plates. "I got you French toast with baked apples and bacon."

I nod appreciatively. "And what did you get for you?"

"Eggs Benedict."

"Ooh, that sounds good, too. I love eggs Benedict."

He smiles. "I know. I figured we'd share, like usual."

I should've known. It's definitely not the first time we've ordered separate meals and split them and I don't know why his consideration and thoughtfulness make me feel different now than it used to, but it does. "Perfect."

———

Once breakfast is wrapped up and Brew's pushed the cart back out the front door, I stand from the sofa and rifle through my suitcase, regretting all the bathing suits I bought. None of them are, in any way, super revealing or anything, but I still might as well go down to the beach in my underwear for all the coverage these small scraps of fabric will give me.

Finally settling on the dark green bikini, I slip into the bathroom to put it on. After I get all the thin shoulder straps adjusted to ensure they won't slide off my shoulders, I examine my appearance in the full-length mirror on the back of the bathroom door. I knew the fit was good since I'd tried it on at the store, but actually wearing this in front of Brew makes something flutter in my belly. I remind myself that he saw me in a thong and tank top the other night and this is covering a lot more of my ass than that thong, but it doesn't make me feel any better.

I feel even more apprehensive when I see the fading bruises from Brew's bites. They've gone more green and yellow, but they're definitely still very visible. And I'm sure he probably saw the ones on my thighs, but he's not seen the ones on my stomach or my breasts and there's a blatant one peeking out from the top of my bikini top. As many times as I've seen them since that morning we woke up together, I still can't help but run my fingers over them and imagine what it was like when I first got them.

I shake the thoughts away and take a deep breath before opening the bathroom door and stepping back into the bedroom. I notice he's put on some swim trunks and pulled his hair up and taken off his shirt. Brew takes me in and I don't miss how his eyes widen slightly when they land on the bites. He says something under his breath that sounds an awful lot like *sweet Jesus*, and I can't help but smile.

"Was that for the bikini or the bruises?" I hope my voice sounds as playful as I intend, but my pulse ratchets up with his eyes on me.

He huffs a laugh. "Maybe both. Shit, Gem, I'm sorry about all *that*."

It's my turn to laugh. "It's okay; I'm sure I didn't mind."

Brew's brow tics up and he gives me a lopsided grin. "Still, it's a lot."

My cheeks heat as flashes from that night play through my mind again. "I'm pretty sure that entire night was a lot."

He doesn't say anything for a long moment and seems to work through some things in his mind. I can't help but wonder what he's thinking, but he just clears his throat. "You ready to go down to the cabana? I've got some towels and bottles of water. Do you have sunblock? I wasn't thinking about needing any, but I don't get out in the sun a whole lot, so I'll probably burn."

I nod. "Yeah, let me grab it out of my suitcase." I do and then pick my phone up off the bed and fish my sunglasses out of my purse before following him out the sliding glass door.

CHAPTER EIGHT

BREWSTER

I should be used to seeing Gemma. Hell, I've apparently seen her naked; even though I don't remember it. But seeing her in that green bikini that makes her hazel eyes pop was nearly enough to end me. Not to mention all those fucking bruises. Faded as they are, they're *there* and are further evidence that we've had sex.

I honestly don't know what to think about them because that's not normally who I am in bed. I might leave a couple on the inside of a thigh when I get a little adventurous, but nothing like that. I can only think that I truly must've wanted to leave my mark on her, so to speak. And fuck if it doesn't turn me on to see them on her. I have to admit, I'll be a bit disappointed when they're all gone.

Our cabana is about fifty feet from the water and is a huge cushioned lounger with a dark blue canvas roof and curtains on all sides. One thing about this place, they give you plenty of opportunities for privacy. I hang our towels on the back of the lounger and set our bottles of water on a small table that sits toward the back of the cabana. Gemma tosses her phone on the chair and opens the tube of sunscreen. She slathers it over her face and body and I can only watch her. For some reason, it feels like she's being more deliberate with her movements and I have no clue how to interpret that.

"Will you do my back?" she asks and gestures to the lotion on the cushion in front of me. I nod and she sits facing the water and I scoot closer to her. I squeeze some into my hands and rub them together before starting at the back of her neck and working over her shoulders and down her back. It should feel strange to be intimate with Gemma like this despite all the time we've spent together over the last ten years working together. All the nights we've hung out and eaten pizza and watched football or basketball games. All the nights we've gone out for drinks after work. All the closeness we've shared.

But I've never seen her like this. We don't live anywhere near the beach and I'm not a pool or lake guy, so we've never done anything like that together. So rubbing sunscreen on my half-naked, incredibly attractive best friend should make me feel at least a little weird, right? Except, it doesn't. It just feels... right.

I probably take longer than necessary to get the lotion rubbed in, but Gem doesn't say anything or move away from my hands, so she must not mind and although I shouldn't dwell on it, it makes me feel good. After a moment, I realize I'm finished and there's no way to make it seem like anything less than me just groping her for my own enjoyment to do it any longer.

"All done."

I squeeze some more lotion into my hands and apply it on my face, chest, stomach, arms and legs. Gemma takes the sunscreen tube into her hand. "Scoot up, I'll get your back. I don't want to hear you whine if you get burnt. You're almost pasty."

Shaking my head, I can't help but laugh, even as I switch spots with her. "Sorry, miss I-live-in-the-water. We can't all be in the pool every single day during the summer. And we can't all have your Italian heritage to not have to worry about being out in the sun for more than five minutes at a time."

Her hands slide across my shoulders and down my back and I try to focus on her words and not on the way it feels to have her hands on my body.

"I am not in the water every single day; once a week, at most. But it still wouldn't kill you to go out and get some color."

"I get out. I help Law build houses, so I'm outside a lot for that."

"Yeah, but I know you. You wear long-sleeved shirts and jeans. So the only thing on you that gets any sun is your face and neck. Alright, all done." She tosses the sunscreen into a small pocket on the side of the lounger and scoots over to let me move back to my original spot. "So, I'm thinking that for today's post, we do it from here. It will mainly just be our ankles and feet with the backdrop of the water."

I nod. "Okay, sure. You're a whole lot better at that stuff than I am, so you just tell me what you want me to do. I'm sure Curtis won't be happy with anything, so I say we just do what we want."

She rolls her eyes. "Yeah, sounds like he's only going to be happy if he somehow gets footage of us making out with me topless or something. He acts like we've got this huge following he can exploit."

I try not to think about her topless or us making out, but I'm not very successful. I don't realize she's still speaking until she nudges me. "Did you hear what I said?"

"What, sorry."

She chuckles. "Okay, so I was saying, you should be fine

like you are; just stretch out a bit. It doesn't matter what you do from the knees up, but you just need to look relaxed."

I nod. "Okay, that's easy enough. This is pretty relaxing." She scoots a little closer to me and stretches out and frames the shot of our feet and the water. She doesn't seem to be able to get the angle she's searching for and sighs. "What, Gem?"

"It doesn't look right." I'm not sure what she means and she must see it, so she snaps a photo and shows me the screen. "It just looks like we're *here*. If I post it like this, Curtis is going to bitch, and I'd rather not have to deal with him."

"Okay, so what do we need to do to get the shot you want?" She bites her lip and looks unsure. "It's fine, Pearl. What do we need to do? I know you have a specific way you want it to look and you'll obsess over it if it's not what you want. It's truly in my best interest to help you get it so we can actually relax."

She sighs and scoots even closer to me and turns her body toward mine and pulls my arm up and around her. I try not to react, even though my pulse picks up with her as close as she is and her tits pressing into my side; not to mention my hand resting pretty close to her ass. She tangles our legs up at the ankle and I instantly see what she's going for. "See, that's all you had to do, Gem. Now, take your picture."

She positions her phone and snaps off several shots from multiple angles and I just enjoy the feel of her next to me. "We could go ahead and get one for tomorrow, too."

I shrug. "Whatever you want."

"Okay, so since I'm already like this, I thought we'd finally do one of our faces, since we're kinda close right now."

I chuckle. "Gem, you don't have to explain it; just fix me however you need me and we'll get it done."

She huffs, sounding a bit frustrated. "It helps me to visualize it if I talk through it. I'm sorry."

I look down at her, suddenly feeling like a tool. "No, I'm

sorry. I know you have to work through stuff like that. I'll keep my commentary to myself. Explain away."

She sighs. "Okay, so I figure Curtis will want at least one shot with a ring, right?" I nod, but don't say anything, because Gemma's not really talking to me. "So, I'm going to kind of rest my head on your chest and you'll bring your left hand up to grip my face and kiss the top of my head. Both our faces will be in profile and it'll look a little more intimate than just your standard straight-on shot."

Even as she's describing it, I can visualize it and can tell, from a publicity standpoint, it'll be perfect. "Damn, Gem. That's pretty good."

She smiles. "If nothing else, it'll get Curtis off our backs for a couple of days."

I nod. "Alright, pose away."

She chuckles and takes off her sunglasses and sets them on the other side of the lounger. She shifts to get a bit more comfortable and lays her head on my chest. And now I'm hoping she can't hear how hard my heart is pounding with her so close to me.

I rest my nose on the top of her head and Gemma pulls my left hand up to her face and I move it to a more natural position, farther back on her cheek. My pinky rests under her jaw and my fingers barely slide into her hair. "Ready?" she asks.

"Sure." I plant a kiss on the top of her head and just hold it since I know she'll want to take several shots. I keep my position, but pull her closer with my other arm. I don't even realize I'm doing it until I've already done it, but I notice the way Gemma's breath catches and I can't help but smile. "Did you ever think with all those promo photos we've had to do for the station over the years we would ever have to do something like this? Gives a whole new meaning to the term 'work wife'."

Gemma laughs against my chest and I kiss the top of her

head again, but this time, when I do it, I know it's not for any photo; it's simply because I want to.

She looks up at me. "Thanks for being a good sport. I know you're not big on all this publicity stuff."

I shrug. "It's probably my fault we're having to do it anyway, so the least I can do is cooperate with your vision."

She grins. "We might never know how it happened; not unless that guy from the casino gets you the footage. And even then, it might not explain how we ended up married. It'll explain how we got the money, but that seems pretty obvious."

I nod and can't help but notice that Gemma hasn't pulled away, even though we're done with the pictures she wanted to take. My hand is still on her cheek and it would be nothing at all for me to lower my mouth to hers and actually kiss her. Despite how badly I'd love to finally share a kiss that we can both remember, I still don't want to push too far, too fast. So I already know I won't.

"You know, my first thought when we got here was that even if we'd planned on getting married and it wasn't something neither of us remembers, we'd never, in a million years, be able to do something like this for an actual honeymoon."

Knowing what I remember about our wedding and haven't told her sends a pang of guilt through me, but I'm just not ready to lay that all out yet. I nod and huff a laugh. "You're not wrong about that. I've gotta say, though, this is pretty nice. You know, as far as crazy Vegas elopements and publicity-seeking honeymoons go."

"It is. Really nice." She bites her lip and her eyes travel from mine down to my mouth and I feel her chest expand against mine as she inhales deeply. And then I'm thinking that my thoughts a moment ago about not pushing too fast can shove it, because I'm definitely about to kiss her. My face is lowering to hers and she's not pulling away. Her eyes even seem to smile as I close the distance between us.

Then it happens.

No, not the kiss. Something else entirely.

Gemma's phone rings and the sound is shrill and jarring. It breaks the spell of the moment because she scoots away suddenly and picks it up. She looks at the screen and slumps and rolls her eyes, and I know without even having to look at the screen that it's her brother. She steels herself, much the way she did when she talked to her mother the other day. "Hey, Graham."

I've never wanted to reach through a phone and punch someone more than I have at that moment. I rise from the lounger because I can't be that close to her right now and think straight. Knowing I don't have anywhere else to go, I step toward the shore and once I get to the waterline, I just stand in the sand and let the waves crash against my ankles. I think back over the last five minutes to make sure I hadn't gotten it wrong. Because I was going to kiss Gemma. I was going to kiss my best friend in the entire world and possibly make things even more weird between us. And unless my eyes and brain were totally deceiving me, she was open to it.

It seemed like our conversations today have been more normal; as though we're getting back to *us*. If I kiss her, will that go away again? If I take her to bed, will it fuck up our friendship? Is that something I'm willing to risk? In a perfect world, it wouldn't fuck things up and what happened would be some crazy, romantic story Gemma and I would tell our grandkids when we're seventy. But this isn't a perfect world. There are feelings and emotions that are bound to get tangled up if we sleep together when we're sober and remember it.

And I know from what I said at the wedding, I already have real feelings for Gemma. I don't have a clue if the only thing she's feeling is our usual chemistry mingled with the flashes of memories she has from our wedding night. Truth is, though, we're stuck in this thing; even after we go home next week. We're going to be expected to live together and work together and do that fucking dog and pony show of a party that Curtis wants.

I'm still standing at the water's edge looking out toward the other islands, my arms folded and I'm rolling the ring that no longer feels foreign around my finger. I don't hear Gemma approach and I'm so lost in my own thoughts that when she puts her hand on my arm, I startle at her touch.

"You okay?" she asks with a grin.

I glance down at her. "Yeah, sorry. I was just looking out toward the other keys. This is really beautiful. What did Graham want?"

She sighs and rolls her eyes. "Want to go for a walk?"

"Sure." We start down the beach and our feet splash in the surf as we walk.

"Graham said that Mom and Dad are appalled by all the publicity we've gotten. That they think we did everything as some big stunt and I ought to be ashamed of myself. That marriage is sacred and I've embarrassed our parents by parading my drunken night like some badge of honor. And continuing to keep up a charade for the sake of sponsorship dollars for the station just flies in the face of what marriage is supposed to be.

"Never mind that I didn't tell him anything about the sponsors and stuff that Curtis expects us to pander to, but Graham's not stupid. He follows me on social media and knows I don't make a habit of broadcasting my personal life or tagging places in my posts because I'm weird about people knowing my location or that I'm not home."

I feel my jaw clench. As much as I care about Gemma, her brother can be a pretentious prick. "What did you say?"

"I told him that the reasons we got married were our own and regardless of what he or our parents, or anyone else for that matter, thinks, we *are* married and if he couldn't accept it, he could fuck off."

Her words shouldn't fill me with pride and something akin to joy, and yet, they do. The fact that she might still be struggling to accept it herself while still standing up for us makes warmth bloom in my chest.

She gives me a sheepish smile. "Sorry if I leaned a little too hard into things. I just couldn't stand to hear him being all judgey and self-righteous. Because he's so perfect all the fucking time and has never done anything spontaneous or remotely reckless. Not that I'm saying us getting married was reckless."

I can't help but laugh. "Pearl, for you, it totally was reckless and completely out of character. But it means a lot that you'd tell off your brother when you're still dealing with everything."

She shrugs. "No matter what, Brew, you're still my best friend, and no one, not even my family, gets to criticize you. I'm the only one who gets to do that." She winks at me and damn if my heart doesn't turn over at the sheer adorableness of it.

CHAPTER NINE

GEMMA

We walk along the beach a little while longer and I don't tell him what else Graham said or what I said to him, because I honestly don't know that I meant to say it, since I hadn't even said it to myself before that moment.

"Gemma, do you know what everyone is saying? That you and Brewster only got married to ink those syndication deals. Mom heard someone say it at the grocery store. Do you know how mortified she was? I can't believe you, of all people, did this just so you could get ahead at work."

My stomach had clenched at his words because they were exactly what Kyle had accused me of, and I can't help but point that out. "And by *everyone*, do you mean Kyle? I know y'all are still friends, but I'm your sister, dammit. Doesn't that mean anything to you?"

"It doesn't matter, Gemma; he's not wrong. You and Kyle were together for three years. He'd proposed to you and you said no and ended things with him right before you go to Vegas and marry Brewster? You know he thinks you cheated on him, right? And that's why you wouldn't or couldn't marry him."

"He's full of shit. I've never cheated."

My brother's voice came out a near hiss. "Then, why, Gemma? Was it only for the publicity? I've always known you and Brewster were ambitious, but I never thought you'd sell yourself out like this. It'd be something if you actually loved him, but Jesus, to do it only as a stunt? That's pretty fucked up."

"I do love him, Graham." The words left my mouth before I'd even thought about them, but I couldn't bring myself to take them back. And maybe more for my benefit, I'd followed it with, "He's my best friend and there are much worse foundations for a marriage than friendship. Maybe if you weren't such a dick, you'd know that." And that's when I'd said the stuff about accepting us or fucking off. I'd also hung up on him, which made me feel good in a very juvenile sort of way.

The truth is, I do love Brew, and he is my best friend, but my feelings toward him are no longer just ones of friendship. If that were true, I wouldn't still be dwelling on those brief flashes of memories from Vegas. I wouldn't relish the way he pulled me toward him in bed last night. My heart wouldn't have stuttered when I realized he was going to kiss me earlier.

I didn't imagine that, right? I have no clue what I'm supposed to do with my feelings, because far above the possible new romantic feelings I have for him, I value our friendship so much more. And if we consciously cross that line, would we survive it? Would our working relationship survive it? There are so many things to consider, my heart not withstanding.

At some point during our walk, we've turned around, and I wasn't aware, but soon, we're back at our cabana. "I think I'm sunned out, Gem. I'm past my five minutes of allotted exposure." Brew gives me a playful smile and I nod.

"Sure. Okay. I could do with a shower and a nap. Vacations make me lazy."

He chuckles. "Sounds good to me."

We take our towels, sunscreen, and bottles of water back to the room and I nearly shiver from the air conditioning. I grab a change of clothes and step into the bathroom and turn on the shower. My eyes linger on the glass doors of the shower and how, if Brew came in to pee this time, he'd see all of me. I can't help but wonder if he'd come into the shower with me or just watch. Both options have their merits.

Stop it, Gemma.

I shake the thoughts from my head. Surely, all this proximity to Brew has muddled something in my brain. It has nothing at all to do with the memories I have of us fucking like horny teenagers. It has nothing at all to do with how I feel his eyes on me and my lips and thighs and tits. It has nothing to do with me liking the feel of his body next to mine while we're in bed. It has nothing to do with the way it feels to wake up with his cock pressed into my ass. It has nothing to do with the way my heart squeezes when he does something for me that he's done a million times before; in a way that it never has until now.

Again, I shake away these thoughts and strip out of my bathing suit and step under the hot spray. I wash my hair and body before shaving and just standing under the water simply because it feels good. But all too soon, I'm shutting off the shower and grabbing my towel to dry off and get dressed.

When I come out, Brew is pacing. His hair is down and he's dragging his fingers through it like he does when he's pissed. "Curtis, you realize what an invasion of privacy that is, right? We're posting photos. Great ones. Gemma is churning out some fantastic content. We don't need your help. I don't fucking care what the sponsors are offering. You know Gemma and I are real people, right, not puppets that you can command at will? Not to mention that we are very private people; we didn't sign up for any of this. We're already going way above and beyond the call of duty with all the shit we've already agreed to."

I sit on the edge of the bed and take my hair down from the towel and watch as Brew listens to whatever new decree our production manager has issued. I squeeze the moisture from my hair and suddenly wish I had a glass of wine to offer Brew for the headache of having to talk to him. He's always taking the brunt of the conversations with Curtis, and I don't envy him.

"No, you listen, Curtis; if we do this, we do it tomorrow and get it over with. I'm not having this hanging over us for the rest of the week. They can have us for thirty minutes and not a minute longer. Otherwise, Gemma and I will hole up in this room for the rest of our time here and no one will see us."

Seeing him be protective of us makes me appreciate him even more. Not to mention the sound of his voice when he goes into full-on negotiator mode. I've never noticed exactly how sexy it is before. I guess I've never noticed how a lot of things Brew does are sexy until just the last few days.

"Okay, sunset tomorrow. Like I said. Thirty minutes. That's it. We walk after that." He hangs up on Curtis, tosses his phone on the couch, and scrubs his face with his hands.

"Let me guess, photographer?"

"Yeah. I'm sorry, Gem, I tried to get us out of it. He wanted all-access for the rest of the trip and I shut that shit down. I wish we didn't have to do it at all, though."

I shrug. "It's thirty minutes; we'll be fine."

"I'm going to grab a shower. Want to look over the menu and decide what we should do for supper?"

I nod. "I can do that. Anything in particular you're craving?"

You know, besides each other.

Fuck.

Stop it, Gemma. Get your head out of the gutter.

He shakes his head. "No, you know what I like. And want to do a full bottle of wine tonight to split? That one glass last night wasn't quite enough for me."

"Okay. Can do." I watch Brew grab his clothes and go into the bathroom and I return my focus back to the menu. I consider getting a myriad of nachos and tacos and a pitcher of margaritas, but then I remember the guy at the casino saying that we'd drunk a lot of tequila and I think better of it. I finally land on beer and pizza since we haven't done that in a while and a bottle of red wine for later if we want it.

After I place the food order, I go over to my purse on the end of the bed and try to find a hair tie so I can braid my hair. I glance toward the bathroom door and my heart lurches when I see that it's cracked. And not just a tiny bit. In the mirror's reflection, I can plainly see Brew taking a shower and my breath hitches. It feels really wrong to look, or worse, stare, but I can't bring myself to move. Either he's not taking a very hot shower or the shower doors are treated with something that keeps them from fogging that I never noticed when I was in there earlier.

I drag my eyes down his body, or what I can see of it, in the mirror. He's washing his hair and the shampoo and suds are running down his chest and fucking hell, why does *that* have to be sexy? I'm not even seeing anything that should turn me into some sort of sex-crazed maniac. It's his chest and arms and hair. That's it.

But what if you stepped closer? You might see more.

My breathing grows shallow at the thought and, like some kind of woman possessed, I take a couple of steps closer and, sure enough, I can see his waist. One more step and I can see everything else.

Every glorious inch of him.

He squeezes body wash onto a washcloth and soaps up his chest and stomach, his arms and underarms, his legs and feet and back up. He seems to take extra time to wash his cock and sweet Jesus, I wish it were my hands lavishing such attention on him. My heart is crashing against my rib cage and my nipples pebble in my thin bra watching him drag the cloth around to wash his back and lower and I still can't stop watching him as he steps under the spray to rinse off. I'm playing a very dangerous game and I know it. Wanting him is bad enough. Actually acting on it? That could be disastrous.

Yeah, but he's your husband.

The shower shuts off and I should step back, because why would I be standing in the middle of the room like this? But it's as if I've been glued to this spot, rooted by some unknown force. It's not until Brew opens the shower door to grab his towel and our eyes lock in the mirror that I'm spurred into motion, my cheeks flaming. But not before I see the smirk on his face.

Thankfully, just as he's opening the bathroom door all the way and comes out fully dressed, there's a knock on the door signaling that our supper has arrived. I quickly answer the door and the resort staff member rolls the cart in. Once he's gone, I pull it farther into the room and remove the metal domes.

Pizza it might be, but it's fancy pizza. It makes me miss our local pizzeria a few miles from my apartment that Brew and I always order from. They know our order by heart and always give us extra cheese. I can't help but wonder if that's something we'll continue doing when we get back home, since I'm supposed to be living with Brew and his house is clear across town from the pizza place.

I finally find the hair tie I had abandoned looking for earlier and work my hair into a quick braid. Brew grabs us each a slice of pizza and I open the beers as we sit on the couch. I take a bite of my pizza and he does the same and we eat in relative quiet. Brew seems to remember something. "While you were in the shower, I booked a massage for you for tomorrow. Thought it might help you be relaxed before we have to do those pictures."

I frown. "It's supposed to be a couple's massage."

"I know, but I just asked them to extend yours."

"No, Brew, that's not fair to you."

"Gem, I don't get massages."

"Yeah, but if this is supposed to be a honeymoon and they've gifted us a couple's massage, Curtis will be pissed if we don't use it. It might get back to the sponsor and they could feel slighted."

He sighs. "I didn't think about that. Shit, I hate this. Okay, I'll call after we eat and change it, I guess. I don't like people touching me." He quirks a brow. "Well, people I don't know, anyway." He grabs the TV remote and finds a basketball game and he gives me a smile. "Just like at home. Beer and pizza and basketball."

I nod. "Yeah, it's pretty nice. Do you think when we get back home, we'll still be able to order from Big Ed's?"

His brow furrows. "Of course. Why wouldn't we?"

I shrug. "If I'm living at your place, that's going to be a hike just for pizza. They don't deliver to your house."

"Well, we can always pick it up. It's not a big deal."

Another thought hits me, and I nibble my pizza. "Do you think we'll get tired of each other?"

"What do you mean? Like, working together?" Something like fear flashes in his eyes and I immediately shake my head.

"No, I love working with you. But now we're going to be living together, you know, at least for the foreseeable future *and* working together. We're pretty much going to be spending all of our waking hours together."

He chuckles. "Gem, I don't know if you know this, but we already spend a ton of our waking hours together. Even when you were with Kyle and I was with Alyssa, we still got together, just the two of us, to have our pizza and ballgame nights. We have cookouts at each other's places. We go out for drinks. Now, I guess we'll just be sharing a bathroom.

"But I think we've already proven we can do that. To answer your question, no, I don't think we'll get tired of each other. We've seen one another and spent almost every day together for the past ten years. And there's not a day that goes by that, even when we're not together, we don't text or talk. I think we'll be fine, Pearl."

I nod, only vaguely bolstered by his words. "Okay."

As if sensing that I'm still uneasy—because he's Brew and he *knows* me—he levels me with a gaze. "Something else bothering you, Gem?"

I let out a deep breath and shrug. "I don't know. I just don't want things to be weird between us."

"Gem, we're us; things have never been weird between us."

"We're *married* now, Brew. It changes people."

He huffs a laugh. "We're still us, Gemma; married or no. Apparently, we've seen each other naked and we can still look at one another, so I think we're okay."

I bite my lip. "Do you think it would be more weird if we remembered what happened?"

His brow tilts up, and he offers me a slow smile. "You do remember; at least parts of it. You told me."

CHAPTER TEN

BREWSTER

Gemma's jaw goes slack and all the color drains from her face. She covers her face with her hands. *"That's* what I told you when I was drunk? Oh, God."

I can't help but laugh. "That's not all you told me."

She peeks out between her fingers. "Do I even want to know what else I said, or am I mortified enough already?"

"I don't have to tell you if you don't want. I can keep it to myself."

She shakes her head. "No, just tell me. I'm sure there's a bridge I can jump off of somewhere on this island."

Laughing, I roll my eyes. "Well, you told me I had an enormous dick and that I was better than Kyle. Gotta say, Gem, drunk you is quite the flatterer."

Her cheeks flame as she hangs her head. "You know what, just take me out on a boat and feed me to the sharks; it might be less painful. I'm sorry, Brew. God, I can't believe I said all that. I actually said 'enormous'?"

I shrug. "Well, the actual word you used was huge, but you know, semantics. You really don't remember?"

"No, I don't remember saying all that."

"Well, at least you remember parts of that night. Seems a bit unfair if you ask me. I only remember when we kissed at the wedding."

Gemma's brows rise in surprise. "You do?"

I nod. Even if I don't yet plan on telling her what I said after that, I can at least give her this tidbit. "Yeah, after we watched the video, it came back to me."

She worries her bottom lip between her teeth. "Was it okay?"

Vulnerability laces her words and makes something squeeze in my chest. I give her a soft smile. "Yeah, Gem. It was. It was better than okay." I put my hand on her arm. "See, it's not weird. We're fine. I think even if we remembered every-thing, it still wouldn't be weird."

"Really?"

I nod, because I truly don't think it would make a differ-ence; except possibly to our emotions.

"Yeah. Listen, over the past ten years, I think it's pretty safe to say that we've seen each other at our worst. You've seen me get food poisoning and shit myself live on the air." She snorts a soft laugh. "You were there when my grandma died and I was in a really dark place for months. You came over and made me get out of bed and go to work every day. We've been there for each other through all our breakups and that time you thought you got pregnant and were so freaked out that you gave yourself hives. And that's not even counting all the hangovers we've nursed one another through or that month that they changed your birth control pills and you were a basket case."

Gemma laughs and I feel a little better, but then her expression turns serious again. "I just don't want things to change between us, Brew. You're my best friend. And there has to be a reason for people to say that spouses shouldn't work together. I don't want us to hate each other at the end of this thing; whenever that is."

Since she's bringing up *the end*, I can't help but be a little serious myself. "And what if we decided it shouldn't end? I mean, who knows what's going to happen, but there must've been a reason we decided to get married; even if we can't remember why. Even if we were caught up in something in the moment, I still feel like there had to be a reason we decided it was a good idea."

Her eyes widen slightly. "So, you're asking what happens if we decide to *stay* married?"

I shrug. "I don't think people get married thinking things are going to end, so maybe we shouldn't either. And if you think about it, we probably know a lot more about each other than most married couples do, even after five or ten years of marriage, so that's a pretty good foundation."

Gemma nods. "Yeah. I think so."

I take one of her hands in both of mine. "And change isn't a bad thing. Look at Pokemon; when they change, it's always for the better. Just because things change doesn't mean it's an inherently negative thing. I know you're still freaked out about this, but I think with all the shit we've weathered over the past ten years, we'll be okay."

Gemma chuckles. "Pokemon? Really? That's your argument?"

I shrug. "You liked that *Detective Pikachu* movie, so don't be hating on Pokemon."

She rolls her eyes. "I only liked that movie because it had Ryan Reynolds in it."

I give her a wide grin. "Feel better?"

She nods. "How are you so calm about all this? And you're so rational and talking me off the ledge at every turn. I feel like all I've done is fall apart."

"Gem, you haven't fallen apart. You've been maybe a six on the Gemma Hopkins Freak Out Scale. None of this compares to that two-month period where we weren't sure they were going to renew our contracts for the show. I feel like I had to reel you back in almost daily with that. And, honestly, I don't know that I have been that calm. I think I've just channeled it into my anger when I have to talk to Curtis."

She nods again. "Well, you've done spectacularly with him. You've turned into quite the protector. Although, maybe where Curtis is concerned, you've always been that way for me and I just never noticed it before." I want to ask her what else she's noticed, because I don't think I'm acting any different, work-wise. I've always gone to bat for her and for us and our show.

After a beat, she seems to consider something. "Did you tell your parents? Do they know?"

I shake my head. "Not unless Lawson told them. But I'm guessing he didn't, or they would've called to comment on the depths of my stupidity."

"Well, they'd have to get in line behind Graham. I swear, I wanted to strangle him. You would think that him being my brother would hold more weight for him than what Kyle told him, but I guess not."

I feel that protective anger she was just referring to settle into my gut. "What did he say?"

"It doesn't matter. I just can't believe how different we can be, considering we have the same parents and grew up in the same house."

"What did he say, Gemma?"

Her jaw clenches and she heaves a sigh. "Kyle accused me of cheating on him with you and, of course, Graham immediately thought that must be true, because Kyle's perfect and I'm an idiot because I ended things with him."

"We never cheated. We didn't even kiss until we got married, for all we know."

She huffs a laugh. "I know that. And that's what I told Graham. Not the kissing part, but the cheating part. You know, before Kyle and I dated, Graham was adamant that I shouldn't date him because they were friends and he didn't trust Kyle with me. But I break up with him and all of a sudden, *I'm* the bad guy."

"Why did you break up with him, Gem?"

She shrugs. "It was a lot of stuff." I know from the way she suddenly won't meet my eye, she's not telling the full truth and I have the thought that it had something to do with me and my heart lurches.

"Stuff to do with me." Her head snaps in my direction and she hears that it's not a question.

"It doesn't matter, Brew."

"Tell me, Gemma."

"What does it matter? I broke up with him."

"Does it have anything to do with the fact that he proposed and you said no?"

She blanches and her breath catches. "How did you know about that?"

"When we were still in Vegas and you were in the shower, your phone got a text and I just glanced at the screen. It was an unknown number, but I knew it was Kyle. Did he really propose?" She nods. "So, all that talk about getting married, it wasn't just in passing?"

She shakes her head and sighs. "No."

"So, why did you turn him down?" She chews the inside of her cheek and I know she's trying to find whatever words she's looking for, so I just wait.

"I need another beer."

"Gemma, just talk to me."

"I will, I just need another beer. I promise, I'll tell you." She goes over to the fridge and pulls out a bottle, opens it, and proceeds to down it in about six seconds. I feel my eyes widen in shock and she tosses the bottle into the trash and covers her mouth with her hand as she lets out a soft burp.

She starts to sit, but thinks better of it and paces in the eight feet of space between the sliding glass door and the food cart. I'm suddenly unsure if I want to hear what she has to say if it's got her worked up like this, but I just lean forward, rest my elbows on my thighs, and give her my full attention.

"Kyle started talking about us getting married about a year ago. We were practically living together, and I wasn't getting any younger and we wanted to have kids, so of course, marriage came up. In about the last six months, he started mentioning things like, 'when we get married, you'll get to stay home since I make plenty of money.' But it sounded more like you'll *have* to stay home. None of the women in Kyle's family work, so I don't know why I thought it would be different for me.

"And then, when I was adamant that I would keep working, he said that maybe I could do a podcast or something so I could work from home. You know, if I wanted a *hobby*. And I said, 'oh, a podcast might be cool, maybe Brew and I could start one and by the time it takes off, we'll have enough of a following that we could give up the job at the station'. And he got really pissed and said that I couldn't do it with you; I'd have to do it by myself.

"I laughed at him because I thought he was joking, but then I saw he was serious. I told him that the only reason that I was successful was because you and I were a team and that it didn't work with just me by myself. I told him we'd worked together for ten years and I wouldn't do a job without you.

"We fought over it for months. But then he dropped it and I thought he understood. The night he proposed, he'd gone all out and covered my apartment in roses. Never mind that roses aren't even my favorite flower."

"No, that's hydrangeas."

Gemma nods and gives me a soft smile. "Yeah, well anyway, the night he proposed, I wasn't really all that shocked since we'd been talking about getting married and, initially, I said yes. I got excited and said, 'oh my God, I have to call Brew', because you and Augusta would always be my first call. And he got all quiet and took my phone out of my hand."

I feel my hands curl into fists. As if I need another reason to hate Kyle. I swear to all that is holy if she's getting ready to tell me he hurt her—like, truly hurt her—I will kill him.

"He said, 'why do you always have to call fucking *Brew*? You realize when we get married, you'll quit your job and you won't have him anymore, right?' I got really angry and I told him, 'First of all, I'm not quitting my job; we already talked about that. And second of all, even if I didn't work, Brew would still be my best friend.' He threw my phone against the wall and said that over his dead body would his *wife* have a man as a best friend. He said he wasn't going to be somebody's cuck and let me make a fool out of him.

"So I told him that he didn't need to worry about it, that I wasn't going to be his wife. I tossed the ring back in his face and made him leave and I threw all the shit he had at my apartment over the railing, including his laptop. But whatever; he broke my phone, so I figured it was fair."

"I wondered why you had a new phone when you'd just bought that one a few months before that."

She shrugs. "So, yeah, Kyle thinks that we must have cheated and that was the only reason I wouldn't marry him. Never mind that he's a chauvinistic piece of shit who only wants a wife who will live to serve him and not have a life of her own."

"I'm sorry, Gemma. I know I always hated him and I'm never going to be sorry that you ended things with him, but I'm sorry I was the cause of so much turmoil for you."

She finally comes to sit next to me. "Brew, you weren't; that was all Kyle. And I feel like every guy I've ever dated has had an issue with me having you as my best friend; Kyle just lasted a lot longer before he blew up about it. But I'd never give you up. You're my person, Brew. And I guess it's a moot point now since you're stuck with me, but any guy would have to be okay with you in my life. I've always considered us a packaged deal."

"I'm not stuck with you."

Her brow furrows. "What?"

I take her hand in mine again, because at this moment, that's the only part of her body I trust myself to touch without wanting to get her naked. Because if I needed confirmation that I'm in love with Gemma, hearing that she's chosen me—our friendship—over every guy she's been with in the past ten years seals it for me. I look into her eyes; those beautiful, familiar hazel depths.

"*Stuck* implies lack of choice. And I guess, in a way, you've never been a choice for me; you're just you. You're just Gemma. Just my Pearl. I don't have to choose you; I just choose not to be without you. Ever.

"And you asked me why I've been so calm through all this. Maybe it's because I'm not sorry we got married. Because it doesn't feel wrong. You're my best friend, Gemma. And I'm terrified of ruining that part of things, but, honestly, I could think of a hell of a lot worse fates than being married to my best friend; even if it was forever."

Gemma looks down at our joined hands and bites her bottom lip. "I don't think I'm sorry, either."

She says it so quietly that I almost don't hear it. But I do hear it and my heart kicks over. I want to kiss her so bad I can't stand it, but I also know she's emotionally spent from telling her story about Kyle and I don't want the first kiss that we both actually remember to be on the tail end of *that*. But very soon, I'm going to kiss this woman. I'm going to do a hell of a lot more than just kiss her.

I pat her knee. "Go get ready for bed, Gem. I know you've got to be tired. I'll put the cart outside. And then I'll call to update the massage."

She gives me a tiny, tired smile as she nods and rises from the couch to go into the bathroom. I set about piling the empty plates onto the cart and stick the bottle of wine on the dresser next the coffee maker. I roll the cart outside and make the quick call down to the spa to leave a message to change Gem's extended massage back to our original couple's one. By the time I come back into the room, she's already under the covers and her eyes are closed.

I step into the bathroom and quickly brush my teeth before turning out all the lights except the single lamp next to my side of the bed. I ensure everything's locked up tight and strip down to my boxers. As I crawl under the covers and roll toward Gemma, I drape my arm around her waist. Somehow, over the past few nights, it just seems natural to pull her to me in bed. To feel her bare legs against mine. To bury my face in her hair and breathe her in. To brush a kiss under her ear.

And the last thought I have before I fall asleep is that however all this happened, I'm thankful.

CHAPTER ELEVEN

GEMMA

Brew's body against mine when I wake up has quickly become familiar and normal and somehow *right*. I was so exhausted after telling him about Kyle's ultimatum and my choice, I didn't even feel him come to bed.

I thought for sure he was going to kiss me and I would've happily let him, but Brew knows me and knows emotional monologues tire me. And although I was a bit disappointed that he didn't, since we'd been talking about Kyle, I feel like the moment would've been tainted by him. But I know one thing for sure: if he tries to kiss me now, I won't stop him. He said the kiss at our wedding was really good and I'd like to find out if that's true.

This morning, Brew's breath is on my neck and his hand is up my shirt and gripping my breast like a small child might clutch some stuffed animal. I could choose to move his hand, but truthfully, I'd prefer he wake up and do something with it.

I have the thought that I could always initiate something, but I won't. *Am I really going to kiss Brew? Am I going to have sex with him again?* I think I am. And Brew's right, just because things change, that doesn't make it bad. We both know we had sex and we're still us. Granted, I don't know what will happen if we both remember every bit of it, but I think we both still want to find out what could happen.

I find myself wanting to snuggle up to Brew because I love lying on his chest, and I pry his hand off my breast and roll to face him. I relocate his hand to my ass and tangle my legs up with his as I get comfortable again. As I breathe in that smell that's just him, I'm struck with another flash.

Brew, standing behind me, sweeping my hair over my shoulder as he unzips my dress. He bites my shoulder, hard enough to bruise, and I hiss as he slips the straps down my arms. He unhooks my bra and guides it down my arms and his hands come around to cup my breasts as he leans in to whisper in my ear, *"So fucking perfect, Gem. I want you so bad."*

I turn in his arms and take his face in my hands and search his eyes. *"Me, too."* He gives me a soft smile that seems to convey what words can't in this moment. I kiss him and it's sweet and perfect and then Brew deepens the kiss and I'm short of breath.

I blink rapidly as the memory stops. We wanted each other. Like, *really* wanted each other. And the kissing. Brew was right; it was good. So, so good.

For once, I try to induce a flash of memory and bury my face in his chest and breathe deep, but nothing comes and I'm instantly disappointed because now, I want to remember every minute of it. And hopefully, someday, I'll have all the pieces. Then I remember that Brew has none of these memories and I'm sad. He remembers us kissing and said it was good, but *this?* This is even better.

I raise up to look at Brew's face, relaxed in sleep, and I want so badly to kiss him, but I'll take just looking at him for now.

My husband.

I find those words no longer fill me with anxiety, because it's Brew. And I meant what I told him last night; I'm not sorry we got married, either. And if I'm not sorry he's my husband, shouldn't I want to act like his wife; his true wife?

Yes.

I trail my fingers lightly down his chest and stomach and over to his hip. I'm pressing soft kisses across his chest, not enough to wake him, but enough for me to feel his skin under my lips, when Brew's phone rings.

I reach over him to see who's calling and nearly groan when Curtis's name flashes on the screen. But I pick up the phone and clear my throat before swiping to accept the call. "Good morning, Curtis." I can tell by the way he stammers, he wasn't expecting me to answer. "Something I can help you with?"

"Oh. Hi, Gemma. Where's Brewster?"

"He's sleeping, Curtis. What do you want?" I realize my words come out clipped and I sound annoyed and I honestly don't care.

"Wow, you wearing him out and he needs his rest?"

"Curtis, you're a pig. You do realize that talking like that is clearly sexual harassment, right?"

"Oh, come on, Gemma; y'all know it's all in good fun. Listen, I won't keep you so you can get back to your *honeymoon.*" The vibe I get when he says *honeymoon* is that he clearly means *fuck fest* or something equally disgusting. "You need to get your hair done at the salon there at the resort. I'm thinking big curls. And make sure your makeup is on point, too. Some of the pictures y'all take tonight will go back to the travel agency and we'll use them as promo for the reception. See if you can get Brewster to do something with his hair and clean up that scraggly mess he calls a beard."

I feel my eye twitch. "Listen, Curtis, you'll get the pictures you get. There's nothing wrong with how either of us looks.

We'll look like ourselves, not some fake version you find appropriate. And if you want us to enjoy our *honeymoon*, leave us the fuck alone." I disconnect the call and lay the phone back on the nightstand.

I drop my head back on Brew's chest and his arms come around me and he pulls me closer. "Curtis should know better than to talk to you before you've had your coffee."

I huff a laugh. "Yeah, I'm pretty sure he wasn't expecting to talk to me. But hopefully, he'll leave us alone now."

His fingers drag lazily down my back. "Well, only you can get away with telling him to leave us the fuck alone."

I shrug. "He's a disgusting worm. What time is our massage?"

"Two. That way, we have enough time to shower and get ready for pictures."

I'm about to nod back off when Brew's phone dings with incoming texts. He groans and reaches for it. "What does Curtis want now?" I ask.

He reads the texts. "You two need to get on board and do what you're told. Visit the salon. G has an appointment at four for hair and makeup." Brew looks down at me. "Sorry, Pearl. Looks like you get to get pampered."

"Fucking Curtis," I say and roll my eyes. "What else does he say?"

Brew scrolls up to continue the text thread. "Your wedding reception is three weeks from Friday. When you all get back to town on Monday, you'll meet with the event coordinator and they'll have cake and catering samples, flowers and rings for you both to look at. G has dress appointment on Tuesday at Bliss. Photographer and DJ are already taken care of. B has tux appointment Wednesday at Grayson's."

I hold my hand up. "Wait, so they're sponsoring *rings*, too? Jesus, this is going to be, like, a legit big production. I guess we should just be grateful we even get to make some choices."

Brew scratches his beard. "If I was going to guess, it's the vendors putting the options forth. If it was up to Curtis, we probably wouldn't have choices. But he's nothing if not accommodating to sponsors, so that's at least in our favor."

"I'm starting to feel like some sort of Nascar car. Like, if the sponsors demanded that we wear labels with their company names, we'd be covered up."

He chuckles and pulls me closer. "Hopefully, that message means that he's finally going to leave us alone until we get back home. So, after pictures tonight, we'll be free." He presses a kiss to the top of my head. "What are you feeling like for breakfast?"

"Omelet and fruit."

"Okay. Pancakes?"

"Sure."

"You've got it." I roll back onto my side and stretch as Brew calls for our breakfast order. Once he hangs up, he rolls to curl his body around mine and pulls me against him. He nuzzles under my ear and his breath on my skin sends goosebumps scattering down my arms. His lips brush the side of my neck and my breath catches. "You smell good enough to eat, Pearl."

I huff a laugh. "I've heard that before."

He freezes. "From me?"

"Uh-huh. Although it was more along the lines of 'I could eat you up' or something like that."

"Fuck, it's not fair that you remember all that."

"Yeah, it's pretty nice."

He continues to trail light kisses down my neck and my pulse tics up. "Next time, Gem, I plan on remembering everything."

Again, my breath catches, but I feign nonchalance. "Oh? That implies there will be a next time."

Brew's hand trails down my stomach and skims under the hem of my T-shirt. "You're my wife, Pearl. I'd very much like there to be a next time." When he says *wife,* it almost sounds like when he says *precious* or *treasured* and something in my chest tightens. His hand begins a slow climb up my torso and I know it's so I'll know exactly what he intends and I'll have plenty of opportunity to deflect or push his hand away, but I don't want to. When his fingers continue inching upward, I feel as though I'm going to die before he actually touches me. But when his thumb grazes my nipple, I can't bite back a soft moan. Brew's hand cups my breast and he nips at the sensitive skin under my ear. "So fucking perfect, Gem."

"I've heard that, too."

He huffs a soft laugh. "Sounds like I need some new material."

"You don't hear me complaining."

His hand moves back down my stomach to rest on my hip. He grinds himself against me and damn, he's impressive, and I reach my hand back to trail down his thigh. Brew leans into me and his mouth is right next to my ear. "Do you want there to be a next time, Gemma?" The tip of one of his fingers slides just under the waistband of my panties and drags slowly along my stomach.

My breathing is already shallow and I feel myself growing wet. I reflexively press my thighs together. "I might be coming around to the idea." I place my hand on top of his and slide it down farther when there's a knock at the door and we both freeze.

Brew lets out a soft chuckle. "Looks like I'll have to convince you after breakfast." He gives me a quick kiss on the cheek and jumps out of bed and I flop onto my back, frustrated.

I hear him tell the delivery guy to leave it and go and I almost laugh because I'm sure Brew answering the door in only his boxers while fully erect would be quite a sight. A moment later, he opens the door and rolls the cart into the room and I sit up and realize I have to pee. I swing my legs over the side of the bed and go into the bathroom to quickly pee, wash my hands, and brush my teeth. The irony that I'm brushing my teeth before I eat isn't lost on me, but the only thing I'm thinking about is the possibility of kissing Brew. And the thought of that sends a thrill through me.

Coming back into the bedroom, I see he's pulled his hair back in a rubber band, which I almost hate to see. He's also already split the food, poured us each a cup of coffee, and opened the heavy curtains a bit to let some muted sunlight into the room. He steps past me to go in the bathroom and I crawl back into bed because I don't plan on leaving it again until we absolutely have to. Another jolt of anticipation shoots through me as I wait for Brew to come back. When he does, he sees me leaning against the headboard and his expression is one of pleasant surprise. "I thought breakfast in bed might be more fun," I explain.

He nods. "Works for me." He lifts a tray I didn't even know was built into the top of the food cart and sets it gently on the bed so our coffees don't spill. I grab our mugs as he climbs back into bed with me. He pulls the tray toward us and I hand over his coffee. I spear a piece of cantaloupe with my fork and happily munch away. He lets out a soft chuckle as he takes a bite of pancake, and I look at him. "What?"

"You always do that when you eat something you love."

"Do what?"

"This little dance." He demonstrates by doing a little shimmy with his shoulders, making me laugh. "Every time. It's how I know if you actually like something you're eating."

"Surely not every time."

He nods. "Yeah, every time. It's adorable, by the way."

I playfully nudge him. "Well, maybe good food is my love language."

"No, your love language is words of affirmation mixed with quality time."

I examine his face. "How do you figure that? I've never taken that quiz. Even when we talked about love languages on the show a few years ago, I never took it."

He shrugs. "I took it. But I wouldn't have had to take it to know what yours are. I just have to know you. It makes you feel good for people to tell you you're doing a great job or validate your thoughts with words. Plus, you like to actually spend time with the people you care about. You're not a super outgoing person, even if we deal with the public, but you go out of your way to make time to connect with the people you care about. Like with Augusta; she loves to thrift shop. You hate it but you go with her so you can spend time with her. And when we first became friends, you didn't like basketball or football, but you knew I did, so you'd watch the games with me just so we could spend time together."

My mouth falls open in surprise. I have no clue why I should still be surprised by anything Brew says or does anymore. He knows me better than anyone else, and apparently, he knows me better than I know myself. Warmth spreads through my chest with exactly how well he knows me and makes me think that he's right and there could be a lot worse fate than us being married to each other.

"For the record, I like football and basketball now; I just didn't understand them back then."

He chuckles. "I know you do. Even so, the fact remains that you spend time with people to show them you care about them."

I nod and think for a minute. "Okay, well I also know your love languages," I say matter-of-factly.

He grins. "You said you didn't take the quiz. Do you even know what all of them are?"

I roll my eyes. "Yes. And like you said, you don't have to take the quiz, you just have to know the person. And yours is primarily physical touch. And what's that other one, where you like to do stuff for people?"

"Acts of service?"

I nod. "Yeah, that's it. You've always been a hugger. Or you'll squeeze my shoulder or pat my hand or my knee. But it's never been a sexual thing, it's only ever been a friendly, reassuring kind of thing. If someone like Curtis did it, he'd get punched." Brew chuckles and I take a bite of my omelet. "And you go out of your way to do stuff for other people. Bringing them coffee or making them cookies or giving someone a ride." I hold his gaze. "Or even taking the brunt of your production manager's disgusting vitriol to protect your friend."

I spear another piece of fruit and pop it in my mouth and yes, I totally do a little happy dance.

CHAPTER TWELVE

BREWSTER

Gemma and I are in bed, both of us practically half naked, and we're eating breakfast and talking. If you had told me a week ago that this was in store for me, I would've said you were insane. But now that we're here, it only feels like Gem and I were inevitable. Because why else would this feel so right? I could be annoyed at the interruption that was our breakfast being delivered, but I'm not above a little—or, as the case may be, a lot of—build up. Ten years of buildup, it would seem.

As we were lying in bed earlier and I could simply run my hands over Gemma's body, it felt like something out of a dream. And as much as I want to get back to it and truly see what sex between us is like, I can't deny that I honestly enjoy talking and eating with her, just like this.

We finish up our breakfast and I pile everything back on the cart and roll it out the front door. For good measure, I slip the "do not disturb" sign over the doorknob and can't help but smile. But as I re-enter the bedroom, I keep my features entirely neutral, not wanting to give away how much my heart is pounding with each step I take back to the bed. Because, yes,

Gemma is still on the bed. And even just her in a T-shirt with everything covered is enough to make my cock swell. And maybe this time, that's an okay thing.

I sit next to her and pull the covers up over my legs, not wanting to make things so very obvious just yet. Gem curls up against me and I wrap my arm around her and press a kiss to the top of her head. Her fingers trail down my chest and her touch seems to spark all of my nerve endings, making my skin feel like it's on fire. When her lips press against my pec, it sends a jolt to my balls.

"Brew?"

I look down at Gemma. Her hazel eyes are wide and maybe a little nervous, which makes me feel better, because I am too. God knows I want her with such a visceral ache it's like I'm about to crawl out of my skin, but I also don't want to screw this up.

Gem's tongue darts out to wet her lips and sweet Jesus, her lips. How are they always so perfect? How do they always look like she's been kissed for hours when there has been no kissing? I can't help but imagine what they'd look like wrapped around my cock; even if in ten years, I've never allowed myself to imagine that. Ever. Not until now. Not until Gemma became my wife.

"We're still us, right? No matter what?"

And I know what she's asking. This marriage and sex and all the shit that's coming down the pipeline in the next few weeks doesn't get to change us. Doesn't change the fact that our friendship is the most important thing to either of us. I grip her face and brush my thumb across her cheek and look into her eyes. "Yeah, Pearl. No matter what. We'll always be *us*. That's never going to change. You're my best friend above everything else. But I'm not sorry you're my wife. Honestly, I'm pretty stoked about it."

She huffs a laugh and bites her bottom lip. "I'm not sorry you're my husband, either; even if I don't know how to be somebody's wife."

"Gem, you just have to be you. I'm not expecting that piece of paper that neither one of us remembers signing or a ring or even this shit show that Curtis is orchestrating to change anything. It's not like I know how to be someone's husband, either. I guess we'll just have to learn on the job."

She smiles. "Wouldn't be the first time."

I chuckle. "You're not wrong. But look at us now; we're pros. Maybe we can become pros at this, too. We never know until we try, right?"

"Right."

Gemma's throat bobs with a swallow and she tilts her chin up in what I hope is an invitation as I lower my mouth to hers. My heart seems to fully stop in the time it takes for our lips to connect, because until they actually meet, I'm not totally sure that it's going to happen; that Gem won't pull away at the last second and say this is a mistake. But she doesn't, and when my mouth covers hers, it's almost achingly tender and makes my chest tighten with how right it feels. How have we waited *ten years* for this? The hand that Gemma was trailing down my chest grips my waist and pulls me closer to her as our kiss deepens.

I slide my hand around to the back of her neck and into her hair and I relish the feel of our lips and tongues and breaths mingling, making for this heady sort of near euphoria. And all I can think is, if kissing her is this good, what will it be like to peel our clothes off of one another and explore each other's bodies? Take our time and remember every second. Every kiss, every touch, every thrust. Surely, it can't be better than this, right? God knows I plan on finding out.

Gemma moans into our kiss and fuck if my cock isn't

already painfully hard. After what seems like no time at all, I'm forced to pull back just to breathe. I can't help but search her face to ensure that I haven't ruined us. "Okay?"

She nods and gives me a sweet smile. "Better than okay." She puts her hand on my chest and rises onto her knees and swings one leg over my hip. My heart lurches as she straddles me. I can't stop myself from resting my hands on her hips and when she lowers herself onto my lap, I'm unable to stop the groan that leaves my mouth as her pussy slots right up to my cock. I can feel her heat radiating through her panties and my boxers and I'm almost sure I'm going to die.

I press my forehead to hers and wrap my arms around her, pulling her close and just holding her there. "Is this real, Gem? Or am I dreaming? This doesn't seem real; it's too good."

Gemma takes my face in her hands. "It's real, Brew." She grinds herself down against me and huffs a breath and I just try to simply breathe. "Really, really real." She reaches up to pull my hair free from its tie and slides her fingers along my scalp as she closes her eyes. "That was one of my first memories of the night we got married; my fingers in your hair. I love your hair."

I can't help but laugh. "Well, here's hoping I don't go bald, I guess."

She shrugs. "That might be alright, too. But it really is unfair how you have such great hair and don't even try."

It strikes me that, still, right in this moment when we're building up to sex, we're still us. We're having a very normal *us* kind of conversation and I'm thankful. I lean in and brush kisses down her neck and Gemma tilts her head to give me better access. "What else do you remember from that night, Pearl?" I ask as I slide my hands up the outsides of her thighs, savoring the feel of them under my hands.

"I think I'll just show you instead of tell you."

I run my hands around her hips to grip her ass. "Damn,

your ass is something else, Gem." She huffs a laugh against my shoulder and presses soft kisses to my bare skin.

I know I could quickly move from point A to point B and get us both naked and be inside her and it would be amazing, but honestly, I can't make myself rush it. I want to run my hands over every inch of her body and know it as well as I do her mind and heart.

Gemma's mouth travels up my neck and jaw to my lips and the kiss she gives me is deep and hungry and filled with need. I have the thought that if any of this is a dream, I never want to wake up.

I skim my fingers up her shirt and cup her absolutely perfect, just-barely-overfill-my-hand tits. And fuck, I need to see them. I've thought about what they look like since she almost took her shirt off our last night in Vegas and even more when I saw her in her bikini yesterday, one of my love bites peeking from the top of the cup of her bathing suit.

I break our kiss and drag her shirt slowly over her head because I want to enjoy the reveal of each inch of her hips and waist and fuck, her tits are gorgeous. Dark pink nipples contrast beautifully against the backdrop of her olive skin.

I take her chin in my hand and shake my head in awe. "Who gave you the right to be so fucking perfect?" My words come out in a low rasp that I almost don't recognize.

Gemma's face colors with the compliment and I capture her mouth with mine, even as my hand returns to her breast to flick the blunt nail of my thumb over her nipple, feeling it rise just before I take it between my finger and thumb and roll it to a tight peak. She huffs into our kiss and writhes against me. I can already feel the pre-cum threatening to drip from the head of my cock. Fuck, I want her so badly; like I've never wanted anyone before. It shouldn't be like this. There's no reason it should be this good already. And yet, it is.

I kiss my way down her cheek and neck, feeling her pulse race under my lips and I love how affected she is. By me. And knowing that Gemma might want me just as badly as I want her offers its own sort of headiness that is better than any drug I've ever encountered. I continue trailing my mouth down her chest and she arches her back as my kisses brush across the swell of her tit as I cup it. And if I thought they felt good in my hands, it's nothing compared to how it feels when my tongue flicks over the nipple and Gem moans. I draw the hardened peak between my lips and suck and lick and nip until she's panting, and the sound goes straight to my cock.

She tangles her hands in my hair and her grip is almost painful in the best way possible. "God, Brew, please. I need you to touch me."

Hearing Gemma almost beg for me to put my hands on her body is enough to make me giddy. You know, if men were ever supposed to be giddy. Okay, fuck it. I'm totally giddy. But I'm also determined to take my time and thoroughly enjoy this. No fucking way am I rushing to finish line without thoroughly enjoying every single second.

I pull my lips from her breast, popping the nipple as the seal breaks, making her gasp. I grip the back of her neck and tilt her head back so I can speak close to her ear. "You don't get to rush me, Gem. I want to know exactly what makes you so wet you can't stand it. I want to know what your face looks like when you come on my fingers and my tongue and my dick. I want to know what sound you make when you take every inch of my fat cock. But what I don't want is for you to think that you get to rush this."

Gemma's chest heaves against me. "When did you get to be so bossy?" Her words come out breathy and I love that even the things I say to her have an effect on her.

I lick a line up the side of her neck before nipping at the

soft skin under her ear. "Oh, Pearl. You know me. You know me better than anyone, but you don't know that side of me."

She grips my face and looks into my eyes. Her cheeks are pink with a flush that travels all the way down her chest. "I want to know all of you; especially that side of you. You're my husband, Brew. I know we didn't plan this, but I'm glad it happened. And I don't know what's going to happen when we go home and real life picks back up, but right this second, I'm so happy we got married."

It feels like my ribs might crack with the breath I'm holding to keep all the things I can't say inside. But hearing Gemma say that she's happy to be my wife makes warmth spread through me and my heart turns over, threatening to spill out all my feelings. But I can't let myself do it; not when we both just got to the point where we've accepted the fact that we're married and plan on acting like it. To where we feel comfortable enough— secure enough—in our friendship that we can allow ourselves to explore one another's bodies and not worry it's going to wreck us.

One thing at a time, right?

And because I can't wait another moment to feel Gemma under me, to access every part of her body, I wrap my arms around her and roll us until I'm above her. She lets out an adorable squeak of surprise and an honest-to-God giggle with the swift movement that has me grinning like an idiot as I brace my hands on either side of her head. I'm between her thighs and it's all I can do to not just rip off both of our remaining scraps of clothing and drive into her. But I don't, because I want to savor every moment of this.

My hair falls over my shoulders and Gem reaches up to push it off my face and behind my ears. She runs her hand along my jaw and her thumb brushes across my bottom lip as her eyes search mine. "You're so handsome, Brew."

I almost want to laugh because although I don't struggle with self-esteem issues and haven't ever really cared what people think about my looks—I work in radio, after all—I've never considered myself a particularly good-looking guy. I'm not overly muscular, even if I am strong. I don't really work out and I drink and eat a lot of beer and pizza. Even though I'm not a father, I am the epitome of the term *dad bod*. And "handsome" is not an adjective I've ever considered being used to describe my appearance.

I like to think that my sense of humor, skills in the bedroom, and, yeah, pretty great hair make up for what I might lack physically, but when Gemma looks at me the way she is, I nearly want to believe her. But I can't forget about the other men she's been in relationships with. Least of all, Kyle, who seemed to be carved from marble and had the trust fund to go with his blonde hair and thousand-dollar suits.

And then, there's Gemma herself, who is like some kind of fucking Roman goddess with her big hazel eyes and olive skin, her full lips and perfect body. She's way out of my league; always has been. I know she wants me, but I don't know that I'll ever feel like I'm good enough for her; to be seen with her.

"Brew?" Gemma's voice brings me out of my thoughts. "Where'd you go?"

I give her a soft smile. "Sorry, Pearl. Just trying not to let you calling me handsome give me a big head."

Her expression turns serious. "You are handsome. Why shouldn't I tell you that? And why shouldn't you believe it? You have the richest blue eyes I've ever seen before and that smile." She levels me with her gaze. "Your real one—not the one you just gave me, because that one was fake—is my favorite smile on the planet." Her hands trail down the backs of my arms. "And these arms are strong. You carried my not insignificant ass to our room the last night in Vegas. I might not remember what I said, but I remember that."

I can't help but chuckle. "Yeah, that smile. That's the one I love." Her fingers drag down my chest. "And do you know that I really enjoy waking up on your chest? It's strong and solid and perfect. And you always smell the same. Like soap and something woodsy. I could pick your smell out of a lineup."

She bites her bottom lip and her cheeks color. "That morning we woke up in Vegas and I started crying and you pulled me in for a hug? Your smell is what triggered my flashbacks. The first one was of me pulling your shirt off, getting ready to suck your cock. Too bad I don't remember the actual act, but I know that's what I was about to do."

CHAPTER THIRTEEN

GEMMA

I've never thought of Brew as someone who lacks confidence or self-esteem and he's the least vain person I've ever met. He doesn't care about trends in fashion or what's expected of him, he just wears what's comfortable and *him*. But when I told him he was handsome, something flickered in his eyes as though he didn't believe it and something in my heart cracked. And while Brew is not some chiseled cover model, he is absolutely perfect, and I intend for him to know it.

His face registers shock when I mention my flashback and his brain seems to glitch. I can't help but laugh and give him a sly smile. "I'm pretty sure that was the first thing I wanted to do when we got to the room. Turns out, black out drunk me might be a bit of a nympho."

He closes his eyes as if in pain and his voice comes out strained. "Fuck, Gem, don't tell me stuff like that. I've got an agenda here and you're going to kill me." The thought of whatever *agenda* he has planned makes my pulse tic up, but I need him to hear me more than I want him to make love to me.

"Well, when I'm satisfied you believe me, I'll let you get

back to it. When I first woke up that morning and rolled over and knew it was you—." I huff a laugh. "Well, at first, with all the hair, I honestly thought it might be a woman, but then I saw the beard, so I knew it was a man."

"A woman?" He asks with a grin.

I shrug. "Who knows what drunk me gets up to? Anyway, as soon as I saw your tattoo, I knew it was you and I knew I was naked and just out of curiosity, I had to find out if you were, too. So, I peeked." I run my hands around his waist and down his back to grip his butt. "And you know the first thing I noticed?" He shrugs and I continue. "This fine ass. I thought to myself, 'Shit, he's got a nice ass. How did I not know that?'"

I lift my head to brush kisses down his neck, and I listen to the way his breathing changes tempo and his hips grind into me just the slightest bit, but I keep going with what I want to say. "And then, when you rolled over onto your back? Yeah, I totally peeked then too and thought, 'no wonder I'm so sore, Brew's cock is huge.'" Brew's cheeks color and I press a kiss to his lips. When he tries to deepen it, I pull away.

"But none of that is what truly makes you incredibly handsome and sexy to me. Granted, they're very, *very* nice perks." I bring my hand up and place it over his heart. "None of that matters if this part of you is ugly. But your heart? Your heart is the most gorgeous part of you. It's big and beautiful and open. Don't get it wrong, though, you are damn sexy and I want your body."

Brew leans down to press a light kiss on each of my cheeks. "So, what I'm supposed to take from all that is that you've possibly slept with women before and you think I have a big dick and you want it?"

I jab him playfully in the ribs and laugh. "No, I've never slept with a woman before. But I've also never been blackout drunk before, either, so who knows what I would have gotten up to? And, yes, I want your huge dick."

"That's all you had to say, Pearl." He brushes a kiss across my lips. "The rest was really nice, too, though, not gonna lie." My skin prickles under his gaze as his eyes scan down my body and he rakes his top teeth as he contemplates exactly what he wants to do to me.

I grip his face and kiss him and hope he can feel every bit of desire I have for him. I hope he can sense how much I want him. I hope he knows that despite my fears, I am happy to be his wife. It's surreal to know that a few days ago I was terrified of what we'd done and now, I can't imagine things being any different than they are. And I can only hope that Brew and I will still be *us* by the time we get through all the shit Curtis is expecting of us.

But I feel like, if we always choose our friendship over everything else, we'll be okay. I honestly never would've imagined it would be like this to kiss Brew and feel his hands on my body, but I never want to feel anyone else's hands ever again.

And maybe it's *because* he's my best friend. I feel safe and cherished and, dare I say, *loved?* I know that I'm dangerously close to falling for him. It's not a shock to me; we've always been so close and have such a deep connection. I'm just shocked I've never entertained the thought of us together before now. Because I can't imagine anything with anyone else feeling this *right*.

My hands are still in Brew's hair as his mouth travels down my neck. His breath is warm and his mouth is wet. His teeth graze my collarbone and I gasp with the sensation.

"I love your noises, Gem. I can't wait to hear all of them."

Overcome with the need to touch him, to feel him under my hands and drive him as wild as he's making me, I drag my hands from his hair and down his neck and chest, splaying my fingers across his stomach as I reach the waistband of his boxers. I dip my hand inside and to wrap around his hard length and nearly want to moan.

Even though I know he's large—I've seen him, felt the aftermath of him—feeling my fingers wrapped around him and barely being able to get my hand all the way around his shaft is enough to make my breath catch. I stroke him in long, easy movements and Brew seems to falter as he kisses his way down my chest. Knowing that my touch affects him sends a thrill up my spine and makes me want to never stop making him feel good. It's enough to make heat shoot straight to my core and wetness pool between my thighs.

I'm not inexperienced in the least. I've had several serious boyfriends in just the time I've known Brew alone. But for some reason, I've never worried about wanting to make sure things are good for my partners like I want to with Brew. That probably makes me a selfish lover, but I have a feeling it's just making me see how much more important Brew is than any of the other men I've been with. Not that I didn't already know that from a platonic standpoint, but now I'm seeing that from a romantic one as well.

I continue to move my hand up and down his length and Brew groans and shifts his hips out of my reach. When I scoff and attempt to reach for him again, Brew grabs my wrist, even as his mouth clamps down on my nipple. "Not fair." But my words come out on a moan as his teeth scrape over the stiff peak.

He raises a couple of inches off my breast. "It's too good, Gem. I let you keep that up, and I'll be done for and I want in your pussy, so you'll live." He blows cool air over my nipple and I huff out a ragged breath as it puckers from the sensation. "Look at these tits, Pearl. Fuck, they're gorgeous." He moves to the other breast and swirls his tongue over the nipple before tugging it between his teeth. I let out a sharp hiss and pull his hair hard enough to sting.

Brew raises up to look at me. "So that's why my scalp was so sore that morning. Jeez, Gem, easy."

I can't help but chuckle. "You, too. I don't want to be covered in bruises again." I quirk a brow. "At least, not visible ones."

He presses light kisses over my breasts and down my stomach. "I can be gentle, Pearl. Is that what you want?" His eyes hold mine even as his mouth moves farther south and his hands trail up my thighs.

"Not particularly. I want you, however you want to give yourself to me, Brew."

He gives me a wicked grin. "I like the sound of that." The mischievous glint in his eye makes my heart stutter, but not with anything close to fear, only anticipation. His fingers hook in the waistband of my panties, but he pauses for a moment.

I run my hand through his hair and down his jaw and he looks up at me. "I just needed to brace myself, Gem. You've already been so much more beautiful than I ever imagined, and I'm in awe of you. So, I needed a minute to collect myself to take in every bit of you. Because I want to remember it forever."

His words make my chest ache with their earnestness and the implication that this is not a small thing we're doing. There's no way, even if this is the only time we have sex, that it could ever be considered anything remotely resembling casual. Not that I thought it was, but still, Brew and his big heart make me feel as though I'm precious and cherished.

And just like that, I'm gone for him.

I want to put my hands on top of his and push my panties down, but he wants to take his time and I can't bring myself to take that from him; regardless how much I want him. So I nod and give him a soft smile and tell him, "I'm all yours, Brew, and there's nowhere else I'd rather be, so we can take as long as you want."

He presses soft kisses along my stomach and slowly—nearly agonizingly so—drags my panties down my hips and off my legs. When his eyes travel up my legs and settle between my thighs, he truly seems as though he's in awe and I only hear a soft *fucking hell* under his breath that makes me blush. I'm not a prude and never have been, but I'm not accustomed to being visibly devoured. But with Brew, I enjoy seeing the way he looks at me. I also definitely enjoy seeing the sizable bulge in his boxers grow even larger.

I let my knees fall open a bit more and give him a slow smile as I drag a finger up my thigh. "Well, *husband*, what do you plan on doing to me now that you've got me where you want me?"

Again, his teeth rake over his bottom lip and his breathing grows a bit more shallow. "Gemma. Damn. You calling me 'husband' is going to end me. Shit." He sets the backs of my knees on his shoulders and kisses and bites his way up my inner thighs and I try to simply focus on the sensations of Brew's—my husband's — lips and hair and beard brushing up the inside of my leg.

His thumbs part my folds and I gasp as his tongue drags up my pussy. He flicks over my clit before he draws it between his lips to suck and swirl and tease. I sink my fingers into his hair as he continues his glorious torture and I can't stop my hips from writhing of their own volition, even as my breathing grows ragged. But then Brew wraps his arms around my thighs and I'm unable to move.

"That's dirty. And mean." My words come out stilted and when he chuckles, I can't bite back a moan from the vibration and I let my head fall back on the mattress and I close my eyes.

Brew raises his head, and it's as though cold water's been

dumped on me. I look down at him to find out why he stopped. "No, Gem, you watch your husband eat you like the feast you are. You taste so fucking good. I want your eyes on me when you come on my tongue."

His words make me grow even wetter; especially as he continues to suck and lick and fuck, the nibbling. All the while, his eyes don't leave mine. And it just makes things so much more intense. I'm never going to be able to sit across from him at work again and look him in the eye without having to change my panties from now on. Not gonna happen.

My pleasure builds and builds and still his eyes don't leave mine and my abs start to cramp with the tension. "Fuck, Brew. Fuck. Fuck. *Fuck.*" His eyes drill into mine, and as if with some sort of unspoken command, my toes curl against his back as I let go with a shudder and deep rasp. Brew doesn't even let my orgasm subside before his fingers enter my pussy and I gasp and my hips buck with the sensation. I watch as he drags the back of his free hand over his beard, shiny with my release. He rises above me and braces his free hand beside my head while his fingers curl as he slides them in and out.

"Do you know how beautiful you are when you come, Pearl? I could watch it for the rest of my life. You feel so good and I can't fucking wait to be inside you."

I grip his face and pull his mouth to mine as my second orgasm takes me so unexpectedly, I cry out into our kiss as I clench around him. He continues to fuck me with his fingers, even after the climax abates and I press my forehead to his. "Please, Brew. I need you. Fuck."

Even as he pulls his hand away, my body mourns its loss as I try to catch my breath. I watch as Brew tugs his boxers off and my heart lurches at the sight of him, a bead of pre-cum at the head of his thick length. "Looks like I should've braced myself, too. Sweet fucking hell, indeed."

If I didn't already know that my body could take him, I might have reservations, but the one flashback I have of him inside me is enough to assuage any need for hesitation.

Brew laughs as he tugs my hips farther down the bed and settles himself between my thighs. He pauses, braced on one forearm and takes my face in his hand. His cock presses against my entrance and I want to move my hips and draw him in, but I want to give this to him the way *he* wants, so I don't. His gaze is tender, and he presses a sweet kiss to my lips. "I know as soon as I start, it'll be over too soon. Even if it lasted hours, it would still be too soon, Gem."

I tuck his hair behind his ear and grip his face. "Make love to your wife, Brew. Please?" His eyes close as he enters me and I gasp from the sheer invasion of him and Brew lets out a soft groan and takes some deep breaths as he lets my body adjust to him. But I need more and I tilt my hips to drive him deeper. He lets out a soft *fuck* as we move together. "Look at me, Brew. You wanted to watch me, so watch."

His hips punch forward as his eyes open and slide to mine. He pulls out nearly to the tip and slams into me and the breath is nearly knocked from my lungs. Brew grips my face and covers my mouth with his for a scorching kiss that has my heart rate ratcheting up even higher before he breaks it and drags his mouth to my ear as his thrusts pound a deep, steady rhythm. "You like to watch, too, don't you? Like last night, when you watched me in the shower. Did you like that?" Brew's tone is a near growl that makes goosebumps rise over my entire body. He raises up to brace my knee on his forearm to drive himself even deeper, and I nearly come on the spot. He gives me a smug smile. "Tell me you enjoyed watching me in the shower, Gem."

"Yes. You left the door open on purpose."

"You're damn right, I did. I wanted you to watch. I wanted

you to want me." A vein in his neck has popped and a bead of sweat rolls down his forehead.

"I did want you. I've wanted you since before we left Vegas." My voice is breathy and the words leave my mouth on jagged exhales as another orgasm begins to build.

Brew's chin drops to his chest, and he reaches between us to work my clit. "Fuck, Pearl, I need you to come. I can't wait. Fuck."

I grab his hair and pull his mouth to mine as I let go one final time. I kiss him deeply and I let out an almost soundless sigh. He grips my face and looks into my eyes as his hips buck a few final, brutal times before his body shudders and he releases a deep, guttural grunt.

CHAPTER FOURTEEN

BREWSTER

I can't move for fear that I'll wake up. Surely this has to have been a dream. Making love—because that's all I can call it—to Gemma is too much. I don't even want to pull out. I want to stay buried inside her forever, but soon, my arms grow shaky and I lower myself to the bed beside her.

She rolls into my arms and I don't know that I trust myself to speak right in this moment, so I tug her closer and pull the covers up around us.

"What time is it?" Gemma asks, and I'm loathe to move from this spot, but I reach over and pick up my phone to see that it's nearly noon.

"Time for a nap, wife." She chuckles, and I set an alarm for an hour from now since we have to do that massage and get ready for pictures. "How pissed do you think Curtis would be if we stood up the photographer?"

Gem laughs against my chest. "Infinitely. And we can drag ourselves away for thirty minutes, right?"

I roll until we're both on our sides. "I'd prefer not to leave this bed for the rest of this trip."

She nods. "Ditto. But at some point, we'd have to eat, right?"

"We proved this morning that we can eat right here in this bed."

"Yeah, but at some point, my vagina will have to have a break, so we'll have to get out of bed."

I can't help but laugh. "Okay. That's fair." I pluck a hair that's plastered to the sweat on her forehead and brush it off her face, then I press a kiss to her lips. "See, Gem, we're still us."

She gives me a soft smile and grips my face. "I'm glad. Although, maybe you were right with your Pokemon analogy. If this is change, it's good."

I grin. "See, you can't hate on Pokemon."

"I'm so glad we were sober for this. It's even better than what I remember from Vegas."

I feign deep relief. "Thank fuck for that. I was so worried your booze-addled memories had made you think I was better than I was."

Gemma laughs. "I don't know, you were really, *really* good both times. I'm just glad you'll remember this one, too."

"Yes, because it was so unfair that you had all these memories that I didn't. I'm still really jealous about that."

She tucks my hair behind my ear. "Well, we can consider this our actual first time. How about that? That way, we both remember it and we were both coherent and know what it meant." She bites her lip. "Because it meant a lot."

I take her hand in mine and kiss her palm. "It meant so much, Pearl. It meant everything."

We lie quietly and I watch as Gemma's eyes flutter closed and then her breathing deepens. I just listen to her sleep and marvel at how this woman—my beautiful Gemma—wants me. It seems unreal. I'll never get over this. I don't care how it happened. Whatever led us to decide to get married in Vegas, I couldn't care less if I ever know. I only know that I wouldn't change a thing. Part of me says I should wish that Gem and I would've always been like this, but I don't know if I could ever want that. Our ten years of friendship are the highlight of my life.

The fact that we were just *us* and we got to know each other outside of what we have now, I wouldn't trade it for anything. I'll tell you this, though, I don't plan on going back; I couldn't if I wanted to. Now that I know what it's like to have her, truly have her, I'd never be able to give it up. It'd be easier to cut out my own heart, because that's exactly what it would be.

———

"Brew. Wake up." Gemma is yelling at me and I realize that I must have nodded off.

"Hmm. Five more minutes," I say with a groan.

"Okay, but I'm going to take a shower. I was going to see if you wanted to join me." Her words come out low since she's next to my ear and her breath tickles the side of my neck. My eyes pop open and she laughs as I scramble from under the covers. "Thought that might get you up. Come on, I've already got the shower going."

I follow her into the bathroom and pull my hair up so it doesn't get wet and I see that Gemma's done the same. She tugs me into the shower with her and we stand with the spray hitting us for a minute just looking at one another. I take her face in my hands and press a kiss to her lips. "I could get used to this. We could take showers together every day before we go to work. We'd conserve so much water."

Gemma chuckles and wraps her arms around my waist. "I think we'd get distracted and be late all the time."

I trail kisses down her neck. "Distractions can be nice. And Curtis does want us to act like we're married. I think it's pretty common for newlyweds to not be able to keep their hands off each other and be late for work." I run my hand down her side to settle on her hip. "I don't think I'm going to be able to keep my hands off you for the foreseeable future."

She presses kisses into my chest. "Yeah, I don't know that I'll be able to make eye contact with you across the console at work anymore."

"Oh? Why's that?"

Her cheeks color and she quirks a brow. "Because all I'm going to be able to see is you looking me in the eye with your face between my legs."

"Well, yeah, that was pretty nice."

"Yeah, it really was, but I can't be thinking like that at work. I'd lose my train of thought all the time."

I can't help but laugh. "Nah, you're too good at your job for that."

She shrugs. "I don't know; I've never had to work with my incredibly hot husband before."

I nod. "Yeah, and I've never had to work with my sexy-as-fuck wife before. I think it might be a struggle for both of us. But if nothing else, it'll just make it really hot for when we get back home."

She smiles, then she seems to consider something and her expression grows serious as her forehead falls to my chest. I lift her chin and force her to look at me. "What's this face about? What are you worried about?"

She sighs and gives a halfhearted shrug. "We're going to be okay when we get home, right?"

I give her a grin and press a kiss to her forehead. "Yeah, of course. Why?"

"I don't know. I can see why it's easy here. It's just us, and yeah, we've had to deal with Curtis some, but it hasn't been real life. When we get back home, it's back to the show and bills and my parents and responsibilities. I think we both want to make this work, right? That's what we decided?"

"Hell yeah, I want this to work. Now, more than ever."

"Okay, but what if, when we get back to our real lives, it's too much? Not to mention all the stuff that Curtis is expecting of us. We're going to be trying to navigate a new relationship and living together and working together and having to jump through all these hoops. It's just a lot of pressure, Brew. Plus, I'd never want to hurt our friendship; it's the best thing in my life. *You're* the best thing in my life."

A single tear rolls down her cheek and I swipe it away with the pad of my thumb. "Pearl, I'm never gonna say it'll be easy, because when Curtis is involved, it's never easy, but we're still us. We've already decided that. And yeah, this is a kind of new us, but not really. The only difference is that now we're legally bound to one another and have amazing sex. But the rest? Work and your parents and living together and stuff; all that's minor. All that is figureoutable."

Gemma chuckles. "That's not even a word, Brew."

I shrug. "Well, you knew what I meant, so it was good. But for real, we'll be okay. I honestly believe that. You're the best thing in my life, too, so I think if we can always remember that, we'll be fine. Listen, I know you like to plan everything and know exactly how things will play out. And on the show, I love it. It keeps us moving along like we're supposed to and reels me back in when I get us off topic when we're having fun.

"And I know that you not knowing what it's going to be like when we get home is a lot for you. I know that I'm usually mister throw-caution-to-the-wind and 'whatever happens, eh, it's fine'. But with this? With you and me and what we're doing here? I want it and I'm not throwing caution to the wind. I want it bad, Pearl. So I'm going to do whatever it takes to make sure it works. I've always fought for us on our show; I'll fight even harder for us in this, okay? I promise."

Nodding, she reaches up to grip my face. "Who knew you were such a romantic? That was pretty good. But you've always been good at talking me off the ledge. I'm sorry I'm still such a basket case."

"Gem, if you weren't freaking out, I'd be worried. But I'll always be there to talk you down. I promise. I've done it for ten years; I'm not about to stop now."

She gives me a soft smile and a quick kiss before reaching over to grab her body wash and squeezing some into her palm and rubbing her hands together. "I guess we better hurry. I'm kinda looking forward to that massage now. I was nervous before when I thought about us having to be naked under a sheet right next to each other. And I'm not quiet when I get massages. There's a lot of moaning when the masseuse gets to big knots and stuff." She gives me a smirk. "It almost sounds down right dirty, if I'm honest."

The thought of that spurs me into action. I grab my own soap and start lathering up. "Well, in that case, we better hustle. I'll happily hear you moan for an hour. I can't promise I won't drag you back in here before you have to go get your hair and makeup done and take advantage of you, but damn, Pearl, now I'm excited about this massage." She laughs and we wash up with only a few wandering hands and get ready for our massage.

When we get to the spa, an attendant gives us each a plush robe and shows us to a small changing room with some lockers for us to store our clothes. As we're getting undressed, I ask, "Do you have to get completely naked?"

She shrugs. "It's personal preference. I always leave my panties on, but I know a lot of people who go without."

I nod and decide to leave my boxers on since I don't know how I feel about someone who's not Gemma touching my bare ass. We pull on our robes and stow our clothes, and when we emerge from the locker room, two women in white scrubs are standing at the reception desk.

The taller of the two, a brunette who looks to be in her forties, with hands larger than mine, smiles at us. "Mr. and Mrs. Lincoln?" Gemma and I nod and her grin widens. "I'm Rhea." She gestures to her co-worker, a small blonde woman in her late twenties. "And this is Hope. We'll be your massage therapists today. If you'd like to follow us, we'll be happy to get started."

The two women turn and as Gemma and I follow, she loops her arm through mine. "I think you'll like this. I'd tell them to do light to medium pressure, though, since this is your first massage. Otherwise, you'll be really sore tomorrow." She looks up at me with a sly smile on her face. "And I don't want you really sore tomorrow."

I chuckle. "Noted. Any other pointers?"

She seems to consider. "You might fall asleep. Or fart. Things happen when you get really relaxed."

I can't bite back the bark of surprised laughter that escapes when Gemma mentions farting. "Well, I'll try not to do that."

She shrugs. "It happens; just saying."

"Well, now I'm going to be really tense trying *not* to fart. Thanks, Gem."

She laughs. "You'll be fine. Besides, I've heard you fart before. I've heard you do a lot worse than fart. We'll be okay."

I pull her into my side and kiss the top of her head. "You're not wrong, but I'll try," I say with a smile.

The women lead us out a set of doors to an open-air room that overlooks the ocean. Rhea gestures to the two massage tables. "We'll step out while you all get settled and relax." She closes a curtain and leaves Gemma and me alone in the small room.

"This is really nice. You don't even have to have any kind of nature sounds or anything since you can hear the ocean."

"So, what do I do; just drop the robe and lay face down?"

"Yeah, and pull the sheet up over your hips. You put your face in that hole at the end of the table and just relax. You'll like it."

I tug off my robe and lay it on a nearby chair and watch as Gemma does the same. She already seems relaxed, while all I want to do in this moment is crawl onto her table with her and make her moan myself. Instead, I crawl under the sheet on my own table and rest my arms by my side as I put my face in the hole.

A moment later, the massage therapists reenter the room and I see feet under the table. "Mr. Lincoln, are there any special areas you'd like me to focus on?" It's the smaller woman, Hope, whose voice I hear.

I'm honestly not sure what I'm supposed to say and I hear Gemma telling her masseuse to focus on her neck and shoulders. "No, I guess just all over? This is my first massage."

"Oh, sure. Okay. Do you have a preference for the amount of pressure you'd like, or do you know?"

"Light to medium?"

"Alright. And you have a choice of aromatherapy oils. There's one for relaxation which has lavender and sage. There's one for energy with citrus and bergamot. And there's one for revitalization that has eucalyptus and rosemary."

I consider. I know Gem hates lavender and I don't have a clue what bergamot is. "The revitalization one is fine."

"Yes, sir." I watch her feet disappear and a moment later, reappear. "I'll start on up here at your neck, but at anytime the pressure is not to your liking, please let me know."

"I will. Thank you." I feel fingers make sweeping motions up the sides of my neck and into my hair, and within minutes, I nearly melt into the table. I can't help but wonder how I've never done this before, because, shit, this is nice.

At least until the therapist gets down to my shoulders and apparently finds where every bit of tension in my body is housed. I never even knew I had any knots, but she manages to find them all. As her thumb kneads a particularly large one, I can't bite back a groan and I hear Gemma chuckle over at her table.

"Yeah, laugh it up over there," I quip with a grunt.

"I wondered how long you'd last before you made any noise. You actually lasted longer than I thought you would. Is it your shoulders?"

"Yeah. I guess all that being hunched over the console at work does actually affect things."

"Yep, that's why I go once a month to get a massage. I wouldn't be able to move if I didn't. We really should figure out how to get Curtis to wrangle us a sponsorship for monthly massages. At least get something *we* want out of this thing."

"There's a thought." My last word comes out with another groan and Gem chuckles.

My therapist asks, "You all work together?"

"Yeah, for ten years."

"Wow, and how long before you started dating?"

Gemma laughs and answers her question. "Actually, we never dated."

"But you all got married? This is your honeymoon, right?"

"Yes, we were at a conference in Vegas and there was a lot of alcohol and when we woke up, there were also rings."

Her surprise is evident in her tone. "Wow. So, what happened?" The other therapist seems to make some sort of disapproving noise, because my therapist says, "Sorry, it's none of my business."

I pipe up. "No, it's fine. Gem and I get paid to talk; we don't mind. We honestly don't know. We have a video from our wedding and we know we went to a casino to play craps and won some money, but it's all a blank."

"But you all decided to *stay* married? Don't most people annul things if they get married on a whim in Vegas?"

Gemma takes over. "We talked about it, but we're best friends. And honestly, that was the only reason we worried about things to begin with, but we've decided we're going to try to make it work. I could do a lot worse in life than Brew. He's my favorite person in the world. And we've always had good chemistry, even if we had never acted on anything in the past. You know, until now."

"Well, you two are very adorable together. And laughter is good. I hope you all are very happy together. Will you still be able to work together?"

I'm trying not to fall asleep, but Gem seems oddly energized. "Oh, yeah. We'd never give that up. Our working relationship is amazing. We play so well off each other, I think our listeners would riot if we split up."

"Listeners?"

"We're have a radio talk show."

"Oh, wow, that's cool."

"It can be. We meet a lot of interesting people and hear really great stories."

CHAPTER FIFTEEN

GEMMA

While I'm talking about the show, Brew starts snoring and I can't help but laugh. His therapist says, "Oh my, I think Mr. Lincoln has fallen asleep."

"Yeah, I told him that might happen. I'm glad he could relax enough to fall asleep. We're having pictures taken this evening, and I was worried he'd be tense."

"Pictures are good. It'll be good to have those memories when you get back home."

"Yeah, that's true."

And I know she's right. Brew and I don't have any memories of our wedding or even photos, so this will be nice to have. I smile thinking about hanging photos of us on the wall of Brew's house. *Our* house? I know we talked about me moving in with him right after all this happened, but I don't know if I can give up my place. What if things don't work out between Brew and me, regardless how much both of us want them to? He's convinced we can weather whatever pressures and obstacles come up, but the thought of the unknown terrifies me. Even if I know I'm in love with Brew.

That's scary, too. Not to say that I haven't been in love before, because I have. I loved Kyle, but this feels so different. It feels bigger somehow. And I don't know if that's only because there's a ring on my finger, or it's just because it's Brew. I suspect the latter. I want to believe him when he says he'll fight for us, because I know that's true. That's always been true. But I'm pretty sure this time, he can't be the only one fighting. I'll have to fight, too.

When my masseuse pulls the sheet up over my back and gives me a final pat, I know our hour is up. I'd zoned out for the last twenty minutes or so, but as she steps away, I come back to myself.

Once the therapists leave the room, I drag myself up to sitting and roll my shoulders. I step off the table and grab my robe, tying it around me before going over to Brew's table.

I bend to speak next to his ear. "Brew, it's time to wake up." He grunts and I press a kiss onto his shoulder blade. "Come on, husband, your massage is over. I have an hour before I need to be down at the salon. If we hurry, you can get me naked before I go down."

Brew pops his head up. "Did you say naked?"

I can't help but laugh. "Yeah, but we'll have to hurry."

He rolls to sitting and swings his legs over the side of his table. He pulls me between his knees and tugs at the belt of my robe. "And what if I don't want to hurry?" I try to keep the robe closed, but then Brew's hand slips inside to cup my breast.

"Brew, we can't do this here. There's not even an actual door and I'm sure they have other massages scheduled." But even to myself, my protests sound halfhearted at best.

Brew stands and turns me until he can set me on the edge of the table. He nudges my knees apart, steps between them, and plants one hand next to my hip. With his other, he grips the back of my neck as he drags his lips up my jaw, making my heart race.

"I don't really care, Pearl. What if I wanted you right here? Would you stop me?"

"You're dirty, Brew. You know that? I think you like the idea of people watching you. It's why you left the door open in the bathroom. Who knew you had an exhibition kink?"

His teeth graze my collarbone as he unties the belt of my robe and parts it in the front and continues to trail kisses down my chest. "Well, you liked watching, so what does that say about you, wife? You like to watch me do a lot of things, so I think you might have a voyeurism kink. Might have to see how far that goes."

I pull his face to mine and capture his mouth in a deep kiss. Brew wastes no time tugging my hips forward toward the edge of the table. His hand glides up my inner thigh and he runs a knuckle over the crotch of my panties. I inhale sharply as he presses against my clit and works it through the fabric.

"You want me, Pearl? Right here; where anyone can come in?" He lowers his mouth to my breast and I lean back on my hands and arch my back. His eyes stay on mine as he moves my panties to the side and slides two fingers into me, making me gasp. "I think you do want it, Gem. Otherwise, you wouldn't be this fucking wet. Jesus."

Brew's tongue swirls over my nipple and as he scrapes his teeth over it, I clamp my lips together to stifle my moan. He brings his face up to mine until our lips are only about an inch apart, close enough to share breath. His thumb works my clit as his fingers continue to work my pussy. "Tell me you want it, Gemma. Tell me you want your husband to fuck you on this table."

My breaths come out labored and I can only nod. Brew

gives me a smug smile as he applies more pressure to my clit, nearly making me gasp. "Say it, Gem."

"Please." I can barely get the word out as my climax threatens to break free.

He quirks a brow. "Please, what?"

More than a little frustrated, I nearly growl, "Fuck me, Brew. On this table. Please. Shit."

He withdraws his fingers and drags my panties down my hips so quickly, I'm sure I'll have some sort of burn from the fabric later. He drops his boxers just enough to free his cock as he gives me a triumphant smile. "That's all you had to say."

"You asshole. I—" He laughs and grips my hips and anything else I was planning to say dies in my throat as he slams into me. I can only let out a sharp cry.

I bring my hands up and slide my fingers into his hair and can only hang on as he sets a brutal pace. Brew braces his hand on the table next to me and claims my mouth, but when he nips at my bottom lip, I pull back. "No biting."

He chuckles, even while maintaining his impressive tempo. "You like it when I bite, Pearl."

"Not visible."

He gives me a wicked grin and his mouth lowers to my breast again. As he sinks his teeth into the fleshy mound, I inhale sharply. But after the sting, he presses a soft kiss to the quickly forming bruise before bringing his face back to mine. "I like seeing my marks on you. It lets me know you're mine."

I take his face in my hands, even as my pleasure builds and builds. "I am yours, Brew."

He lifts my leg and presses it back, driving himself deeper and I bite down on my lower lip to keep from crying out as my release claims me so suddenly, tears spring to my eyes.

Brew joins me after a few more powerful pumps of his hips

and his head falls to my shoulder with a low groan. "I'm yours, too, Gem."

After we allow ourselves just a few minutes to come down, we hurriedly clean up using the rumpled sheet on the table. I find my panties, slip them back on, and retie my robe as Brew slips his on. We make our way back to the locker room and quickly redress, with just enough time to grab a quick bite to eat before I have to be at the salon.

Brew walks me over and gives me a kiss before I go in. "What do you want to wear? I can make sure it's ready when you get back to the room."

I try to think. "One of those new sundresses I bought in Vegas? And you have a button-down, right?"

He nods. "Yeah, it's light blue."

"Okay, then I think the cream-colored one."

"Alright, I'll get it ironed for you."

"Thank you. You spoil me."

He takes my face in his hands. "I'm happy to spoil you, Pearl. Always. I'll be happy to keep spoiling you later tonight, too."

"Promises, promises. Alright, give me one more kiss so I can get all Curtis-afied."

He does and gives me a playful slap on the ass as I head into the salon.

A little over ninety minutes later, I'm coifed and made up to within an inch of my life. I know from some of the promo photoshoots Brew and I have done in the past, they do heavier makeup for photos since it shows up better, but I hate feeling like I have a mask on. I count the minutes until I can wash my face again. My hair is in large curls, just as Curtis requested, but it feels stiff from all the hairspray and I can't wait to wash it, either.

When I get back to our room, I knock on the door and Brew opens it, already dressed. As someone who is only ever casual, I never get used to seeing him in anything even close to dressed up. He's had to wear very few suits over the years since we've worked together, and only if we had to go to an awards dinner or something like that. It's definitely not his default to wear dress slacks and button-downs, but damn if he doesn't clean up good.

He's wearing what are probably the only dress pants he owns—a black pair—along with the light blue button-down he'd mentioned earlier. He has the sleeves rolled up to the elbow and he looks so handsome. His hair is the same as always, past his shoulders and light brown with a slight wave that gives him such great texture and volume, any woman who meets him is instantly jealous of his hair—me included. But he's trimmed his beard to a shorter, neater length.

"You look amazing, Brew."

He gives me a shy smile. "Thanks, Pearl. Your dress is hanging in the bathroom. I hope it's the right one. The photographer texted and she'll be here soon. We're supposed to meet her at the cabana."

I nod and hurry to change. Ten minutes later, I'm ready and slipping on a pair of earrings and a dainty gold chain necklace, but I'm having issues getting the clasp closed. Brew comes up behind me and takes it from me. Once he gets it fastened, he presses a kiss to my bare shoulder. "You look beautiful. As much shit as I gave Curtis for making us do these, I'm kinda glad we'll have them."

I turn to face him and wrap my arms around his neck. "Me, too. Maybe we can hang them up at your house."

Brew levels me with a gaze. "*Our* house, Gem. Although, if you'd prefer, we can live in your apartment."

I shake my head. "No, your house is a lot bigger. You have a yard. My apartment would be a definite down grade for you."

He grins. "Okay. Whatever you want." I don't tell him that in this moment, I want whatever he wants to give me; even if that's forever. His phone dings and he pulls it out of his pocket to read the screen. "That's the photographer. They're ready for us."

We'd promised Curtis a half-hour, but honestly, Brew and I were having a great time and the photographer was a sweetheart. We ended up lasting over an hour, ending the session only when we completely ran out of light. She promised to send us the link to a gallery so we'd have them and I smile, thinking about them hanging on our walls.

We ordered supper and decided on steaks to have with the wine we hadn't drunk the night before, along with a chocolate lava cake with ice cream. As we sit eating our dessert, I look at Brew. "You think we could consider this our wedding cake since we didn't get one in Vegas? I know we'll have that one when we get back home or whatever, but I like this one."

Brew smiles and nods. "Absolutely. Steak and wine and chocolate cake. I'm thinking it should be our anniversary dinner every year, too."

I can't help but return his smile. "I think I'd like that." He leans over to give me a kiss that tastes like chocolate and red wine.

"I can't believe we got married," I mutter. Brew brushes kisses along my neck as his hand slides up the outside of my thigh and under my dress to grab my ass.

"I can't believe they gave us this room. I can't believe we won fifty grand. Fuck, Gem, your ass is perfect."

Unable to stop myself from running my fingers through his hair, I drag his mouth to mine for a deep kiss as the elevator continues to climb. Short of breath a moment later, I ask, "Damn, Brew, where'd you learn to kiss like that?"

"I use my mouth for a living, Pearl. I'm happy to show you what else it can do." The elevator dings and we tumble out on our designated floor, kissing as we slowly make our way to the room the casino comped for us. When we finally get to our room, I stop at the door and put my hand on his chest. "What, Gem?"

"Are we really going to do this? You're not worried about our friendship?"

Brew takes my face in his hand as he unlocks the door. "No, Gemma, I'm not. I love you. It just took me ten years to see it." He tugs me into the room and presses me back against the door, his knee wedged between my thighs. He kisses me deeply and I trail my hands down his waist to settle on his hips.

He grinds himself into me and shit, he's huge. He pulls back and I see his face in the dim light spilling through the large window. "After I broke up with Alyssa and I went on all these dates, I would always wonder what you'd think of these women because if you didn't like them, I couldn't be with them. But then I started outright comparing them to you, Gem. Even that woman I had drinks with yesterday, I compared her to you.

"And I realized, none of them are you. None of them will ever be you. Which made me see it could only be you. I love you, Gemma. I know this was rash and impulsive and I know that's not who you are, but when you asked me, I wasn't about to say no to you. I'm so happy you're my wife."

I wake with a start, noticing that it's still dark, so I roll over to curl up next to Brew. *I asked him?* Well, I'll be damned. Why would I have done that? Not that I care, because I'm here with Brew and I'm happy, but I can't help but wonder what led up to *me* asking *him*. We both assumed that this was his idea, since impulsivity is pretty much written in Brew's DNA, but I almost want to laugh.

And then another thought hits me: Brew told me he loved me that night. I'm almost giddy with it. Brew loves me. But he doesn't remember saying it, so I don't want to tell him. Not that I don't think he'd believe me if I tell him he said it, but because I want him to remember that he's said it if he tells me again.

How do we not sound drunk, though? We weren't slurring our words or stumbling around or anything. And I know from our last night in Vegas, after only a few glasses of wine, Brew had to practically carry me to our room. Neither one of us does drugs. Well, maybe a little pot every once in a while, but not hard drugs.

Is it possible we did that night, though, and that's why we don't remember anything? Not that it's going to change anything, but I'd still like to know how everything transpired. And yeah, we were both hungover, but now that I think back on it, I didn't really have any of my normal hangover symptoms like I normally do. I had a headache and was nauseated, but I didn't feel as dehydrated as I normally do and I've never, in my entire life been so drunk that I don't remember *anything* from the night before when I wake up the next morning. I've never lost huge chunks of time before.

I know we might never know, but I'll will probably always wonder; even if I'll never be sorry.

Because apparently, I'm the one who proposed.

In truth, I am deliriously happy and so in love I can't stand it. I snuggle closer to my husband and even in his sleep, he pulls me tighter against him. I breathe in his familiar scent as I drift back off.

CHAPTER SIXTEEN

BREWSTER

Gemma is still out when I wake up. Secretly thrilled, because she's almost always awake before me, but vacation Gem must like her sleep. She's lying on her stomach, her face turned toward me, her hair falling over her bare shoulder. Her left hand rests next to her face and a pang of possessiveness settles in my gut seeing her wedding ring; knowing that she's mine. I'm nowhere near the content creator that Gem is, but I can't resist grabbing my phone and taking a photo of her like this.

Once I snap the picture, I put away my phone and get up to go pee and brush my teeth. I'm struck with the thought that we only have a few more days left here before we have to go home and back to reality. I was truthful when I told Gemma that I'll always fight for us. I'm never giving her up; I couldn't if I tried. I'm so in love with her, I would be irreparably damaged if something were to happen to what we've got going on—our marriage.

Marriage.

It's still such a foreign word, but it feels right when I think about being married to Gemma. I want to be married to her forever and if I have any say in it, I will be.

When I come back to the bedroom, Gem has rolled onto her side and the covers are down below her tits. Seeing her like this instantly makes my dick harden, especially when I see the bite mark I left on her breast.

I crawl back into bed and curl up behind her, pushing her hair off her shoulder. I brush kisses down her neck and even in her sleep, she tilts her head to give me better access and I can't help but smile.

I trail my fingers down her arm and I lift our left hands and examine them side by side. I can't help but wonder if Gemma feels that same possessiveness I do when I see these rings. She curls her hand around mine and brings it around her waist as she wiggles her ass against me as she stirs.

"Morning, wife," I say as I nip under her ear.

"Hmmm. Morning, husband." Her voice is husky from sleep. And not that her normal voice isn't sexy, because, duh, she works in radio and has this textured and raspy kind of voice that everyone compliments her on. But her sleepy voice is a whole other level of sexiness and it hits me as just another thing that only I will get to hear from now on. That thought makes warmth spreads through my chest.

"I love the way you sound when you wake up. Your voice is so fucking sexy, Pearl."

She chuckles. "I'm glad you think so. I'm gonna go brush my teeth." She starts to get up and I hold her still.

"Don't you dare move from this spot."

She raises my hand and presses a kiss to my palm. "I have to pee, and then I'll happily let you seduce me before breakfast."

I groan and release her. "If you must." She laughs and I watch her walk naked into the bathroom.

When she emerges, she crawls under the covers and retakes her place as the little spoon. She trails her fingertips down my thigh before bringing my hand to place it low on her abdomen.

I return to kissing her neck while running my hand over to her hip and down the outside of her leg before moving to the inside of her knee and slowly sliding my fingers up her thigh.

"Guess what?"

"Hmm?"

"I remembered something else." Gemma turns her head toward me and I stop moving my hand.

"What's that?"

She bites her bottom lip. "I proposed to you."

My eyebrows rise in surprise. "What?"

She nods. "Yeah. I don't remember doing it, but when we were in the elevator on our way up to the room, we were making out and stuff and I said I couldn't believe we'd gotten married. You said you couldn't believe we'd won all that money or that the casino comped our room.

"When we got to our room, I asked if we were really going to do this and I asked you if you were worried about our friendship." She rolls on to her back and stretches her neck from having to look at me over her shoulder. "You said you weren't worried. You said that you knew it was rash and impulsive and that you knew that wasn't who I am, but when I asked you, you weren't about to say no."

I can't help the laugh that escapes me. "Well, I'll be damned."

She laughs. "That's what I thought when I woke up. So, totally not your fault. It was all me. I got us into this. I've never done anything remotely exciting in my life and I proposed to you. And you said yes, Brew."

I nod. "Yeah, I did. I'm pretty sure I was already thinking about asking you out, though, once we got back from Vegas. Although, I was terrified about it."

She bites her lip and rolls to face me. "You were?"

"Yeah. After I broke up with Alyssa, I went on some dates,

even though I didn't really want to. And I knew with each one of them that you wouldn't like them, so I couldn't like them." She laughs and I quirk a brow and continue, "Packaged deal, isn't that what you said?" She nods. "Yeah, so since none of those women passed the Gemma test in my mind, they didn't even warrant a second date, let alone a trip to pound town."

Gemma rolls her eyes. "Seriously, Brew? How old are you?"

I can't help but laugh as I press a kiss to her lips and settle my hand on her hip. "But anyway, the more dates I went on, the more I started just comparing the women to you, not just as far as if you'd like them, but you as a person. One would say something and it was funny, but it wasn't funny like you're funny. Or they'd choose something for supper and it wasn't something that I'd be okay with sharing and I didn't like that, because I love how we split food. And even their looks. Their hair wasn't as shiny as yours or their lips weren't as pretty as yours. And then I flat out realized that none of them are you, Gem. No one is ever going to be you."

She lays her forehead on my chest and presses kisses into my pecs. After a moment, she seems to consider something else and her head pops up, her expression serious. "Did your hangover seem weird to you?"

I furrow my brow in confusion. "What do you mean? We were hungover as shit."

She nods. "Yeah, but did it seem like your normal hangovers, or did it seem like your symptoms were different?"

I'm totally thrown by her question. "I don't know, why?"

"We lost an entire night, Brew. Both of us. Does that not seem strange to you?"

I shrug. "I mean, I don't know; I've had some pretty hazy nights before."

"Yeah, hazy, but not *gone*. And I know I keep getting

flashes, but why, if we were so drunk, do we not seem drunk? We seem entirely coherent in my flashes. In the video from the wedding, we both seem completely sober. If we had nearly as much to drink as we think we did, there's no way I'd even be upright, let alone able to say vows and sign a license. I also don't think I would've been able to get off that night, but I did. When I'm drunk, I can't orgasm, but I did that night."

"So, what are you saying, Gem; you think we took some kind of drugs? We don't do drugs."

"I know. But I don't know, maybe. It doesn't matter; it just bugs me."

"Even if we did, if it was something recreational, like molly or something, I don't know that it would account for memory loss. And neither one of us was super dehydrated or anything. If you want, we can go get drug tested, but I don't know if anything would even show up. I think most club drugs have such a short half-life, they're metabolized so quickly. And honestly, I can't see us taking drugs. It's just not us."

She nods. "I know. Like I said, it just irks me, is all. It doesn't change anything; I just hate not knowing how we got from point A to point B."

"I know. Maybe one day, all these flashes you have will equate to an entire picture. And maybe if that guy comes through with the footage, it'll fill in some of the blanks, too."

I reach over to the nightstand and pick up my phone. "What are you doing?"

"I'm going to check my email to see if that casino guy sent me anything."

She takes my phone out of my hand and puts it back on the nightstand and levels me with a gaze as she straddles me. "No, you're not. If you start checking emails, you'll go through them all. I know you, Brewster Lincoln. You can't stand to have unread emails. And right now, you have a naked wife who needs your attention more. If that guy sent anything, it'll still be there on Monday when we get home. We're on our honeymoon, remember? We've tied up all the loose ends Curtis assigned us, so I expect you to treat this vacation with the respect it deserves. And that means you don't check your email."

I rest my hands on her hips. "Yes, ma'am. I really do like calling you my wife, you know that?"

She nods and guides my hands up to her breasts. "And I really enjoy calling you my husband." She braces one hand beside my head and grips my face with her other. "And I'm really, *really* happy I asked you to marry me."

"Me, too, Pearl." I run my thumbs over her nipples and they rise to my touch. My cock jerks, already painfully hard with Gemma's pussy so close and hot.

She lowers her mouth to mine, kisses. me and tugs my bottom lip between her teeth. I pull back. "You said no biting."

She shrugs. "I figured you were owed." She gives me a slow smile. "Honestly, I think you're owed a lot." My wife lowers her mouth to my chest and trails her lips down the valley between my pecs. She tugs my skin between her teeth as she makes her descent and the sting is enough to make me hiss, but my eyes don't leave hers.

I let out a soft groan when her pussy slots over my cock as she continues kissing her way down my stomach and she kneels between my legs. She plants a kiss on both of my hips before running her hands slowly up my thighs. My heart is pounding with anticipation, especially as her eyes land on my dick. She smiles as she lowers her mouth to the head of my cock and licks the bead of pre-cum off the tip.

I blow out a steadying breath and curl my fists into the sheets as Gemma drags her tongue down the side of my shaft and comes back up to flick the underside before closing her lips around the head and sucking and swirling her tongue around it. "Fuck, Gem."

She chuckles and my hips buck, but I manage to hold back enough to not gag her. Her hand comes to work the shaft and my head falls back on the bed as I try to concentrate on not finishing. She raises her head and when I snap my head up to look at her, her smile is smug.

"No, Brew, watch. Watch your wife suck your cock. And I'm not cruel like you. You can move your hips," she says with a quirked brow.

I watch as her mouth lowers back around my cock and her eyes are there. I see now what she meant about not being able to make eye contact at work from now on, because I'm only going to be able to think about this, too. I give my hips a small shove forward and Gemma's eyes seem to almost smile.

Fuck, my wife is dirty.

She brings her free hand to one of mine and guides it to her hair and I nearly come right then; especially when she lifts that brow again. "You want me to fuck your mouth?" She gives me a tiny nod. "You going to swallow me down like a good girl?" Again with that tiny nod. It's enough to make my balls draw up.

I slip my fingers into Gem's hair and her eyes close as I hold her head in place. I slowly push my hips up, allowing her to get used to my size. "Open your eyes, Gem. Watch me take your mouth. You should see what you look like. So fucking perfect." When she makes a small gagging noise, I make a mental note to not go deeper and pull out to the tip before driving back in.

Her eyes still don't leave mine and I can feel myself growing closer, that tale-tell tingle beginning at the base of my spine and my breathing becomes more and more labored. "I'm close, Pearl." And again, her eyes smile and I let go with a final buck of my hips and a low grunt. Gemma grips my thighs as she swallows me down before slowly pulling off my cock and kissing her way back up my stomach and chest.

I grab her face and pull her mouth to mine, giving her a deep kiss as I roll us over until she's on her back and I look down into her eyes. "My turn," I say with a smile. She huffs a soft laugh as I trail kisses down her neck and she slides her fingers into my hair as my mouth makes its way to her breasts. I swirl my tongue around one nipple and then the other before nipping and sucking them both until they're pulled to stiff peaks and Gemma is panting.

I continue kissing down her stomach and sink my teeth into her hip and she gasps, "Brew!"

"Sorry, Gem; you just taste too good. I can't get enough."

She pulls my hair until I lift my head to look at her. "That's not where I taste good."

I shake my head. "You taste good everywhere, Pearl. I'll prove it." I tug her hips farther down the bed and put her knees over my shoulders. I flatten my tongue against her pussy, licking a hard line up to her clit and fuck yes, she tastes good. When my teeth close over her clit, she hisses until I draw it between my lips, soothing the sting with the flick of my tongue.

I suck her swollen clit until Gemma's breathing grows more and more shallow. She holds my head in place and grinds her hips against my face and I let her use me. All of me. My nose and lips and tongue. And I'll be damned if I'm not already getting hard again as she shudders and lets out a ragged sob, her head falls back onto the pillow. I gentle my movements and brush kisses down her thighs before coming up to her face.

My cock nudges at her entrance and her eyes pop open. "You're hard again?"

I nod. "You want it?"

She huffs a laugh. "Is that even a question? Of course I do." She sits up. "But I want on top."

"As if I'd ever say no to that." I roll onto my back and Gemma rises onto her knees to straddle me. I grip her hip with one hand and hold my cock with the other as she lowers herself down my shaft.

"Fuck, Brew, you feel good," she rasps and shifts her hips until I'm sunk to the base. Her pussy pulses around me and I have to take some calming breaths. She rolls her hips and I just watch her for a moment, so struck by how beautiful she is. Her cheeks and chest are flushed and her teeth are clamped down on her bottom lip and a line of concentration has formed between her brows. Her nipples are pebbled and I can't resist dragging my hand up her waist to cup her breast. And because I can't not take her, even if she is on top, I grip her waist, my thumb and fingers digging in as I thrust my hips up into her.

She gasps and braces her hands behind her on my thighs. I buck my hips again and she lets out a deep moan as she moves against me. I bring my hand back down her waist to thumb her clit as I continue driving up into her. "So fucking perfect, Gemma. I want to see you come for me. I want you to make a mess of me."

Sweat rolls down my forehead and chest as I continue my relentless pace even as Gem's breathing sounds more like stilted, short rasps. I know when she stops moving on top of me and her mouth falls open and her pussy clenches so tight I think I might die, she's spent.

I pull out quickly and roll us until I'm on top and drive into her once more. "Brew, shit," she says with a gasp. I pull her left leg up and rest her calf on my shoulder as I pump into her.

She pulls my face to hers and I press her knee back farther as my hips slam against her. Her hands are in my hair and she huffs into our kiss. I rest my forehead to hers as grow closer and closer to my release. "So good. So fucking good, Gem."

"Don't stop Brew, I'm so close."

"Come with me. Please. Fuck. Can't hold off."

She reaches between us to work her clit and a moment later, she clenches around me again and cries out. I finally, thank fuck, give myself permission to let go and as I do, it's with a near growl as my hips buck one final time.

My ears pops and my chest hurts from my ragged breathing and I'm pretty sure my abs will never stop cramping. I can only collapse next to Gemma, entirely spent. The last thing I say before I'm pretty sure I pass out is, "I think you're trying to kill me, wife."

CHAPTER SEVENTEEN

GEMMA

Brewster is out about three seconds after he pulls out, and I can't stop myself from laughing when he accuses me of trying to kill him. I'm pretty sure he's trying to kill me, too, but I'm not about to complain about it. I just lie and watch him sleep for a while and I can't get over how in love with him I am. Yeah, I know I'm probably on some kind of sex-addled high, but I don't care. And I know it probably won't always be this hot, but, then again, maybe it will.

After a little while longer, I drag myself out of bed and to the bathroom. I pee, then start the shower and examine my reflection in the mirror. I'm awash in bite marks again, but at least this batch is in more inconspicuous places. Honestly, though, I don't mind. I like that Brew leaves his mark on me.

Once the shower is hot, I take my braid down and run my fingers through my hair before stepping under the spray. After getting clean, I just stand under the water until the growling in my stomach makes me cut off the shower and hurriedly dry off. I slather on some face and body lotion and pull on some panties and a bra, along with a pair of shorts and a tank top.

I glance at the clock on the nightstand and see that it's after eleven, so I open the room service menu to see that they have a mixed brunch that includes pastries, breakfast meats and fruits, along with coffee and mimosas and I pick up the room phone to place the order.

Once I hang up with the resort kitchen, I take a moment to pick up mine and Brew's dirty clothes and fold them and stack them next to our suitcases. I make a mental note to see if the resort offers laundry service, so that's one less thing we have to do when we get home.

Home.

The thought makes me smile. I'm struck with a thought and as I make myself a cup of coffee, I call Augusta.

"Well, she is alive," she says when she answers. "How's the honeymoon? Are things weird?"

"Nope, not weird," I say.

She must hear something in my tone, because she gasps. "Oh, my God. You two have totally boned. So, was it as good as you remember from those flashes?"

"God, Auggie, it's amazing."

She laughs with blatant glee. "Wow. Okay, I want to hear everything. Spare no details because I'm in dire need of some action, even if it's vicarious. Where is he right now?"

"Sleeping."

"What, he's not been up yet? Damn, I knew he wasn't a morning person, but come on."

"No, he's been up. A couple of times," I reply with obvious innuendo. I step out to the deck so I won't wake Brew in the event he's not sleeping that deeply—even if I'm pretty sure he's dead to the world—but leave the door cracked so I can hear the room service delivery.

"Twice? You're kidding. You mean at, like, seven this morning and then again at ten, right?"

I huff a small laugh. "No. I mean that I gave him head and then when he was returning the favor, he was ready to go again."

"Holy shit. Who knew he had it in him? So, other than that, how are things?"

"I love him, Augusta, and I'm the one who proposed."

Her inhale is sharp. "Okay, so that's a lot of information in one sentence. You *love* him? When did that happen?"

"Maybe I always have. He's my person. I've always loved him as a friend, you know that. And the leap from platonic to romantic isn't as far as one might think. Especially when the sex is as good as this. But, for real, I knew the other day. We were about to get naked and I still had my panties on and I wanted him to just hurry and rip them off, but he seemed like he was needing to take a minute. He said that I was already more beautiful than he could've ever imagined and he needed to brace himself because he wanted to remember this forever. And I just knew."

Augusta lets out a slow breath on the other end of the line. "Damn, he's good. Okay, so what about the proposal? I thought y'all didn't remember any of that?"

I go through my memory dream and the part about me proposing, but leave out the part where Brew told me he loves me, because I want to keep that just for me, but when I get done with the story, she laughs. "Wow. That's something."

"Tell me about it. Alright, so I had another reason for my call other than just to gloat about fantastic sex with my insanely sexy husband."

"You've officially crossed into disgustingly gross and in love, but what is it? I can tell by your tone that you need a favor, so you can consider it your wedding gift, whatever it is."

"It's a big ask. Are you sure? You don't even know what it is."

"Okay then, tell me."

"I was going to see if you could pack up my apartment, at least the clothes and bathroom stuff. I don't know what else I'll need for Brew's house, but I still haven't given notice at my apartment, so I have time to figure out what else I'll want."

"Whoa. That's... You're going to give up your place? Are you sure about that?"

"Well, even if Brew and I hadn't decided we were going to try and make this work, we were going to have to live together for a at least few months until all the publicity died down. But we are going to make this work, so I need my stuff. Brew's place is a lot bigger than mine and he has a yard, so it just makes sense. So, will you do it?"

"Yeah, of course. Just the clothes and bathroom?"

"Yeah. And just let me know how much I owe you for the boxes and stuff and I'll Venmo you."

"Okay. I'm guessing you want this done before you get back to town on Monday?"

"That would be amazing. If you can just pack the stuff, Brew and I will come by and get it. You are the best." Hearing a knock sound from the front of the room, I walk back inside and make my way toward the door. "Alright, well, food is here, so I have to go. I want to see you when we get back, but my schedule is going to be really crazy with work and all this reception shit that Curtis is making us do."

"Sure, just call me, okay?"

"Will do." I disconnect the call and open the door, rolling the cart into the room before shutting it back. I pull it over next to the couch and go to the bed and brush Brew's hair off his face. "Brew, honey. Breakfast."

I press a kiss to his cheek and he stirs, but doesn't open his eyes. "Yeah, Pearl?"

"Breakfast, husband. There's danish. And coffee."

"Okay. Give me about four years. I'm pretty sure it's gonna take me that long to recover from you. I promise, I don't have a lot of life insurance. I'm worth more to you alive than dead, so your career as a black widow is off to a sorry start."

A soft laugh falls from my mouth. "Trust me, I know how much money you make. And besides, your dick is no good to me if you're dead, so it's in my best interest to keep you alive."

He slowly drags himself up to a sitting position. "How are you so awake?" He rubs his eyes with the heels of his hands and yawns.

"I had a shower. It was pretty refreshing. You should try it."

"No, I need coffee. And food. And a kiss."

I grin. "In that order?"

He shakes his head as he pulls me down on the bed and covers my mouth with his. Despite how tired and sore I am from the past few days, desire instantly spreads through my middle. I break our kiss. "Alright. Now then. Coffee or food?"

He stretches his arms over his head and his face blanches. "Nope. Totally a shower first. Damn."

I laugh and give him a swat on the ass as he heads to the bathroom. Ten minutes later, he emerges with a towel wrapped around his waist. He pulls a pair of boxers and shorts from his bag and slips them on before tugging a T-shirt over his head and rubbing his hair with a towel.

I take the metal domes off the food and he smiles. "You didn't have to wait on me; I know you have to be starving."

I shrug. "It's fine. You can make yourself useful, though, and open that champagne so I can make a mimosa."

He nods and deftly pops the cork on the bottle and pours me a drink. I set about making us each a plate with a danish, some fruit, and bacon and sausage. Brew pours himself a cup of coffee and brings both or our drinks over as we sit on the couch.

We dig into our food and I sip my drink. "I talked to Augusta this morning."

He nods. "What did she have to say about all of our amazing sex?"

I roll my eyes. "How do you know we even talked about sex?"

He quirks a brow. "Because I've heard you and Augusta talk before. You're very happy to talk to her about the good and bad of your sex life. I'm not assuming that I'm exempt from that."

"Okay, well, I might have told her you are a wild sex god who I can't get enough of."

He laughs. "Alright, I can live with that."

"I also asked her to pack up my clothes and bathroom stuff at my apartment. She's going to box it all up and we'll just need to go by and get them."

His brows rise in surprise. "Really?"

I nod. "Is that okay? I probably should've talked with you before I did it; it just hit me and I thought it would be nice to have my stuff when we got home. With all the stuff we're going to be forced to do before this reception thing, I don't think I'll have a lot of time to pack up, so—"

He puts his hand on my arm to cut me off and gives me a wide grin. "Pearl, that's perfect. I can't wait to have your stuff and my stuff all together. I know it'll be a huge adjustment for both of us, but I'm good. And if you want to use any of your furniture instead of what I've got, we can totally figure that out. I know your taste is a lot different from mine."

I lean over and give him a kiss. "Okay." We continue to eat and drink and as we're finishing up and piling the dishes back onto the cart, Brew's phone rings. "Go ahead, I'll put this back outside."

He walks over to the nightstand and I hear him sigh, but it's not the same one that he usually has when it's Curtis, so I don't think it's him. I push the cart out the front door and hear Brew answer the call. "Hey, Dad."

I sigh because I know he'll probably be in a sour mood for at least a little while when he wraps up the call with his father. My relationship with my parents is complicated to say the least, but Brew's is on a whole other level. He and his brother spent most of their childhood with their grandmother because both of their parents worked so much.

They were older when Brew was born, both already in their mid-forties, and I think by then, they were just tired. They thought Lawson would be an only child and when Brew came along, they'd decided they weren't really invested in raising another child.

They worked and provided, but they were absent, and Brew and Lawson were at their grandma's almost all the time. They retired when Brew was in high school and then decided to travel the country full-time in an RV, leaving Lawson to essentially parent his younger brother.

They're not my favorite people for a myriad of reasons, least of all the fact that they basically abandoned Brew during his formative years. And God knows he tries with them, but they're around so little, I don't know that they even know him as a person, but still expect him to live up to their expectations; regardless of the fact that he's thirty-three years old. They consider a job in radio to be low-class work; especially since Brew has a degree in broadcast journalism and could work in TV if he wanted, but he doesn't want that.

I watch as he paces, his expression tense. So far, he's said very little, his father obviously opting to do most of the talking. "No, Dad, it wasn't a publicity stunt. Gemma and I are really married. Happily so... I hardly think that marrying my best friend of ten years constitutes jumping into things." He laughs, but it's bitter. His brow furrows as he drags his hand through his hair. "Yes, we're doing the reception. It's in three weeks; will y'all be in town?"

A muscle tics in his jaw and he nods."Okay, well we'll probably need an accurate headcount, so if you could let me know, that'd be great... No, I don't need you to hook me up with that guy at CNN. I'm very satisfied with my job... Yeah, because money is the most important thing. Gemma and I have a great show... Of course we're still going to work together..."

He hangs his head, and I come over to wrap my arms around his waist. He pulls me against him and rests his chin on the top of my head. He seems to relax a little; even as his father continues to drone on.

"You know what, Dad? I can't do this right now. I appreciate you calling to congratulate me on getting married... Well, you should have; I'm your son. I'm not a kid and I'm capable of making my own decisions. I chose to marry Gemma. You can get behind that or you can just not see your future grandkids... No, Dad, she's not pregnant. Jesus. But I'm sure we'll probably have kids someday."

I chuckle against Brew's chest, and he presses another kiss to the top of my head. "Dad, I have to go. I'm supposed to be enjoying my honeymoon... We're at a resort in the keys." He stands up straighter. "I don't know; I'd have to talk to Gemma... Monday... Alright, I'll let you know. Bye." He disconnects the call and tosses his phone onto the bed. For a long time, we don't move and he just wraps his arms tighter around me.

"You threatened your dad with not seeing our hypothetical children?"

He snorts a laugh. "Yeah, well, you use what tools are at your disposal. As shitty as they are as parents, they love Law's kids like crazy and are wonderful grandparents. They Face-

Time them all the time and take them on weeks-long excursions in the RV during the summer."

"Well, I don't know if I'd want that for our kids. That's a lot of time away from us."

He laughs. "Okay. Maybe just weekend trips. You know, so we can have really loud animal sex." I jab him playfully and he grabs my hand, brings it to his mouth, and kisses my palm. He sighs. "My parents are in Key West. They want us to meet them for dinner."

I look up at him. "Really?"

He nods. "We don't have to go, but if we don't, it'll just be one more thing they'll hold on to and throw back in my face whenever they feel like they need ammo for something."

"Okay, well, we can go. Not that I really like the thought of leaving this room, but for you, I'll brave it."

He presses a kiss to my forehead. "Thanks, wife."

"Anytime, husband. Although, if they give you shit, I will lose it. As much as you stand up for me and us, you don't stand up to them like you should. You let your dad steamroll you a lot of the time, and I'm not about to put up with it."

"Ooh, fierce Gemma. Been a while since she made an appearance. Okay."

"I just don't like the people I care about being hurt. And I don't know if you know this, but I care about you an awful lot."

He grips my jaw. "I care about you an awful lot, too, Pearl."

I give him a soft smile. "Okay, so let's do it tonight if they're available. Get it over with. I swear, every time I think we'll just get to relax and enjoy ourselves, something else pops up. And I don't really feel like having this hanging over us. You're already going to be in a bad mood for a while after you see them."

He quirks a brow. "What makes you say that?"

I scoff. "History, dear husband. I always dread when your parents are in town because you have lunch with them and then we have to do the show and you're always a little off your game because of them. So, I'd rather your bad mood be confined to this one day. Maybe when we get back, I can help you come out of it faster." I wiggle my eyebrows and he chuckles.

He finally sighs and presses a kiss to my lips. "Okay. But I can already tell you that now that you're family, you won't be exempt from their judgement."

I roll my eyes. "Oh, please. I have a very traditional, Italian, catholic mother. She makes judgement an art form. I ain't scared of the WASPy likes of Sandy and Delilah Lincoln."

He laughs. "True. Alright. At least we know the food will be good. My parents are nothing if not consummate foodies."

CHAPTER EIGHTEEN

BREWSTER

I'm anxious the entire two-hour drive from our resort to the restaurant my parents picked in Key West, and Gemma can tell. She takes my hand in hers like it's something we've always done and brings it to her face and kisses my palm. As if, until a few days ago, we weren't only friends, and this type of casual intimacy was entirely foreign to us. But I love it. I love how easy this transition has been. Not that I don't think we'll have growing pains at some point; I know we will. But for now, I'm enjoying the ease.

When I sigh and drag my fingers through my hair for what seems like the hundredth time since we got in the car, Gemma squeezes my hand. Hard. "Ouch, Pearl."

"Well, if you keep doing that, you're going to pull all your hair out and I really like your hair. So stop it. You're going to be fine. We'll eat. We'll weather their pointed questions. We'll come back to the resort and I'll let you get me naked. It's one night, Brew. If you want, I can be designated driver so you can drink and not have to worry about getting drunk."

I shake my head. "If I get drunk, I won't be able to get it up later and I'd much rather fuck you than get drunk."

She rolls her eyes and laughs.

"Okay, see, that, too," she says after a moment, her tone inquisitive.

"What?"

"You just said if you got really drunk, you can't get it up. You didn't have any trouble on our wedding night, so how could you have been really drunk? I'm really beginning to think we must have taken some drugs or something; even if it's not something we'd ever normally do."

I hadn't thought about that before and she's right. I know myself. If I have more than a buzz when I try to have sex, I can't perform, so her drug theory is starting to make more sense. "Maybe. But I just don't see it. Especially not you. I can barely ever even get you to smoke a joint with me."

"That's because pot makes me paranoid. Not because I don't like it."

"Okay, I'll remember that. But I don't know how we'd find out. Like I said, I don't think anything would still show up on a drug screen after all these days."

She shrugs. "I don't know, either, but it's probably always gonna bug me. You know I don't like mystery; it stresses me out. It's the reason I can't watch whodunnits. I get so caught up in trying to figure out the mystery, I can't enjoy the show or movie."

I can't help but laugh. "Yeah, I know. When we get home, I'll see if we got the video footage from the casino. If, and that's a big, huge *if*, we took anything, it had to have been while we were at the craps table, since we remember everything up to that point, right?"

She nods. "Yeah. Okay. But for real, we're going to be fine

tonight. I'll turn on my sweet side and your parents will love us together. They've only ever seen us as friends with all of our goofy shenanigans. They've never seen us all gross and lovey-dovey."

"True, and you look very beautiful tonight. We both know my dad is nothing if not charming to the ladies, so I'm sure he'll turn it on for you. And I'm sure Mom will already be buzzed, so she'll be pretty sweet, too."

The GPS alerts me to turn onto the next road and we pull in at the oceanfront seafood restaurant a few minutes later. When I park, Gemma pulls the mirror down and applies some lipstick. I'm again struck by how beautiful she is. And she's mine. Every bit of her. I love it. And I love her.

I step out of the car and walk around to her side to open her door. When she exits, I take her hand in mine and we walk toward the restaurant. Once inside, I check with the hostess, who tells us that my parents are already seated and leads us out to a deck overlooking the water.

My parents stand when we get to the table and I shake my father's hand and give my mother a kiss on the cheek. Sure enough, she's already hitting the rum, and I brace myself for the evening. Gemma greets my parents the same as she always has, with a sweet smile and a kiss on their cheeks. I hold her chair for her and sit after she's scooted in. My father doesn't waste any time before starting in on us with questions. We haven't even ordered drinks yet, and he's demanding to know how we ended up married in the first place.

"Well, Dad, Gemma asked, and I said yes."

My mother sips her rum and Diet Coke. "Oh. How... Modern."

Gemma gives them both a syrupy smile. "I couldn't help myself. I mean, just look at him. He's so handsome and sweet, I can't imagine feeling for anyone what I feel for Brewster. Your son is an amazing man." I take her hand under the table and give it a squeeze.

A server comes by to take Gem's and my drink orders and once we have our glasses of wine, my father asks, "So, I take it you didn't confirm with your human resources department that something like this is even approved with the station before you jumped into this?"

"No, we didn't, but our production manager was thrilled, actually."

"Is that why they're throwing you this big party? And is it truly all sponsored? A bit tasteless, if you ask me." His tone drips with disdain and Gem squeezes my hand to remind me to think before I speak.

"Well, to be honest, if we had our way, we wouldn't have anything this flashy, but Gemma's parents were already going to have a party for us and just with her family alone it would've been a pretty big thing, so this isn't much different. We just don't have to pay for any of it. Which is pretty nice, if you ask me."

My mother finally steps into the conversation. "So, you're just content to take all these things, no strings attached? Did they also pay for this honeymoon you're on?"

I nod and take a sip of my wine and Gemma jumps in. "It's pretty common, actually. Not to this degree, of course, but we get perks from sponsors all the time in exchange for promos or doing live remotes and stuff like that. This is definitely the largest perk we've ever gotten, but I'm not going to complain. There's no way we could've afforded something like this on our salaries, so we're actually really enjoying ourselves. Granted, it's been more of a working vacation for the past few days, but we're hopeful the rest of the trip will be relaxing for us."

My father sips his beer. "Well, it seems to me that you all

did this just for the publicity. Everyone knows you all have this great working relationship with some pretty great banter and stuff. What better way to increase your chances of syndication than a viral wedding video and big reception? I know that's something you two have been working towards. But to get married just to get ahead? That's pretty tacky, son."

I feel my jaw clench and I level my father with a stony glare. "Dad, hear me when I say this. Gemma and I may have made the impulsive decision to get married, but it was never with any ulterior motives or anything remotely related to our careers. We got married because we wanted to. No other reason. And we are very happy. So, I would appreciate it if you'd get on board with that. It's not as though I married someone I've known for two weeks. This is Gemma. I've known her for ten years. She is my best friend and I love her.

"We have no illusions that things are going to be easy, but we've weathered a lot just as friends and I'm sure we'll figure this out, too. We've always made a good team and I don't see that changing just because I put a ring on her finger. If anything, it's even more reason for us to be on each other's side. And anyone who can't support us doesn't have to be a part of our lives."

I certainly didn't mean to tell my parents I love Gemma before I've even told her, but I was on a roll, I guess, and she doesn't react. I'm not sure how to take that, but I can think about it later.

My father simply nods and sips his beer. "Alright, son. Well, how about you let your mother and me buy you all supper to celebrate?" He looks at Gemma. "Gemma, welcome to the family. I always wondered when Brewster would pull his head out of his ass and finally recognize what a good thing he had right in front of him. And we'll be at your reception. We wouldn't miss it."

Gemma snorts a shocked laugh and my mouth falls open and my father turns back to me. "What, son, surprised? I've seen this coming for years, but I honestly thought you'd never step up and it was one of those things your sleazy production manager put you up to. I'm glad to hear I was wrong. Congratulations."

My mother looks from Gemma to me. "I hope this means you won't keep any future grandchildren from us?"

Gemma laughs. "No, ma'am, we promise."

It's after midnight by the time we make it back to the resort. I can't deny that I'm pleasantly shocked by the things my father said. We ended up having a very pleasant meal with my parents; which was a surprise in itself. Granted, Gemma was there, and she's good with people and knows exactly how to turn on the charm.

As we walk into the room, she slips off her heels and tucks them into her suitcase. She struggles to get the zipper on her dress down, so I come up behind her and tug it free, brushing a kiss onto the back of her neck. I watch her walk into the bathroom after slipping out of her dress to take her makeup off and pull her hair up on top of her head.

I slip off my own shoes and strip down to my boxers before going into the bathroom to brush my teeth. Gem's finishing up brushing her own and puts her toothbrush back into her toiletry bag after she rinses her mouth. She hops up onto the sink to watch me.

"Your parents surprised me tonight. They seemed so different after you told your dad off." I nod as I brush my teeth and she continues, "I was really proud of you."

I finish brushing and dab my face with a towel before

coming to stand between her knees. I rest my hands on her waist and give her an affectionate squeeze. "I was proud of me, too." She winds her arms around my neck. I look into her eyes; even as my heart seems to be trying to escape my chest. "About what I said at dinner."

"What about it?"

I blow out a breath. "I said I loved you and I'm sorry if it sounded like I was just saying it to make a point to my parents, because that's not why I said it. I didn't mean to say it like that, but I don't want you to think I didn't mean it because I do, Gem. I — I love you."

Gemma offers me a sweet smile. "I know. You told me on our wedding night."

I feel my eyes widen. "I did? Why didn't you tell me?"

She huffs a laugh. "I didn't want you to feel like you had to say it again just because I'd told you that you'd said it. I enjoyed having it as my little secret. I was going to tell you if you ever said it again. Which I did." She takes my hands in her face. "For the record, I love you, too, Brew."

I can't resist pressing my forehead to hers. "How did we get so lucky, Gem? This just doesn't seem possible."

"I don't know, but I'm not about to question it. I'm just going to choose to be happy." She presses her lips to mine and wraps her legs around my waist to pull me closer. "Take me to bed?"

"Gladly."

Over the next few days, we're actually able to relax and have a fantastic remainder of our honeymoon. We don't have to field anymore requests from Curtis and it's extraordinarily nice to just wake up next to one another every morning.

And the truth is, we're still Gem and Brew. We're still *us*. We were both so worried about how a physical relationship might change us, but it hasn't. If anything, it's made us stronger and I cannot wait to see what the future holds for us.

I don't know that either of us really wants to go home tomorrow, but we know we have to get back to our regular lives. I suppose marriages can't be successful in a vacuum, so I'm sure the real tests won't start for us until we resume our normal routines.

Gemma talks me into lying on the beach for a few hours every day in the cabana and her golden skin deepens in color, whereas I just freckle. And this, our last day, is no exception. We've brought out some fruit and champagne to have as the sun goes down.

"What time is our flight tomorrow?" Gemma asks as she nibbles a strawberry.

"A little before noon. So we'll have to leave about eight-thirty to get to Miami and through security and stuff."

She pouts. "Do we really have to go back?"

I can't help but chuckle and pull her against me. "Yes, wife, we do. Curtis would probably just track us down and drag us back. We make him too much money. To be honest, I'm excited to go home with you as my wife. I want to take you home and carry you across the threshold and make love to you in my bed."

She rolls on her side to face me. "Ooh, that sounds nice. Can I get that in writing?"

I pull her left hand up and kiss her ring finger. "I think you already did."

"True. Okay. What do you think work's gonna be like when we get back?"

I consider and blow out a breath. "Who knows? I'm sure Curtis will have a big show planned for us on Tuesday when we get back to the station. I know he's probably going to want us to meet with him as soon as we get back tomorrow."

"I don't want Curtis to be the first person we see when we get back. He's totally going to kill my vacation high."

I press a kiss to her forehead. "I know. But he should have some good information about the syndication offers. I'm really hoping for one on satellite radio."

"That would be amazing. What are the chances, you think?"

I shrug. "Who knows, but that's the pinnacle, right? So, shoot for the stars and all that. Even if we only get a bigger market share, that's still pretty good. Plus, our record and ratings speak for themselves. We're a known commodity and people love us as a team. That guy I met with when we first got to Vegas seemed pretty interested, and he's out of Dallas. That would be a huge market for us to get into."

"You're really sexy when you talk about work stuff. You've got a really big brain and I love it."

I quirk a brow. "Well, you're really sexy all the time."

"Yeah, but you didn't know that until we got married."

I laugh. "Yes, I did. I've always known you were sexy. From the first day we met. Even if I never would've ever acted on it until just recently, I've always thought you were sexy as hell, Pearl."

"Do you remember the first day we met?"

I nod. "Yeah, don't you?"

"Yeah, of course. But I was just wondering what you remembered versus what I remembered."

"Well, what do you remember?"

"I asked you first," she says with a smirk.

"Okay, well, you showed up at the station that summer after your sophomore year of college. You were this young little thing. It was when you still wore glasses and your hair was short, just to your chin, if I remember." She nods. "You were all bright-eyed and ready to change radio.

"I'd just been handed a new show. I think mainly to see if I actually had the chops to hack it, so of course, they give me the shitty time slot. I should've been grateful for it, since it was a shot at my own show, but I was pissed. I'd been working as an assistant on the drive time show and people liked me, but they stuck me in the overnight slot. Which, if we were music radio, wouldn't have been bad, but talk radio on overnights can be brutal and boring.

"They told me I was going to have a partner. A sweet college intern who didn't know jack about the business. When they introduced us at our first planning meeting, I remember thinking you were so young, even though I was only three years older than you.

"And you wore an honest-to-God suit on your first day; even if it did make your ass look fantastic. I kept thinking, 'there's no way she's gonna make it, she's too soft'. I just knew you had to be this uptight little thing because you had this notebook with these cute, girly flowers on it and your phone was pink.

"And I was me. Granted, my hair was shorter then, and I barely had a beard, but I was definitely still my slouchy self. I think I still have that flannel I wore that day."

She snorts. "Remind me to burn that when we get home."

"Not happening. It's my lucky flannel. But anyway, I thought for sure our show was going to be a disaster. I thought you wouldn't even be able to stay up that first night. You looked like someone who valued an early bedtime.

"But then, after our planning meeting, about an hour before we were scheduled to go on the air, you asked me what was one thing I wish I had known on my first day on the job. At first, I thought you were just being a suck-up or whatever, but you had this expression on your face and it was just curious; as if you really wanted to know."

"Do you remember what you said?"

I nod. "Of course. I told you not to take things too seriously. I could tell, even then, that you were pretty serious, just by watching you take notes and the concentration on your face and how committed you seemed to be to learning the entire console in about five minutes. So, I told you not to be too serious. That it was supposed to be fun. Then I asked you why you wanted to get into radio in the first place. Do you remember what you told me?"

She laughs. "Yeah. I said that I figured that in radio, it didn't matter about looks and stuff. People couldn't care less what I look like, as long as I was good at the job. I'd always been prematurely judged because of my appearance. I didn't want to be just a pretty face. And you told me to prove that I wasn't just a pretty face. Prove that I could think on my feet. So, you took my script away."

I laugh. "Yeah, and you were so pissed."

"You're damn right I was. I kept thinking what an asshole move it was and that you'd really only done it because you wanted me to fail."

"But you didn't. Your first few calls were a little stiff, but I knew it was just because you were nervous and so on that commercial break when we were in-between segments, I asked you to tell me something you could talk about unscripted for twenty minutes. I knew Curtis would probably kill us for getting off topic, but I really didn't give a shit because it was the overnight show and nobody cares. You told me you could talk about Girl Scout cookies, so I said prove it."

"And I did. I think most of all, just to wipe that smug smile off your face. And we got into that really heated debate about Samoas versus Thin Mints, which we both know I won. But it really helped me to not be so nervous. It was just like having a conversation."

I nod. "And that's what it's been like for ten years, Pearl. Thousands of hours of conversations. And I've loved every minute of it."

She smiles. "Me, too."

CHAPTER NINETEEN

GEMMA

"Do you remember when we actually became friends?" I ask.

Brew thinks for a beat. "I don't know; I'd say it was this gradual thing. But I know when I realized you were my best friend."

"Really?"

He nods. "Yeah. We'd been working together for about eighteen months, I guess, and I had an opportunity to go to that championship football game. You remember that?"

"Yeah, of course. I still didn't know a lot about football at that point, but it was a lot of fun."

He smiles. "So, I had a girlfriend at that time, but not serious enough that I felt like she warranted a ticket to a big game. And I could've asked Lawson, but the only person I wanted to ask was you, because we always had fun together. At that moment, I realized then that I have more fun with you than anyone, and a lot of my favorite moments since I started working at the station were with you."

"You want to know when I knew you were my best friend?"

"Of course."

"When I was dating Sean, what, seven, eight years ago? When I thought I was pregnant, and yeah, totally gave myself hives with my freak out." Brew chuckles. "But the person I wanted with me when I found out for sure wasn't Sean, or even Augusta. It was you. Because I knew you'd know what to say to make it okay, even if I didn't know if it would. Granted, I've never been more relieved in my life to find out I wasn't pregnant, but I was thankful you were with me. Just like I'm thankful you're here with me now."

Brew extricates himself from our embrace and I glance at him, my brow quirked as he rises from the lounger and starts shutting the curtains on the cabana. "What are you doing?"

It's nearly pitch dark with all the curtains closed, but with the ocean breeze, sporadic slivers of moonlight filter in. "Just trying to give us a little privacy."

"That's what we have a room for."

He shakes his head, reaching toward the back of the lounger and lowers the head until it's flat. My heart rate tics up as Brew returns to sit next to me. "Nope. It's our last night, Gem. I've thought about what it might be like to take you in this cabana since that day when we were taking pictures in here. When I almost kissed you. And now, I'm gonna kiss you the way I wanted to then."

He grips the back of my neck and lowers his mouth to mine as he lays me back. I don't know that I'll ever get used to kissing him. Although, it honestly feels like he's exactly the person I should've always been kissing. As if our lips and tongues were made for one another. They just fit so perfectly together.

I pull him closer and his knee wedges between my thighs. I crook my leg around his hip and roll my pelvis against him and let out a soft moan as I'm able to create a bit of friction with the movement.

Brew kisses down my check and neck and I tilt my head to

give him better access. As his tongue swirls over the hollow of my throat, I let out a sigh and slide my fingers into his hair.

When his mouth winds a hot path down my chest and he pulls the cup of my bikini top to the side, I could protest. I could make us take this back to the room, because fucking in public is not my thing. I like the idea of getting caught fucking in public even less.

But my husband seems to enjoy it quite a lot. He likes the thrill and the risk and maybe he's rubbing off on me, because as he draws my nipple between his lips and I gasp, I don't even try to be quiet about it.

Brew shifts until he's between my legs and grinds his hips into me. I don't know that I'll ever get used to that, either. His size and how good he is.

He reaches between us to sweep my bottoms to the side and thumbs my clit. I exhale sharply. "You want my mouth, Pearl? You want me to eat you out here where anyone could come by and hear those filthy noises you make?"

"You're dirty, you know that?" My words come out in a huff as he works my clit in sure, steady circles.

"That's not an answer, Gem. Do you want my tongue on your pussy?"

My breathing is already turning ragged as he slides two fingers into me and crooks them as he moves them in and out. He smiles against my skin as he presses kisses into my stomach. "It sure feels like you like that idea. You call me dirty, but when I talk about people catching us, you almost gush. I think you're dirty, too." He sinks his teeth into my inner thigh and I hiss, but then he kisses the pain away just as quick. "Are you dirty, Gemma?"

He thrusts a third finger into me and I let out a moan, my hips bucking with the pressure. "Only with you."

"Fuck, Gem, that's hot. If I kiss this pretty pussy, are you going to be quiet, or are you going to let people know exactly how dirty you are?"

My orgasm begins to build, and he must be able to tell by either the way I feel or my breathing, because he slows down and pulls his thumb off my clit and I can't bite back a frustrated whimper. "You want me, Pearl? You want me to finish you off with my mouth and then fuck you senseless, the way I know you like it?"

"Yes, Brew. Please."

He drags my bottoms off my legs and a second later, his mouth has replaced his fingers. I gasp and tangle my hands in his hair. His nose nudges at my clit as his tongue dips into my pussy and I rock my hips, trying to get more friction. It doesn't take long before he's built me back up to where I'm on the verge of letting go. When he reaches up to roll my nipple between his fingers as he sucks hard on my clit, I let go with a strangled cry. Once again, I'm not a bit quiet about it.

I feel Brew's absence as he rises off me, and I hear more than see him taking off his swim trunks. "Get on your hands and knees, Gem."

I scramble to obey and once I get into position, his knees bracket mine on the cushion of the lounger. He leans over my back and rubs the head of his cock up and down my pussy. "You're so wet for me, Pearl. Do you know how much I love it?" He guides his cock past my entrance and I exhale sharply. He feels so much bigger from this angle.

His fingers dig into my hips as he begins a slow, pounding rhythm that has me moaning softly with each thrust. "Do you know how much I love to fuck you? How good you feel. How well you take my fat cock. Like you were made for me. You're so fucking perfect, Gemma."

His fingers settle into the hair at the nape of my neck and he tugs my head back. His mouth is close to my ear, his breath warm on my skin, sending goosebumps scattering down my arms. "I want to hear you, Gem. I want people to know how much you enjoy it when your husband fucks your sweet cunt. Or do you need it harder?"

"Harder." The word comes out strained and when he pounds into me, I let out a deep moan as he hits me so deeply, I nearly come from the impact alone.

He continues his relentless pace and his breathing grows more shallow . All I hear is the slap of his skin against mine combined with the sound of the waves and the jagged rasps that fall from my lips with each deliciously punishing slide of his cock.

When he reaches around to work my clit, I completely shatter, my orgasm hitting so hard, a sob wells up in my chest and my body completely shudders as I clench down. "Fuck, Gemma." Brew's words come out on a loud grunt as his hips buck twice more and his cock jerks inside me, his forehead falling to rest on my shoulder blade.

My arms grow shaky and after a moment, he pulls out and I nearly collapse onto my stomach. He lies down beside me and I turn my face toward him, still only barely visible in the dark. "And you think I'm trying to kill you? Fuck, husband."

Brew laughs and presses a tender kiss to my lips. "God, I love you."

I scoot over and snuggle up to him. "Love you, too. But I think I'm dead."

"Nah, you'll recover. You might feel it tomorrow, but then you'll remember how good it was and you'll want it again."

"You sound awful cocky."

He snorts a laugh. "Gem, I am all kinds of cocky. I think you like me that way."

"Okay, yeah. It's pretty nice. But I'm pretty sure you're going to have to carry me out of here. I have no legs."

"I can do that." He grabs his phone and uses the flashlight app to locate his trunks and pulls them on. He rolls me over and helps me put my bottoms back on and fixes my bikini top. He sticks our phones in his pockets and opens the curtain on the cabana before scooping me up into his arms and starting back toward our room.

I laugh. "Brew, I was joking. You don't have to carry me."

"Nope. I don't have much going for me to show you I'm worthy of you, Gem. Brute strength and a big dick are about all I've got, so I'll use what weapons I have in my arsenal."

His tone is playful, but I don't like to hear him being self-deprecating like that. I put my hand on his chest. "Whoa. Put me down."

He stops and gently sets my feet on the ground. "What's wrong? Was I hurting you?"

I take his face in my hands and pull him down until we're eye level. "You listen to me, Brewster Lincoln. You are the most amazing person I know. I don't ever want to hear you put yourself down or say that you're only good to me for your ability in the bedroom. Because while that is substantial, it's never going to be why I love you. I love you because you have a big heart. You are the person who knows what buttons to push to rile me up. You also know exactly how to calm me down.

"You are incredibly intelligent and talented at nearly everything you do. You are kind and generous and I know I give you shit about your tattoo, but I know exactly why you got it; even if you think I don't. And it's precious. You are my favorite person in the entire universe. And that was true before I ever knew how good you were in bed. So, I don't ever want to hear you talk like that, okay?"

Brew's smile is soft, and he gives me a small nod. "Alright, Gem." He gives me a kiss and then pulls back, his brow furrowed in confusion. "What do you mean, *nearly* everything?"

I roll my eyes and release his face to start walking back to the room. "I think you must've forgotten about that time you tried to skateboard and broke your elbow."

"Oh, that. Yeah, okay, I'll give you skateboarding. I was just trying to relive my glory days."

I scoff. "Playing *Tony Hawk* on Playstation does not constitute 'glory days'." I put the last words in air quotes for emphasis. "Especially when you're trying to skateboard for the first time at thirty years old."

Brew laughs and pulls me into his arms when we walk through the sliding glass door into our room. "You're something else, you know that?"

I shrug and wrap my arms around his waist. "Yeah, but you love me."

He nods. "You're right, I do. A lot." After a beat, he asks, "How did you know about my tattoo?"

"Because I remember the day you got the idea for it. I was there."

"How come you never said anything?"

"Because you didn't want anyone to know why you'd gotten it, so I wasn't going to let on that I knew. After you got it, you were so proud of it and whenever anyone asked, you told them it's because you just liked geese, but I remembered us doing that remote for the children's hospital and that really cute little girl was giving all of us temporary tattoos. You asked her what her favorite animal was. And she said a goose.

"And then when she didn't get to go home, and you'd found out she died, you went that weekend and got the goose. I knew exactly what it was for, but I knew you'd expect me to give you shit because if anyone else had gotten a random tattoo of a damn goose, I would have. But it just broke my heart, because I knew your heart was broken that she'd died."

Brew swallows thickly and gives me a sad smile. "You know, I went back to visit her a few times after we did that remote. She was such a cute kid. When she told me that a goose was her favorite animal, I asked her why and she just said, 'because they bite people'. I couldn't argue with that. But she was so serious about it. Her mom was a single mom, and she was an only child, and after she died, I checked in on her mom. I think she thought I was hitting on her, but when I explained who I was, she understood. I told her I didn't know her, but I had really been rooting for her daughter to get well. I still go by and put flowers on her grave on her birthday."

"What was her name?"

"Collier."

I nod. "Pretty name."

"Yeah. I always said if I ever had kids, one of them would be named Collier."

"Okay." I rest my forehead on his chest. "See, big damn heart. It's even bigger than your dick."

He laughs and kisses the top of my head.

CHAPTER TWENTY

BREWSTER

We're not even on the ground for five minutes after we get off the plane before my phone starts ringing. Gemma and I are attempting to make it to baggage claim to pickup our suitcases and she says, "I bet he was watching the arrivals to know exactly when to call."

I pull out my phone and sure enough, it's Curtis. "What, you got trackers on us or something? We literally just landed," I grit out.

"Yeah, I know. Listen. I need y'all to get to the station. We need to talk about these syndication deals."

"I thought we had to go to do stuff for the reception?"

"That's not until seven. You've got three hours. Get here."

We've been back less than ten minutes and already, the tension is returning to my shoulders.

Jesus Christ.

"What did he want? Oh, look, there are our bags." Gemma points to our suitcases and I lift them off the belt and we start toward the exit.

"We have to go to the station. He wants to talk about the syndication deals."

"Now? We're not dressed to go to work. I was hoping to go home and change before we have to go to do all that stuff tonight. I'm wearing travel clothes, Brew."

"You look great, Pearl. What you have on is fine. You're all tan and sexy."

"Yeah, yeah. Whatever. Let's go deal with Curtis, I guess. I was really hoping we wouldn't see him until tomorrow."

"Yeah, I know, but we'll survive. At least he left us alone those last few days. And they were really, *really* good days."

She smiles. "You're right. They were." We make it out to Gemma's car and put our bags in the backseat. "I hope Curtis knows that I'm going to expense the cost of parking." I laugh as she backs out of the parking spot.

Thirty minutes later, we're pulling up at the station and both our mouths fall open when we see the huge banner plastered on the side of the building. There's a photo of Gem and me from the session we did in Florida along with a date and time for the reception with the tag line: *Gemma and Brewster, WXOR's own fairy tale love story, ten years in the making.*

"Please tell me I'm hallucinating that," Gemma says with fury in her voice. "I'm going to kill him."

I place a hand on her arm in an attempt to calm her. "I mean it's not wrong, Gem."

Her head snaps in my direction. "You're okay with this? Having our picture on the side of a building like some kind of sappy billboard? Curtis is exploiting us. I agreed to do the stupid reception. I agreed to do the honeymoon. I agreed to do the fucking pictures. I didn't agree to having those pictures being hung on the side of the fucking building."

"No, I'm not okay. We know Curtis is a dirtbag. This is what he does."

"I don't know if I can keep working for him, Brew. He's awful. We've put up with this shit for ten years. He's gross and manipulative and even when he's blatantly sexually harassing us, it's *all in good fun*. I'm so over it."

I take her face in my hands. "Gemma, listen to me. We'll be fine. Nothing has changed. We're still us, even if there is a stupid picture on the side of the building. We've known he was exploiting this. We've known it since we woke up that morning in Vegas. We will be okay. Once we get the syndication deals done, we can look into requesting a new production manager. We'll be a lot more valuable to the station than Curtis at that point.

"And if any of the contracts have anything at all relating to requiring that Curtis be part of the deal, we don't accept those. You trust us, right?" She nods and I kiss her on the forehead. "Alright then, we'll be okay. I promise."

She pulls back and levels me with a gaze. "I swear, if he says anything sexual, I will lose it. I'm getting ready to start my period and I'm cranky, I'm tired, I'm crampy and I'm in no mood for Curtis's shit."

I try not to smile since Gemma's on the warpath, but in this moment, I just want to give her a kiss, because even angry like this, she's adorable. "Alright, Pearl. I will run interference and when we get home after the tasting and stuff tonight, I'll go out and get you some of that chocolate and caramel ice cream you like and some Cheetos."

She nods. "Okay." She takes a deep breath and we step out of the car. We walk toward the building and I take her hand in mine as we enter the door. The station is pretty busy since it's peak time and we wind our way through the building as everyone greets and congratulates us.

By the time we finally make it to Curtis's office, I can tell Gemma is already over being here and I steel myself before we enter the room. I knock and Curtis says to enter. He's on the phone when we come in. "No, it's going to be huge. It's two weeks from Friday at the Claremont. Seven-thirty. Black tie. Dancing, cocktail hour, the whole shebang. Listen, I'll send the invite over. You and the missus will come, right? Great. See you then. Bye."

We take the chairs opposite Curtis's desk and he looks from Gemma to me, a smarmy smirk on his face. "Looks like Florida agreed with you two. How was the honeymoon?"

Gemma's hands curl into fists in her lap and I hurry to speak, lest she decide to verbally eviscerate him before we've even gotten started. "It was fine, Curtis. Can we get on with the reason we had to come in today? How many offers are we looking at?"

"Seven."

I blink rapidly. "Really?"

He nods, a huge grin on his face. "Yeah, I fought really hard for you guys, too. I think you'll find the contracts to be to your liking."

I level him with a gaze. "We'll have our lawyers look them over and get back to you." And by lawyers, I mean Gemma's brother Graham. He might be a prick, but he's still a great lawyer.

"Oh, come on, Brewster, I wouldn't let y'all get screwed. I'm sure you got enough of that in Florida, am I right?" He smirks at me and wiggles his eyebrows.

Gemma jumps to her feet and looks at me. "I told you, Brew. I'm out. I'll be in the car." She storms out and slams the door and Curtis looks entirely oblivious as to why she's just left.

"What?"

"Curtis, you're disgusting. That's the last time you do that. Ever. Do you know how often I have to talk her out of quitting because of you? And I'd follow her if she ever did. Then where would you be; having to explain that to the station execs? We're already putting up with way more than we ever should have with you. If I hear you ever say anything inappropriate in front of Gemma, we'll walk."

"Oh, lighten up, Lincoln. It's not a big deal."

"Bullshit, Curtis. I have text messages, you know. I'm sure your bosses would love to hear about how you talk to and harass your talent. Try me."

He holds his hands up as if in surrender. "Okay, I hear you. I'll try to rein it in."

I stand to leave. "There is no 'try', Curtis. This is your only warning. Email me the offers for Gem and me to look over. We'll be back to work tomorrow." I don't wait for his response as I shut the door when I leave his office.

Gemma is on her phone when I get out to the car. "Yeah, Mom. I know. I'm sorry. We were still in Florida... No, we had to go for work. We just got back today... Okay, yeah. We'll be there on Sunday... I'll let him know... Alright. Listen, Mom, I have to go. Brew and I have to go to this thing for the reception... No, work is throwing us one. They've got all these sponsors. But I have to go to look at dresses tomorrow. Will you go with me... Okay, I'll text you the details... Love you, too. Bye."

She disconnects the call and pinches the bridge of her nose. "I'm going to need so much wine when we get home. I just want to drink and go to bed. We have to go to Sunday dinner next week or my mother will kill us."

I nod. "We can do that. Well, not the bed part. Not yet, anyway." I check my watch. "We probably have enough time to go by your apartment and get some of your boxes, if you want.

That way, you'll have your comfy pajamas and any bathroom stuff you might need, so we don't have to buy all new tonight."

She nods. "Sorry I'm in a bad mood. And I apologize in advance for my shitty attitude over the next couple of days. I hope you'll still love me when I'm biting your head off."

I take her hand in mine and kiss her palm. "Gem, you act like I've never been at the mercy of your PMS before. I've known you for ten years. I know exactly what you're like and I promise I'll still love you. Do you want me to drive?"

She hands me her keys and we get out of the car to switch seats. I start the engine and pull out of the parking lot to head toward Gemma's apartment.

What seems like five hours later, we've made our choices of cakes—a strawberry cake with cream cheese frosting, as well as classic vanilla with Italian buttercream. We also sampled many dinner items and settled on brisket and roasted chicken, along with baked or mashed potatoes and grilled vegetables. Honestly, neither Gemma nor I really cared about the food, but the cake was actually really good. She did her little happy dance when she tasted the strawberry cake and I knew that was a definite choice. I left the flower choices completely up to Gemma, who I knew would want something with hydrangeas.

We also settled on our rings, which I feel a little strange about. I'm sure if we hadn't eloped, I would've wanted to get Gemma a nice engagement ring, but honestly, I like our simple gold bands. But I know this is all part of it for work, so I picked one; a simple hammered white gold band.

I knew which ring Gemma was going to pick as soon as I saw the selection. It's exactly the ring I would've picked out for her; which somehow made me feel like maybe this was all meant to be. Hers is a yellow gold band with a round diamond flanked by two sapphires. It just looks like *her*.

When we get home, Gem seems dead on her feet, so she tugs on one of my T-shirts and I get her tucked up into bed before bringing her boxes into the house. In truth, she didn't have nearly as many clothes and shoes and bathroom stuff as I expected. I deposit her things into the guest room, so they'll be out of the way.

I take some time to go through all the mail that's piled up over the last week and toss out the expired food in the fridge and run the trash out to the curb for pickup before getting ready for bed.

She doesn't stir when I crawl under the covers and pull her against me, but it's so very nice to have her in my bed. I press a kiss under her ear and listen to her steady breathing as I drift off.

When I wake up, Gemma's already out of bed and I hear cabinets opening and closing. I climb out of bed and pad into the kitchen to see her making coffee. I come up behind her and plant a kiss on the side of her head. "How'd you sleep?"

"Fine. I should've brought my pillows from my apartment, though." She stretches her neck and rolls her shoulders.

"Sure, Pearl, we can get whatever you want from your place. If you want to make me a list of anything you can think of, I can go by there and pick the stuff up. I know you've got to go look at dresses this evening."

"And you've got a tux fitting tomorrow."

I sigh. "Yeah, I know. I don't need a tux. Maybe I can do a suit instead. I would actually wear a suit again."

Gemma nods as she continues to make coffee. "You'd look

fantastic in a charcoal gray suit. Are you going to get Lawson to go with you, or do you want me to go? I didn't know if maybe y'all would want to go out and have some drinks after, you know, do a guys' night or something. Mom and Augusta and I are going out to supper after we look at dresses. So you'll be on your own tonight. Sorry."

I give her a smile. "Don't worry about it. I'll hang out here and make room in my closet and dresser. Unless you want the guest bedroom closet. We'll probably want to think about enlarging the primary bedroom's closet, just so we have plenty of space. I'll talk to Law about that."

She chuckles. "Sure. I'm fine with the guest room closet for now."

I nod. "Okay. I'm gonna go grab a shower. I put all your boxes in the guest room if you're looking for your clothes and suitcase and stuff."

"Thanks, Brew."

"Gem, it's nothing. And whatever you need to do to make this place feel like your home, too, we'll do it, okay?" I give her another quick kiss and head to the bathroom.

After my shower, I find Gemma in the guest room, pulling out a pair of jeans and a top from her myriad of boxes, along with some of her bathroom things. "Shower's free, Pearl."

"Okay, coffee's ready, too. I'm gonna grab a quick shower, but then we'll have to hurry. We have to be at work in an hour. Augusta is going to pick me up at the station to take me to my dress appointment and she'll bring me home after, okay?"

I can't help but smile at the fact that she's calling this *home*. "Sure. Want me to fix you some coffee to take with us? And I'll go grocery shopping after work. Is your spare key still in the same place at your apartment?"

"Yes. And coffee would be great. Do we have anything for breakfast here?"

I shake my head. "No. Sorry. I had to toss a lot of stuff when we got in last night. I guess we can grab something on the way to the station."

"Alright."

An hour later, we're pulling up at the station and heading to our booth and I inwardly curse the fact that I didn't check my emails yesterday. I know I'm going to have hundreds to get through. Gemma and I go through our normal routine of reading over the talking points we're scheduled to discuss and we make notes on any we feel like could be fleshed out into an entire segment.

This process used to take us over an hour, but now we have it down to about twenty minutes because of the shorthand that we've developed over the years.

"Brew, are you noticing a theme with the outline today?"

I huff a laugh. "Yeah. Curtis is really cashing in on the wedding thing. Elopement horror stories, drunken Vegas weddings, crazy honeymoon stories, favorite wedding memories. And don't forget about all the plugs for the sponsors. Ugh. I'll be glad when we get through all this. Two more weeks, Pearl."

"Have you checked your email, to see if the guy from the casino sent anything?"

I shake my head. "I haven't had time. I'm going to put in a couple hours tonight to go through them all. Fingers crossed, we'll have something."

Our assistant producer and call screener, Rosie, sticks her head in the booth. "Ten minutes, y'all."

Gemma smiles. "Thanks, Rosie. We'll be ready."

CHAPTER TWENTY-ONE

GEMMA

"I don't know if y'all have noticed, but today's show has had a bit of a theme. And I'm sure by now, most of our listeners are aware that Brewster and I embarked on our own crazy Vegas wedding adventure last weekend and got married.

"So, during this hour, we wanted to hear from you. If you got married in Vegas on a whim, give us a call. The crazier your story, the better. You know us, we like all the drama. Keep it clean for radio though; Brewster already gets us in enough trouble with his mouth. But the phone lines are open and we'll take our first call as soon as we return from this quick commercial break."

I click my mouse over the commercial segment designated for this time slot as I sip my water and stretch my neck. I can see just by looking, the phone lines are already full and I don't know whether to be excited or dismayed. We've fielded so many questions about our own wedding weekend, we've heard very few actual stories from listeners today.

"Pearl?" I glance up at Brew over the console and he gives me a grin. "See, we're still us," he says with a wink.

I return his smile and nod. "Yep. It would seem that we are. Truth be told, though, I think I'm vacation hungover or something. I'm on the struggle bus today."

He smirks. "See, and here I thought it was just all that really great sex that had you like that."

Heat climbs up my neck and Rosie's voice comes through my headphones. "Y'all realize I'm still here, right? I'm really glad y'all are all hot for each other now and that it hasn't seemed to affect your work one bit, but if I have to hear about all your countless orgasms, I might just barf."

I can't help but laugh. "Sorry, Rosie, we'll try to keep it to a minimum."

Brew shakes his head. "I can't promise that. Have you seen my wife, Rosie? She's fucking hot."

Rosie snorts on the other side of the plexiglass separating her small console from our larger one. I glance down at my monitor. "Thirty seconds."

When our buffer music starts back up, I take one last sip of water and Brew leans in closer to his mic. "Wow. Looks like a lot of you have some crazy stories to tell about your shenanigans in Vegas. Our first call today is from Phil. You have a Vegas story for us?"

The caller, an older man, pipes up. "Oh, yeah. My wife and I eloped to Vegas while I was in the service. Craziest weekend of my life."

"Did you do any gambling while you were there?" Brew asks.

"Only with my heart. My wife was a blackjack dealer at a casino and it was my last weekend of furlough before I had to go back to base. She was the most beautiful woman I'd ever seen. Love at first sight, for sure. I stayed at her table all night long and kept losing money even though I'm great at blackjack."

I'm already smiling. "So, did you win any of it back?"

Phil chuckles down the line. "I was down to my last chip and I bet her if I won that hand that she had to have a drink with me after her shift. She thought for sure, she had me, but I won that hand and one drink led to another, which led to a chapel."

Brew huffs a laugh. "Yeah, those drinks will get you. So, did you stay married?"

"For almost thirty years. Best thirty years of my life until she passed last year. But I wouldn't trade our time for anything. So, I wanted to let y'all know, sometimes those impulsive decisions you make can be the best decisions of your life."

My chest tightens with emotion. "Thank you, Phil. I know I speak for Brewster and myself when we say that we're sorry to hear about your wife. I can only hope Brew and I are as happy as you were with your wife."

Brew disconnects that call. "Next on the line is Carrie. You have a crazy story, Carrie?"

A woman with a nasal voice answers, "Oh, yeah. I was in Vegas for a bachelorette party and there was a group of guys across the bar. We struck up a conversation and a few drinks later, we were in front of Elvis. Craziest night of my life."

I chuckle. "I'm beginning to sense a pattern with these stories. Looks like everyone's a bit uninhibited in Vegas. So, did you stick with the guy?"

"Hell, no. When we woke up the next morning, we couldn't even remember each other's names. We annulled that thing faster than you can order a cup of coffee. And I haven't been back to Vegas since."

Brew laughs. "Why's that? Are you worried about a repeat performance?"

"Most definitely. I'll just stay right here, thanks."

I disconnect the call. "Alright, looks like we can take one

more call before we have to make the station some money. Next on the line is Smith. Hi, Smith. Tell us about your crazy Vegas weekend."

"Well, not my weekend, but the girl I was supposed to marry ran off to Vegas and married some loser." I look over the console at Brew, all the color draining from my face. Because I know this voice. While Smith is his name, it's not his first one. *Kyle.*

Brew mutes his mic. "Is that Kyle? You okay?"

I nod and take a deep breath. "Oh, really? Are you sure that wasn't the guy she wasn't always supposed to marry? I doubt he was a loser."

"No, he totally is. And she'll see it soon. I'll get her back."

A muscle tics in Brew's jaw. "Come on, buddy, this is supposed to be about crazy Vegas stories. If you don't have one, we'll have to take the next caller."

"Lincoln, you think just because you caught Gemma in a weak moment that you'll be enough for her? That you could ever be enough for her. Everyone knows y'all only did this for the publicity. Soon—"

I disconnect the call. "Oops, looks like we lost him. Sorry about that. We'll be back right after this quick break." I click the audio files for the ads and pinch the bridge of my nose.

Brew takes off his headphones and rounds the console to put an arm around me. "You okay, Pearl?"

I nod and Rosie comes into the booth. "I'm so sorry, y'all. I didn't know that was Kyle. I never would've put his call through."

Brew gives her a weak smile. "We know. He's just bitter. He hasn't been able to get a reaction out of Gemma up till now. It's fine, Rosie." He returns his attention to me. "What do you want to do about him? You think he'll leave us alone, or do we need to pay him a visit? I'm not going to put up with him harassing you like this."

"I'll take care of it."

Brew takes my face in his hands. "Gem, I don't want you to see him. Not by yourself. He's angry. There's no telling what he'll do."

"Brew, I'm fine. I can handle Kyle. I'll call him and tell him to leave me alone. He'll get over it. He's just jealous."

He gives me a lopsided grin. "Not that I'm not happy to know that Kyle Smith would ever be jealous of me, but I still don't like the idea of you getting anywhere near him; even if it's only on the phone."

"Like I said, I'm not scared of him. He's a blowhard and a dumbass." I glance at the monitor. "Sixty seconds."

Brew plants a kiss on my cheek and returns to his side of the table.

The rest of the show passes uneventfully and I give Brew a kiss before climbing in the car with Augusta to meet my mother at the dress shop. "Augusta, keep her out of trouble. I expect my wife back in one piece," he says with a smile as he bends down into the open door of her car.

Augusta rolls her eyes. "Please. You know I take care of my girl."

I tug the front of his shirt until we're eye level. "You're still going by my place, right?"

He nods. "Yeah. I've got the list of stuff you wanted me to get. I'll make sure to get you some chocolate when I go to the store, too."

I pull him to me for a kiss. "See, this is why I love you."

"And here I thought it was for my big dick." He wiggles his eyebrows and I can't help but laugh.

Augusta scoffs. "Y'all. Seriously? Gross."

He gives me one more kiss before backing away to shut the door.

I glance over at Augusta. "I mean, I didn't know it was so big when we got married, but I'm not mad about it."

She laughs. "Jesus. And here I can't even get a date. You hit the jackpot with the perfect guy. Brains, great hair, totally adores you, apparently a horse cock. I am entirely jealous."

"It's pretty nice, not gonna lie," I say with a smile. A moment later, I sober. "Did you listen to the show today?"

"Yeah, of course. I always have it on."

"So, you heard Kyle's call?"

She nods as she pulls out onto the highway. "Yeah, he's such an idiot. Does he honestly think that earns him any sort of grace with you? Embarrassing you at work like that?"

"Right? I was so angry. Brew was really pissed. He's always hated Kyle, so this is just one more thing for him that puts him on his shit list. I'm going to call and rip him a new asshole. I won't have him calling me at work."

"That is your right. So, what are you thinking as far as dresses go? Have you looked at any online or anything?"

I shake my head. "Haven't really had time. I was a little busy this past week."

"Yeah, yeah, we all know. You were busy getting massive amounts of good dick. Stop rubbing it in. I wonder if this is one of those bridal places that offers you champagne while you look at dresses. That might be nice."

"Yeah, except my mom will be there. And not that I don't want her to be with me when I find a wedding dress—a reception dress? Whatever. I'm happy she's going to be there, and I'd never

take this away from her, but her taste and mine are totally different. She's going to want me in this big ballgown or some shit, and
it's just not me. I'd never be comfortable in something like that."

"Well, we'll just have to remind your mom that this is your
day, and she's not paying, so it'll be fine. And if not, we'll go to
dinner and get tipsy and have Brewster come and pick us up
after."

"There's a thought."

Augusta pulls in at the bridal salon a short time later and I
notice my mother's car is already in the parking lot. I steel
myself to see her as we walk in. It's not that I don't love my
mother; I do. It's just that she has the mom guilt thing down to a
science and she doesn't even have to speak to make me question
if what I'm doing is right or whatever. She can make a small
noise in the back of her throat and I immediately second guess
myself.

But when we walk through the door, she walks up and
throws her arms around me. "Gemma, sweetheart. I'm so glad
you're doing this."

I huff a small laugh and return her hug. "Hey, Mom.
Although, it wasn't really a choice. I'm just glad I get to pick my
dress."

My mother turns us, takes my hand, and tugs me toward
the back of the store. "I've already been talking with the clerk
and had her pull some great numbers that I think you'll love."

I feel my right eye twitch. "Mom, I appreciate that, but I'm
not sure what I'm looking for yet. I'd like to talk to the clerk and
tell them a little about my style and see what they pull before
we start picking things willy-nilly. I'm happy to look at the
options you've pulled, but my style is different than yours,
okay?"

Even though I try to keep my tone as even and devoid of

annoyance as possible, my mother's expression still looks pained.

Cue the mom guilt.

"I know. I still think you'll like what I picked, but I'm sure you'll find something you like better."

"Like I said, Mom, I'm sure everything you've pulled is beautiful, but let's just see what the store clerk says, okay?"

She gives me a quick nod and then we're greeted by a clerk named Ashley. "Gemma, welcome. We're so happy to have you. We all listen to your show in the afternoons. We love it. So when we heard that you and Brewster got married, we jumped at the opportunity to do our part for your reception. Y'all have such great chemistry together."

I give her a genuine smile. "Thank you so much for the support. Brewster and I can't believe all the people who want to help us celebrate."

Her grin widens. "Yours and Brewster's story is like something out of a movie. Co-workers turned best friends turned husband and wife. It's amazing."

I nod. "I'm a very lucky woman. Brewster is an amazing man."

My mother clears her throat, and Ashley seems to come to attention. "Oh, my. Of course. You're here for a dress, not to hear me drone on about how much we love your show." She gestures to a sofa near a large pedestal and a wall of mirrors. Mom, Augusta, and I sit while Ashley takes a nearby wingback chair. "So, tell me a little about your style. I know your mom picked a few pieces for you, but I'm interested to see if I can pull some that you'll like as well. I always feel like it's a personal challenge to myself to find *the* dress. When you've worn formal dresses in the past, what sort of fit did you gravitate towards, or do you have a preference?"

"For any type of awards dinners or anything we've had to

do in the past few years, I normally go with something fitted, like a sheath or something like that. I'm not an overly modest person, so I don't mind plunging necklines or low backs or anything like that. I'd prefer not to wear white."

"Gemma, you have to wear white. It's a wedding," my mother interjects.

I look at her. "Mom, it's not a wedding. It's a reception. White dresses are for virgins and that ship sailed a long, long time ago. Not to mention the patriarchal value that society places on virginity is not something I care to emulate by supporting that kind of message. So, no, I will not be wearing a white dress." I look back at Ashley. "I'd prefer something with some black or silver. I don't mind looking bridal, but I'm not a traditional kind of person."

She smiles. "I like a woman who knows what she likes. Alright. Just so I have my information correct, you like a sheath silhouette, but don't have a preference in the neckline and you're a bit edgy. Is that about right?"

I nod. "Sounds right to me."

She confirms my dress size and heads off to find some dresses for me to try on.

I catch Augusta's eye in the mirror and she gives me an excited grin. My mother touches my arm. "You'll still try on the ones I picked, right? Even if you think you won't like them?"

I nod, trying not to appear annoyed. "Yeah, Mom, I'll try them on."

She gives me a soft smile. "Thank you. It just feels like none of this is how I pictured it would be when you got married. I thought whoever you married would come to your father and me and ask for our blessing. Like Kyle did."

"Mom, I wouldn't have married Kyle anyway. I know you and Dad really liked him, but he wasn't the right guy for me. Brewster is my husband and I love him."

She nods. "I know. I just wish your father and I had been a part of it. We love Brewster. We've always loved him. And we're thrilled you're happy; we're just feeling a bit left out is all. And now we don't even get to buy your dress or pay for your wedding or anything the bride's parents are supposed to do. I've looked forward to your wedding day since you were a little girl. I'm just a little sad, sweetheart."

And whether it's mom guilt or just the mournful expression on my mother's face, I wrap my arms around her and give her a big hug. "I'm sorry, Mom. I promise, if we had planned this at all, you and Dad would've gotten to pitch in all the ways you wanted. How about this; you and your ladies' group can throw us a shower and you can go with me and Brewster to register for stuff, okay?"

Her eyes brighten. "Really?"

"Yes, really. I'll even let you plan the menu and I'll do my best to not complain."

She smiles and returns my hug. "Okay, I can live with that. And when you have babies, I can throw showers then, too, right?"

I laugh. "One thing at a time, Mom. It'll probably be a little while before we have kids."

"I don't know. Marriage has a way of making people baby crazy. Your father and I were only married two years when Graham was born. Of course, it could've been our inability to keep our hands off one another that contributed to that." She winks and I blush.

"Mother! I don't want to hear about that."

Augusta laughs. "Oh, she and Brewster already have the whole not keeping their hands to themselves part down, Mrs. H. It's totally weird considering that just a couple of weeks ago they were only friends. They've flipped some sort of switch, and now they're all over each other."

I level my friend with a glare. "Augusta. I don't need my mother knowing things like that, thanks."

My mother dismisses my admonishments with a wave. "Oh, please, that son-in-law of mine is quite yummy. I can totally see the appeal. I've never really liked long hair on a man, but it works for him."

Augusta pipes up, "Right? He rocks it. I bet it feels great to run your fingers through, doesn't it, Gem?"

I cover my face with my hands. "I'm not talking about this right now."

"That's a yes," Augusta says with a laugh and my mother joins in.

I've never been more grateful for an interruption as I am when Ashley comes out of a back room, arm loaded down with dresses, none of them white. "Alright, Gemma, I've got several to get us started, if you want to come with me."

CHAPTER TWENTY-TWO

BREWSTER

After seeing Gemma, I head back into the station to take a bit of time to go through my emails. Most are simply for company-wide distribution that were valid last week, but don't serve a purpose to me now, so I delete them.

When I get my inbox cleared out, I'm disappointed to see I don't have one from the casino employee. A quick online search nets me the phone number for the casino, so I decide to give Edward a quick call.

Ten minutes later, after I've been routed through seemingly every employee at the casino, I'm connected with Edward's company voicemail. I leave him a brief message and my number, hoping to hear from him soon.

Once I leave the station, I go by the grocery store to get enough groceries for the week, including Gemma's favorite caramel and chocolate gelato and a bag of Cheetos, knowing those are her preferred PMS foods. I can't help but smile that I've known Gemma long enough to know exactly what all her favorite things are.

In the past, whenever I thought about marriage, which, to

be honest, wasn't a lot, I always dreaded the thought of having to combine houses and learn the habits of someone, knowing there are some things you never truly know about someone until you live with them.

But I don't feel that with Gemma. We've spent so much time together over the last ten years, I've yet to be surprised by anything in the week we've been married. Granted, working closely with someone, you learn the ins and outs of their bathroom habits after a while, so not even that part of our relationship has been a surprise.

The thought of women's periods has never bothered me. I mean, what's the point in being grossed out by something that's completely natural? So there have been several instances where I've gone on supply runs for Gemma. And since she's not a prude, she's never been ashamed of her cycles, anyway. She's always been good to tell me when she's PMSing since we met, but anymore, I've almost got her cycle memorized since I've known her for so long.

So, I throw some tampons in the cart for good measure, just in case she's low, and finally head to the checkout. The clerk, a woman in her fifties, rings up my order and when she gets to the tampons, she gives me an impressed nod. "How long have you been married?"

I chuckle. "A week."

Her eyes widen. "And you're comfortable enough to buy your wife's tampons and she's comfortable enough to let you? Wow, that's something."

I can't help but laugh. "I've known my wife for ten years. We were best friends before we got married."

She nods. "Well, that's good. Not a lot of men, even ones married for a long time, will venture into that territory. I applaud you."

I grin. "Nothing to applaud. It's the least I can do for what she has to go through. I don't know what I'll do when we have kids. I'll probably need to buy her a new car or something for that."

The clerk laughs and tells me my total and I swipe my debit card. She hands over my receipt and congratulates me on my marriage. I thank her and roll my cart out to my car to load the groceries.

Knowing Gemma's going to eat with Augusta and her mother after they visit the dress shop, I swing in and grab a fast food burger and fries to eat on the way over to her apartment to gather the things on the list she gave me.

When I pull in at the complex, I look over the list one last time before sticking it in my pocket. I nearly laugh out loud when I read Gem's neat script and see that she's underlined and circled the word "pillows".

I'm guessing if I go home without those pillows, she's gonna be pissed.

As I reach the door to her apartment, I run my fingers over the frame for the spare key and head inside. And although she didn't ask me to, I clean out the fridge of expired items so they won't start to smell, and also toss out some shriveled apples and black bananas.

I glance around her kitchen to see if any of her small appliances are better than mine, and unplug the coffee maker since I know for a fact it's practically brand new, as I was with Gem when she bought it last month. I set it on the table next to the front door and grab a trash bag from under the sink to put her pillows in.

I walk into the bedroom and bag them up, along with a few other items Gemma must've overlooked when she was here. I pull the list out of my pocket to double check that I have everything and see that she's also listed the books on her nightstand. I grab the bag and books and start back toward the front door. When I'm halfway down the hall, it opens with a soft groan.

My first thought is that Gemma must've forgotten something on her list, so she had Augusta run over to see if I was still here and she could just ride home with me. But when I get to the living room and see Kyle sitting on the sofa, I stop in my tracks.

He has a bottle of what looks like bourbon in his hand and it's over half empty, so I'm sure he's got to at least be buzzed, if not completely drunk. I set the bag and books down on the floor. "What are you doing here, Smith?" I try to keep my tone level, even though I'm pissed. I know for a fact that I locked the door when I came and I have the spare key in my pocket.

"How did you do it, Lincoln? Was it like some kind of long-term plan for you? You'd bide your time and then, as soon as we got in a fight, you'd pounce? We were supposed to get married."

He stands, and he's not too steady on his feet, but I still keep my distance, because I know myself and I've always itched for a reason to put my fist through Kyle's face.

I still keep my tone even, but I level with him. "Actually, Gemma proposed to me, and I said yes."

"Bullshit," he literally spits out, droplets flying from his mouth.

I shrug. "I'm not saying you have to believe me, but that's what happened. Now, I'll ask you kindly, just this once, to leave whatever key you still have and go. I know for a fact Gemma wouldn't like you being here. You have no reason to be; you have nothing here. She threw all your shit out with you the night she turned down your proposal."

He tips the bottle up to his lips and takes a long drink before wiping his mouth with the back of his hand. "Yeah, and that's your fault, too, fucker."

I shake my head. "Whatever you need to tell yourself, man.

I get it. Gemma's the best woman I've ever met. If I lost her, I'd be torn up, too."

"I never should've lost her. If it hadn't been for your stupid ass, I wouldn't have."

I can't help but smile. "From what Gemma said, you fucked yourself on that. You should've known better than to give her an ultimatum. She's not some bird to be caged. Now leave, before I make you leave." My phone rings in my pocket and I know, without even having to check, it's Gemma. Probably wanting to make triple sure I got her pillows. "Listen, man, I'm sorry your life is shit right now, but it's not Gemma's fault or mine."

He throws the bottle against the wall and I'm just thankful it doesn't shatter. I square my shoulders as he takes a couple of steps toward me. Knowing that he has a temper, seeing as how he threw Gemma's phone when he got pissed, I wouldn't put it past him to charge me or try to get physical. "One of these days, Gemma's gonna see what a loser you are, you know that? She's going to realize how little you offer her. I wonder, does she still let out that little sigh when she comes? I always loved that."

I laugh and his eyes narrow. "Kyle, I'll tell you this. Nothing I offer Gemma is small by any stretch of the imagination. And as far as the sound she makes when she comes, it's never been anything as quiet as a sigh. Most of the time, it's my name that she absolutely screams."

Even though I'm expecting it when he lunges at me, I'm not expecting his speed. He's either not as drunk as I originally assumed, or he's just an angry drunk. But somehow, the punch he throws merely glances off the side of my mouth. I still taste blood, but thankfully, it's not a straight-on hit.

I manage to get a good right hook on his chin, but I'm not a fighter and apparently, Kyle is, because he comes in with a punch that lands square on my left eye and pain radiates through my cheek. He loses his balance after the second blow and while he seems to be a bit unsteady, I get a lucky shot off that hits him in the nose.

His hands fly to his nose and blood pours down his face as he stumbles back. "Enough, Kyle. I don't want to fight you. You're not worth it. You can go or I'll call the cops."

He falls to his knees, and a sob works its way up his throat. "I just miss her so much. And if it weren't for you, I'd still have her."

I wipe away the line of blood that runs from my bottom lip and I can tell it's already starting to swell. "I was never your competition, man. I never would've gone after her while she was with you or anyone else. She's still my best friend and all I've ever wanted was for her to be happy. Even if that meant she ended up being with you. But you never understood that."

"It was always so easy with you two. Even after three years, I never felt like I *had* her the way you did. I was so jealous of you. When we'd all go out, you all had this shorthand and all these inside jokes. People always thought y'all were a couple and I was a third wheel. It made me feel like a fool."

I nod. "Yeah, but if you had just let Gemma be herself, you might still have her. Like I said, I feel bad for you. Now that I've had her, I'd never be able to give her up. But you need to go. Also, hand over whatever key you've got. This is the last time you come here and you won't call or text Gemma or harass her anymore. You also won't harass us at work. If it happens again, we'll file a restraining order."

Kyle digs in his pocket, pulls out a key, and tosses it on the floor. He climbs to his feet and blood still pours from his nose. I walk over to the kitchen and pull out a towel and extend it toward him. "Do you need a ride or are you good to drive?"

He scoffs and snatches the towel from my grip. "I'm good."

"Okay, then go. Like I said, don't bother Gem anymore."

He walks out the door and my phone rings again. I pull it out and answer it. "Hey, Pearl."

"Hey, I thought you'd be home by now."

"Yeah, I'm getting ready to leave your place. I'll be there soon, okay?"

"Alright. Love you."

"Love you, too."

When I pull in at the house twenty minutes later, I carry in the cold groceries first since they've been sitting out for a while. As soon as I walk in the door and Gemma glances up from where she sits on the couch watching *Hell's Kitchen*, she jumps up from the sofa and runs over to me. "What the hell happened to your face?"

"You should see the other guy," I say flatly. I put away the ice cream, milk, lunch meat, cheese, and eggs and Gemma steps in front of me.

"You're home so late because you got in a fight?" After a beat, color rises to her cheeks. "I told you I would handle Kyle. I asked you to let me take care of him. You went and started a fight? You know I'm not some fence post for you to piss on, right?"

I slam the fridge shut and round on her. "I didn't start shit, Gemma. Kyle came to your apartment. I was getting ready to leave and he was sitting on your couch, drunk. Although, I guess not too drunk to throw a couple of punches. I was happy to let you handle it. I wasn't going to get involved if I didn't have to. But *he* attacked *me*, Pearl. I wasn't going to willingly take a beating just because the guy's in bad shape. I even tried to be civil. I asked him nicely to leave. And until the point that he wanted to talk about our abilities in the bedroom, I was cool."

She rolls her eyes. "Fucking male ego. I swear. I bet you wanted to get out a ruler and measure your dicks, didn't you?"

I can't help the smile that crosses my face. "Not directly. But I made sure he knows that you're very satisfied."

She sighs and shakes her head. "Sweet Jesus, Brew. Your eye looks bad. And your lip. What did you do to him? We both know you're not a fighter."

I chuckle. "I got a lucky shot off and I think I broke his nose. But then he just cried. It was a really shitty first fight. I thought I'd always feel this rush of adrenaline, but turns out, I just felt bad for the guy." I put my hands on her hips and pull her to me and look into her eyes. "I know if I lost you, I'd be distraught, too, so I can't really blame him. But he shouldn't bother us anymore."

Gemma grips my jaw, her expression serious. "Are you okay?"

I nod. "I'll be fine. I just hope this black eye goes away before the party."

"It better, or Curtis will say you got in a fight on purpose to ruin the pictures." We laugh and she presses a kiss to my lips and I hiss. She gives me an apologetic smile. "Sorry. Put some ice on that. I'll get the rest of the groceries."

I shake my hand. "I'm fine, Gem. But you can come get these pillows and stuff that I had to literally fight my way out with."

She rolls her eyes. "Sure. Although, I think you'll like these pillows."

"I like my pillows just fine, thanks."

"That's just because you haven't slept on my pillows."

While we lay in bed later, Gemma draws lazy circles on my stomach with her fingertip. "Did you find a dress today?" I ask as I drag my fingers down her back.

She presses a kiss to my pec. "Yep. It's so perfect, even Mom liked it. She'd picked out some traditional dresses, and I still tried them on for her, but as soon as I put on *the* dress, even she knew it was the one."

"So, what do you mean by traditional, just a white one or whatever?"

"Yeah, I told her up front I was not wearing a white dress. And the one I got is nowhere near white."

"Ooh, sounds interesting. Want to tell me about it?"

"Nope, I want to surprise you."

I run my hand down her arm and intertwine our fingers. "Okay. Do you still want me to get a dark gray suit? Isn't that what color you said?"

"Yeah. I mean, you could do black, but gray looks better on you."

"You've got it. Lawson is going to go with me, and then we're going to go out for beers."

"That'll be fun. I'm sorry about Kyle, and I'm sorry that I assumed you started the fight."

"It's okay, Gem. If it was up to me, there would have been no fight. Fighting is overrated. I can't believe people actually do that for a job. My eye hurts like a bitch."

Her laugh vibrates through her chest and into my skin. "Oh, poor baby. Want me to kiss it and make it better?"

"You can kiss any part of me you want, Pearl. Always."

Her hand slowly skims down my waist. "Is there a particular part you would like me to focus my kisses on?"

I huff a laugh. "No. If they're kisses from you, I'd be happy to have them anywhere you wanted to put them."

Her fingers slip under the waistband of my boxers. "Do you need kisses here?"

"That might be nice," I say with a smile.

Her hand dips into my boxers and she runs her fingers along the length of my cock and taps the head. "What about here? Do you need kisses here?" My cock hardens under her touch and I hear her smile in her voice. "I'll take that as a yes," she says as she pulls her hand out.

She presses kisses into my chest and down my stomach before tugging the waistband on my boxers between her teeth. When she lets it go, the elastic snaps back against my skin, sending jolts of awareness to every molecule south of my belly button. I run my hand up her back and slide my hands into the hair at the base of her skull. "What about you, Gem; where do you need kisses?"

Her mouth moves side to side along my stomach as she shakes her head. "No, you can't give kisses right now. Your lip needs to heal." A beat later, her fingers hook in the band on my boxers. "Lift your hips."

I do as she requests and my dick pops free as she tugs the underwear off my hips. "You need so many kisses, husband." She wraps her fingers around my shaft and presses her lips against the side before trailing kisses up to the head. "Do you want to fuck my mouth, Brew?"

"Shit, Pearl, when you ask it like that, how can I say no?"

CHAPTER TWENTY-THREE

GEMMA

"Shit, Pearl, when you ask it like that, how can I say no?"

Brew's fingers are kneading into the back of my neck and I know it won't take much for those fingers to grip the hair close to my scalp and use me.

The truth is, I've never been one who enjoyed giving head. I've always used it as a means to an end when I didn't feel like having sex or if I was on my period and the guy whined about not being able to have sex. Although, I honestly have no qualms about having sex on my period, most guys—in my experience—are put off by it. While the topic of period sex has yet to come up with Brew, I don't get the feeling he's squeamish about it. I'm interested to see if that's the case.

But giving Brew head, it's different. Again, maybe that's because I was selfish before, but I think it's just because it's him and I love every part of him and showing him how much I love him.

I lick my lips and lower my mouth onto his cock. Brew lets out a soft groan that makes heat settle low in my belly. I love that he's not quiet in bed. I love his filthy mouth and his words of praise. And yeah, that probably has something to do with words of affirmation being my love language, but I think Brew is just exceptional at dirty talk. Whatever it is, I love it.

His hand grips my hair and he thrusts into my mouth, but it would seem that even in the dark, he knows just how deep to go without making me gag. I don't bother trying to be ladylike about getting him off. Spit trails down my chin and the sound that emanates from our motions is wet and sucking. I can't bite back a moan as I take him in my mouth.

Brew's breathing grows more and more shallow, and when he speaks, it's through gritted teeth. "Fucking hell, Gem, your mouth was made for my cock. Shit. You're gonna have to stop. Fuck. I want inside you. Right fucking now."

I pull off him, but continue stroking him with my hand. "I started my period today, so we don't have to. I can just finish you off." Even though my flow is barely enough to warrant a panty liner, I'm not about to not at least give him a heads up, even if I don't think it's that big a deal.

"Fuck that. I'll get a towel." He practically leaps off the bed, and I can't help but laugh. He's back before I have a chance to miss him and he places the towel on the bed. I roll onto my back, and even in the near pitch dark, I can feel him. Even though he's not touching me, I can still sense him. And as if he can see in the dark, his hands land on my hips and he works my panties down my legs. "Are you wet for me, Pearl?" he asks, his hand trailing up the inside of my thigh.

"Yes." I drag my hands down his waist and he stills their movement. He pulls them away from his body and pins them above my head. My heart rate tics up, but I don't try to pull away.

"Did it make you horny to let me use your mouth?"

"Yes."

"You want me to touch you, Gem?"

"Please, Brew."

He nudges my knees apart and settles between my thighs. I feel the head of his cock sliding up and down my pussy and I shift my hips to nudge him deeper. He gives my clit a gentle pinch with his free hand and I gasp. "I want you to be good for me, Pearl. Can you do that? Can you lay here and let me get you even wetter?" He continues to drag his cock up and down, occasionally rubbing my clit just enough to make me moan, but then he moves it away and I huff. Brew lets out a soft laugh. "Your pussy needy tonight?"

I let out a frustrated sigh. "You were the one that said 'right the fuck now'."

"You're right, I did." He punches his hips forward and slams into me and I exhale sharply and my hands reflexively pull against the restraint. But his one hand is nearly larger than both of mine and it's futile. "No, you don't get to touch tonight. Only I get to touch."

As if to prove his point, as he pounds against me, his free hand slides up my waist to knead my breast, his thumb flicking over the nipple and I can only whimper. I rock my hips forward, grinding my clit against his shaft as he thrusts into me.

Brew lowers his mouth to my breast and his tongue swirls around the nipple before he tugs it between his teeth. My breaths come as short, raspy pants with his movements.

He seems to lose himself in his pleasure, because he releases my hands to grip the back of my neck and crash our mouths together. For the briefest second, I worry about his busted lip, but then his tongue invades my mouth in a claiming barrage and I moan into our kiss. My heart bangs against my ribs and I fist my fingers into Brew's hair, knowing there's no way it doesn't sting.

When I think I'm not going to be able to breathe, he breaks

our kiss and I drag in a lungful of air. "So fucking sweet all the time. I could fuck you every day and it'd never be enough. Jesus, Pearl." I can tell by how strained his voice sounds that he's close and I reach between us to work my clit. He presses my knee back and I gasp at the sheer depth of his thrusts.

My climax builds and builds and builds. "God, Brew. I'm coming. Fuck. Oh, fuck." My words come out between ragged breaths and I let out a guttural sob, my entire body shuddering with my release.

"Gonna fill you up, Gem. Fuck. Coming. Shit." His hips buck one last time and his groan is deep. His forehead falls to my chest as he lets out a soft laugh.

I run my hand down his back. "What's so funny?"

"I'm pretty sure I could only get out about half my words there at the end."

I laugh against the side of his head and press a kiss into his hair. "How's your lip?"

"I don't even care right now." He rolls over to his side of the bed and pulls me into his arms.

The two weeks leading up to the party are punctuated by dress and suit fittings for me and Brew, compiling music choices for the DJ, and picking up our rings from the jewelers. We're both just ready to get the whole thing over with and settle into what we hope will be some sort of normal life.

Our lawyers—okay, Graham—looked over our syndication offers, but they all stipulate having Curtis as our production manager and I've shot them all down, which we both knew I would. We were truly hoping to get an offer from satellite radio, but unfortunately, it didn't happen.

I've given notice to my apartment and slowly, we're swapping some pieces of furniture at Brew's house—our house—with pieces from my apartment. The rest we're placing in storage for now, but we'll probably end up having a yard sale soon to get rid of things we don't need.

When I walk into the kitchen after getting ready for work, Brew's on his phone pouring a cup of coffee. "What do you mean, you already sent it? I never received it." He hands me the coffee and pours himself a cup and takes a sip. "Okay, well, can you send it to my personal email? Maybe our station's spam filter caught it or something."

He's quiet for a minute and then his eyes go wide. "What? Why not?" His mouth falls open in blatant shock as he listens. "Okay, so you sent the other footage to them as well, right? The surrounding areas and the hallway to our room and things?" I surmise he must finally have connected with the guy from the casino. "Okay, yeah, can you send me his name and info? You can just text it to this number if that's possible... Thank you, Edward. Have a good one."

Brew disconnects the call and doesn't wait for me to even ask. "Okay, so that was Edward. You know, the guy from the casino."

"About time. What did he say?"

"He said he sent us the footage from the craps table the day we requested it, but that he also had to send it to the police."

I feel my own eyes go wide. "What?"

"Yeah, he said that after he sent it to me, he rewatched it. In the video, it looks like someone slips something into our drinks, so their policy is to always file a police report."

My mouth falls open. "So, we were drugged?"

He shrugs. "I don't know. He just said that's what it looks like. A Vegas detective has the footage as well, but Edward said they had to turn everything over to the PD, so he can't send me anything. But he is going to send me the name and number of the detective so we can connect with him."

I shake my head. "See, I knew there was something weird about the hangover. We'll probably still never find out what it was, but I guess it could have been worse." I have the awful thought about what would have happened if Brew or I had been alone when we were drugged.

He comes to stand in front of me. "Hey, what's that face about?"

I blow out a deep breath. "I just had the horrific thought about what could've happened if I was alone and had been drugged. Or you. Anyone could have done anything to us. Thank God we just got married and only had sex with each other."

His expression sobers. "Jesus. I didn't even think about that." He checks his watch. "Shit, we're going to be late. Thank fuck that party is tomorrow and then all the jumping through hoops is done."

I nod. "Definitely. Although, I'm kind of looking forward to seeing you in a suit, not gonna lie. You're going to look so handsome."

Brew pulls me to him. "And I can't wait to see you in this amazing dress you picked out." He lifts my left hand with my new ring. "You know, I knew this was the one you were going to pick. It's exactly what I would have picked for you."

I give him a soft smile. "I was really okay with my plain gold band, too, though. I may wear them both."

He nods. "Go for it, Pearl."

"Is it weird that tomorrow feels like a wedding, even if we're not going through all the vows and stuff? I'm still wearing a wedding dress and we're going to have a first dance and cut a cake and dance with our parents and stuff."

He shrugs. "I have a feeling it would be very similar if we'd had an actual church wedding."

I huff a laugh. "Yeah, except my mother would have insisted on a full catholic mass and we would have been so tired by the time the reception rolled around, we would have collapsed into the nearest chairs."

Brew's phone dings and he looks at the screen. "Good. I've got the number for the detective. As bad as I'd like to call him now, I don't have time. Looks like I'll have to wait until Monday morning."

I nod. "Well, hopefully, we'll find out what really happened."

"I'm not entirely hopeful, but maybe."

Our show ramps up and winds down like it always does, but by the end of the day, I'm so exhausted, I can barely keep my eyes open. Brew practically has to carry me out to the car. "What's up, Pearl? You need a nap?"

I shrug. "I don't know. I think it's just work and the party and stuff catching up with me. Can we just order pizza tonight and have a chill night?"

He nods. "Yeah, except you have to go pick up your dress and I have to get my suit."

I groan and pull out my phone. "I'm going to see if Mom can swing by and pick it up for me. The shop is closer to her house anyway and she'll be coming to the hotel tomorrow to be with me while I get ready, so she can bring it with her. My shoes and stuff are at the house, so I can just take them with me. The tux place is on our way home; we can just pick it up, right?"

"Yeah, of course."

I lean over and give him a kiss on the cheek. "Thanks. I'm sensing a really early bedtime for me tonight."

"Sounds good to me."

After swinging by the tux shop before picking up pizza and beer for supper, Brew and I head home and I'm still struggling to keep my eyes open. It seems as though I haven't pushed myself like this, spread myself this thin, since college, and it's all catching up with me.

We sit on the couch, each with a slice of sausage and pepperoni and a beer, and Brew turns on *Hell's Kitchen*. I can't help but smile. "You know, we can watch other stuff. I know you know I have a thing for Gordon Ramsey, but I'm good to watch something else."

Brew grins. "Nah, you always get so amped up watching this and I like to see you. It makes sex hotter."

I roll my eyes. "*Hell's Kitchen* does not get me hot."

He shrugs. "If you say so, Pearl, but I've taken you to bed enough after you've watched it to know."

I nudge him playfully with my elbow and he pulls me closer to him and plants a kiss on the top of my head. "You know, I had the thought the other day that I never really thought about marriage much. Well, until we got married, and then it was pretty much all I thought about." He gives me a sheepish smile and I laugh.

"But I didn't look forward to living with someone else or sharing a bathroom or moving around my kitchen with someone else. I always thought that it would be a hassle. Anytime girlfriends would spend more than a night or two here, that's what if felt like. I thought the adjustment of having someone in my life that much would cause fights and there would be a lot of growing pains."

"I'm not sure if I'm supposed to ask if I'm a terrible house-mate or if it's better than you expected."

Brew sets his plate on the coffee table and turns to me. "See, that's the thing, Gem; with us, there hasn't been an adjustment. I don't know what to think about it, except that we're pretty much the same people at home as we are at work, so our transition was easier. But what I mean is, I never thought about marrying any of the women I dated over these last ten years.

"I know now, it's because it was always supposed to be you. I never saw it until after we got married and I'm not saying it's always going to be this easy because I'm sure we're still in our little honeymoon love bubble, but loving you is easy, Gem. Loving you has always been easy."

He takes my face in his hands and looks into my eyes. "That morning, when we woke up, freaking out and trying to piece things together and we found out about the video? I had a flash from our wedding. And not just of me kissing you."

I frown in confusion. "Really?"

He nods. "After I kissed you, you remember how it looks like I went in for a hug?" I nod and he smiles. "I'd actually whispered something in your ear."

"Was it dirty?" I ask with a grin and pump my eyebrows.

He chuckles. "No, it wasn't dirty. I told you I was so happy you were gonna be mine forever. And I guess it took you asking me to marry you to make me see that. Because, like I said, I didn't really think about marriage. I wanted kids, but marriage was this abstract thing to me. But marriage to you is my favorite thing in the whole world."

Tears burn my eyes. "You and your damn big heart. Jeez. But please don't ever stop saying things like that to me. You are the best man, Brew. Better than I could have ever deserved and I love being your wife. Now, you can take me to bed."

He laughs. "I thought you were really tired?"

I shrug. "I got amped up."

He chuckles. "Remind me to send a shout out to Gordon Ramsey to thank him for the boost in my wife's libido."

I shake my head and pull him off the couch as I stand. "Or, it could be that my husband makes me deliriously happy and the only place the happiness has to go is straight to my vagina."

Brew lets out a deep, full belly laugh and he tugs me toward the bedroom.

CHAPTER TWENTY-FOUR

BREWSTER

"Well, a wedding it might not be, but you still look good, baby brother. And it sounds like it's going to be a hell of a party. I'm really glad you're not making me do a whole best man speech, though, if I'm honest."

I grin at Lawson as we sip tumblers of bourbon while we wait to go down to the party. "What would you have said if you did have to make a speech?"

He takes a drink, sits back in his chair, and thinks for a minute. "It'd probably be something suitably embarrassing, like the time you burnt off all your sack hair trying to light that fart on fire when we went camping when you were fifteen."

I groan. "Oh, God, I'd totally suppressed that memory. I walked funny for a week after that."

Lawson laughs. "Yeah, it was great. I'd also probably have to tell about the day you met Gemma."

"What about it?" I ask, unsure what he'd be referring to.

"You don't remember?"

"Remember what? Of course I remember the day I met her.

She was still in college and I made fun of her for wearing a suit, then I took her script away and she was pissed."

My brother nods. "Yeah, but I knew that day that she was gonna be special to you. You'd had other new broadcasters they'd paired you with before her and you never went out of your way to make sure they did well. You just let them sink. But with Gemma, you took her script, but you also made sure she had a tool to succeed. You asked her, what was it, something she could talk about for twenty minutes?" I nod. "And I was listening during that first show y'all did together."

I can't hide my surprise. "It was like one in the morning."

He nods. "Yeah, Holly was up with the baby and I was trying to be a supportive husband, so I got up with her when she nursed. I knew you were doing the overnight show, so I turned it on just to have as background noise in the nursery.

"Anyway, you and Gemma got into that really great debate about cookies or something, and she just seemed to come to life when you all started bantering back and forth. It was really something. You'd never know it was your first show together. After y'all finished that segment, you said something like, 'well, looks like she's not just a pretty face after all.' But the way you said it, it was as though she really impressed you." He laughs, as if the memory is coming back in full force. "And then she said, 'pretty is a social construct designed by the patriarchy to place value on a woman based on her physical appearance.' But she was so serious. And you said—."

"Well, would you look at that? Brains, too. Man, I'm in trouble," I finish the line from my memory. "Wow, I'd completely forgotten that. She was so pissed that I'd said something about her looks. When we went to commercial break, she tore into me. She was so cute with her short hair and glasses, I almost wanted to laugh, even as she ripped me a new one."

Lawson nods. "So, yeah, I knew even back then that y'all were going to go the distance. I didn't know that meant you'd end up together, but even then I could see that y'all had this special connection. You've always been able to bring out that carefree side of her and she grounds you. You guys are the real deal, brother, and I'm happy for you. So, yeah, that's what I would've said."

My chest tightens with emotion. "Thanks, Law. That would've been great." I check my watch and see that we're supposed to be down to make our entrance in a bit, so I walk over to the mirror to give my appearance one last look.

Lawson comes up beside me to check his own tie in the mirror. "Honestly, I can't believe Curtis didn't try to make you cut your hair off."

I laugh. "Gemma would have rioted. She loves my hair. I think she might be a little obsessed with it. She sure likes to put her hands in it. A lot," I say with a wink.

He rolls his eyes. "Yeah, well, let's see how much that hair serves you when your six-month-old baby has learned to grab things and finds your hair. You might reconsider."

I chuckle. "That's what man buns are for, brother."

He grins and seems to be struck by a thought. "I meant to ask, how did all the offers go? Didn't y'all get several?"

I nod. "Yeah, but all the ones we received were predicated on Curtis staying our production manager and Gemma wants to be done with him, so we shot all of them down. We thought for sure we'd get one from satellite, especially after a meeting we took in Vegas with this guy from LA, but nothing. I've been meaning to follow up with him, but with how we've been scheduled to the hilt these past few weeks, I haven't really even had time to breathe. After today, it should die down and I've got a lot of things I need to follow up on."

Lawson claps a hand on my shoulder. "Well, let's go give you away or whatever. I'm so glad you're someone else's problem now," he says, affection lacing his tone.

"You're such a sweetheart, Law."

As I turn, he places both hands on my shoulders. "For real, though, I am thrilled for you and Gemma. And I wish you guys all the best."

"Thanks, man. I'm happy for us, too. I also can't wait to see how hot my wife looks in her dress." We walk out of the room and head toward the elevator, and I adjust my cufflinks as my brother pushes the button.

"You haven't seen it?"

I shake my head. "No, she wanted it to be a surprise. All I know is, it's not white. That's all she told me."

"Well, if I know Gemma, it'll be beautiful."

"If I know her, it'll be sexy."

He lets out a soft laugh as we step onto the elevator. "Well, I wasn't going to say that, but that's what I meant."

When we get to the ground floor, we make our way toward the ballroom of the Claremont Hotel, a historic Knoxville hotel. I don't even want to think about what it would've cost Gem and me if we were paying out of pocket for this. As we get closer to the room that's been designated as a sort of staging room for Gemma and me to wait until we're announced, Lawson splits off to go on to the party to join his wife and our parents.

As I reach the door, I'm suddenly nervous; as if this really is our wedding day and I can't help the butterflies swarming in my guts. I give a small knock and I hear her voice as I enter, but I don't see her right off. "Pearl?"

She steps from beside a wall, adjusting one of her earrings, and I stop in my tracks. She's absolutely gorgeous in a formfitting dress made of black tulle over silver satin with a short train and detailed beading along the bodice. If you had asked me before Curtis made us do all these segments on weddings and shit, I'd never even know what tulle is.

Although it's black, it's a very soft black with a silver underlay and it has thin shoulder straps, along with a deep V in the front. Her hair is in soft curls swept to the side and her makeup is a dark smoky eye that makes her hazel eyes pop.

I must look dumbfounded or equally shocked, because after a beat, Gemma walks toward me. "I take it by the look on your face, you approve?"

I shake the fog from my brain and close the distance between us. "Gem, you look fucking stunning. Jesus, I don't even have words."

She blushes with the compliment. "You look pretty damn hot yourself. God, you look handsome in a suit."

I make a little twirl motion with my index finger and I know before I even see it how fantastic her ass is going to look in this dress. But I'm definitely unprepared to see the back. The dress is practically backless, so low you can nearly see the divots at the small of her back. "Shit, Gem, this dress. Wow."

She faces me with a smile on her face. "I'm glad you like it. I love it. I feel sexy and I'm ready to party. Now, give me a kiss. I waited to put on lipstick because I wanted to kiss you before we had to go out. I happily oblige her and lift her chin to press a soft kiss to her lips.

A door opens on the other side of the room and the event coordinator enters the room. "It's showtime. Curtis is going to announce you all in just a minute and you'll walk out to the middle of the dance floor and do your first dance."

I nod and watch as Gemma swipes on some dark red lipstick before stepping back to examine her appearance one last time in a full-length mirror. "Pearl, no one is going to be able to take their eyes off of you; least of all me."

She grins and walks up to me, linking her arm in mine.

"Well, I'll be happy to let you look at me all night as long as you promise to take this dress off me when we get up to our room."

I lean into her and press a kiss to her temple. "I'll rip it off you if that's what you want. Me getting you naked was already a given for tonight."

She blushes and looks up at me. "I love you, Brew."

"Love you, too, Gem."

Through the open door, we hear Curtis taking the microphone. He drones on for no less than five minutes, thanking all the sponsors for the event. Then he finally seems to remember he's supposed to introduce Gemma and me. "Finally, for the reason we're all here tonight. I knew when I first paired Brewster and Gemma up all those years ago, they had chemistry. It comes across the radio and in their personal relationship. They say you shouldn't work with your spouse, but it seems to have only improved their working relationship. Without further ado, I'm very pleased to introduce WXOR's own Brewster and Gemma, a love story ten years in the making."

As we make our way out to the floor amidst cheers and rounds of applause, Gemma says with a smile, so only I know she's speaking, "I'm honestly shocked he didn't completely take credit for our relationship."

I can't help but chuckle as I take my wife in my arms as we begin to dance once the first bars of a One Direction song that I can't remember the name of. I'm not a pop music kind of guy in the least, but the lyrics of the song definitely fit for me and Gemma, so I didn't hesitate when she suggested it.

We sway on the floor, and I rest my forehead on hers and hold her hand against my chest. "I know we've done this party thing kind of begrudgingly, but I'm not gonna lie, Pearl, I love showing you off as my wife and dancing with you."

She smiles. "Yeah, this is alright. Can I ask you something?"

I chuckle. "Of course."

"I don't think I've ever asked, but why did you call me Pearl all those years ago? I've never questioned it, and honestly, I've always loved that you have a nickname for me, but why Pearl? Did you have a specific reason, or you just liked it, or what?"

I think back to when I first called her that and can't help but smile. "Well, I'd gone with Lawson to look at some jewelry for Holly for her birthday or Mother's day or something. I can't remember what it was for, but the jeweler was talking about the different kinds of gemstones and things and he asked Law if Holly had any pearls. That pearls were classy, and every woman needed a set of them.

"Lawson asked why the ones they were showing us were so expensive, because they were a lot, and the jeweler told him that the ones he had were all natural, not farmed and therefore, rare. He said that pearls—real, natural pearls—are exceedingly rare these days. And unlike gemstones like diamonds and rubies and stuff, they don't have to be polished or cut before they can be used. They're perfect, just as they're found in nature. Their beauty is entirely organic. He explained that pearls are formed through a mollusk getting a grain of sand or particulate deep enough in their shell that they can't get rid of it. So, they're formed by the discomfort of their environment. Yet, despite that discomfort, something beautiful is the end result."

I bring my hand up to Gemma's face and cup her cheek. "*You* have always been organically beautiful, without any polish. You turn any uncomfortable situation you're facing into something beautiful. And you are rare and precious, Gem. I've always known that. Even on the day we met, I knew you were rare. So, when the jeweler described pearls and how great they were, your face immediately came to my mind. Even if I didn't know that I loved you back then, I still knew you were special to me."

Gemma's eyes shine with unshed tears. "I swear, Brewster Lincoln, you should've been some sort of poet. Jesus."

I lean in and press a kiss to her cheek and whisper in her ear. "Listen, lady, I get paid to use my mouth. I'd be happy to show you what else it can do."

She laughs out loud and pulls back from me. "I've heard that one before."

My brows press together in confusion. "You have?"

She nods. "Yeah, when we were in the elevator going up to our room, you kissed me and I asked where you'd learn to kiss like that and you said that bit about being paid to use your mouth." We both laugh, and as the song ends, I bring her hand up to my face and press a kiss to her palm.

Over the next few hours, we're greeted by so many sponsors and party goers, Gemma and I are both a bit punch drunk by the time we cut the cake, but we manage to not shove it in each other's faces and share a sweet, frosting-laden kiss.

We dance with our parents and endure a champagne toast from Curtis, who uses his time to again thank all the sponsors for a great evening. After he leaves the stage, he winds his way through the crowd and comes to stand in front of Gem and me. "You all did real well tonight. Enjoy the rest of the party, okay? On Monday, it's back to the grind. And listen, we're going to talk about those syndication offers. I can't believe you guys turned those down. They were lucrative deals. You're not going to get much better than that."

I see a muscle twitch in Gemma's jaw. "Be that as it may, we'd still like to see what else is out there before we settle on something we're not a hundred percent happy with."

He considers. "Well, that's your right, I guess. Enjoy the rest of the party; I'll see y'all on Monday, okay?"

We nod and I watch as Curtis walks over to the other side of the room. I notice a tall guy looking very much like Vin Diesel's body double leaning against the wall and as he sees Curtis approach, he pushes off the wall and grabs our production manager roughly by the lapel of his jacket. He practically drags him out of the room and the hairs on the back of my neck stand up.

I glance at Gemma, who's talking with Rosie, and I lean over to her. "I'll be back in a minute." She shoots me a quick grin of acknowledgement before returning to her conversation.

I head toward the door that Curtis exited, thankful to not be intercepted by anyone. Once I get out into the hall, I follow the sound of voices, one of which I recognize as Curtis. I peek around a corner and see Curtis and the Vin Diesel lookalike engaged in some sort of heated discussion. I make sure to stay out of sight; especially when the guy punches Curtis in the gut.

"Where is my money, Curtis? Did we not agree that I'd have my money by today?"

I'm not sure what makes me do it, but I pull out my phone and begin filming the exchange around the corner. Curtis holds his hands up defensively; even as he's almost doubled over in obvious pain. "I'm working on it. I'm trying to get them to sign a deal and then I'll be flush and you'll have your money. I swear."

I can't help but wonder with a sinking feeling if the "them" he's referring to is Gem and me, and I'm immediately pissed.

The lookalike grabs Curtis's shirt and gets in his face. "Listen to me, you smarmy little shit. I followed through on my end of the deal. I cloned their phones, I made it so they wouldn't remember, I made sure the video leaked. And just because they didn't do the crazy shit you hoped they would, my services still aren't cheap, Curtis. We agreed on a sum and today was the arranged date. I'm beginning to think you don't take me or my employer seriously."

Fear is plain on Curtis's face and I'm trying to reconcile the things I'm hearing. *Cloned phones? He leaked the video?* Not to mention the talk about making sure we didn't remember. Rage and so many questions roil in my gut.

"I'll get your money, I swear. I just need more time. I thought they would've signed a deal by now. I'll put more pressure on them. As soon as they sign one, I'll get my finder's fee and you'll have your money."

"You have one week, Curtis. And I'm adding twenty percent interest. You better come through or there might be some very interested parties who will want to find out all the shady shit you've been up to. Least of all, the bride and groom. How do you think they'll take it if they knew all the things you've been doing to keep them down just so you get to keep your job?" He delivers one final punch to Curtis's middle, and he goes down in a heap on the floor. "One week, Curtis. Don't make me come find you again."

The guy starts walking back toward me and I book it to a nearby alcove to hide. I wait a few minutes and peek out to ensure he's gone and book it back to the ballroom. Looking around, I try to find Gemma, only to find her on the dance floor with Augusta. They're singing at the top of their lungs to a Spice Girls song, clearly having the time of their lives. Despite the way my brain is swimming with questions and the anger I feel toward Curtis knowing that he's at least partially responsible for Gemma's and my forgotten night, looking at her across the room, having a blast with her best friend, some of my anger fades.

Struck with a thought, I search for Graham. I finally spot him across the room at the bar, sipping a lowball glass of clear liquor, his gaze fixed somewhere in the direction of his sister and her best friend, an amused smile on his face. Honestly, it catches me off guard because I don't know if, in the ten years I've known him, I've ever seen the man smile. Maybe tonight is the night for all the shocking revelations.

I make my way over to him and field congratulations from partygoers. When I finally reach him, I tap him on the shoulder. "Hey, Graham, can I talk to you for a minute?"

He blinks, his expression returning to its customary scowl, and he eyes me for a beat before finally shrugging. I jerk my chin toward a quiet corner and he frowns. "What's with the secrecy, Brewster?"

I show him the video and his eyes go wide. After it concludes, he shakes his head in disbelief. "Shit. That's serious."

I nod. "Yeah, and not that I wasn't already planning on calling the detective in Vegas on Monday, because the guy from the casino said it looks like someone slips something in our drinks, but now, this pretty much confirms that we were drugged, right?"

"That's what it looks like to me."

I think for a second. "In all those contracts we had you look over, was there mention of any kind of finder's fee for Curtis as our production manager?"

He sips his drink. "Yeah, all of them had at least a twenty to thirty percent yearly commission based on your and Gemma's combined salary. I get why y'all didn't want to be tied to him. He's a sleaze ball."

I nod. "Yeah. So, what do you recommend I do, from a legal standpoint?"

"Hell, Brewster, I'm not a criminal lawyer. I deal mostly with family law and litigation. But, if I were you, I'd get you and Gemma new phones and back up that video. If he went through all the trouble to clone your phones, there's no telling what kinds of emails and things you've missed."

"Okay. Thanks, man. Can I email this video to you, just in case? I don't know that I even trust my personal email now."

He nods. "Yeah, sure. You realize Gemma's gonna shit a brick, right?"

I sigh and glance over at her. "Yeah, I know."

CHAPTER TWENTY-FIVE

GEMMA

Brew is already up and dressed the day after our reception. I'm hungover and bleary-eyed as he sets a cup of coffee on the nightstand, brushes a kiss across my cheek, and sits on the edge of the bed of our hotel suite. I reach for him and run my hand down his arm. "Why are you up so early?" I nearly panic, thinking I've overslept. "Shit. I'm supposed to take Augusta home at ten."

He chuckles. "You're fine; it's not even nine. Listen, I need you to get up; I've got to show you something. I wanted to show it to you last night, but you were having such a good time and I didn't want to ruin it for you."

Suddenly on high alert, I sit up, trying to focus on him. "What's wrong?"

"I need you to watch this video. But drink your coffee first. If it was much later, I'd offer you wine."

I sip my coffee. "What's going on?"

"I don't know, honestly, except that we might have to make a trip back to Vegas."

I'm trying to rub my few sober brain cells together. "What? Why?"

"I called that detective."

"It's Saturday."

He nods. "I know, but he still answered. He wants us to look at the videos to see if we recognize the guy who put stuff in our drink. And I'm thinking it's gonna be the same guy from a video I took last night."

I frown in confusion. "What video from last night?" I set my coffee down and he hands me his phone and hits the play button on his screen.

I watch in confusion as a large bald guy assaults our production manager. When the guy says that he cloned our phones and made sure our video leaked, I gasp. As soon as I hear him say he made sure we didn't remember anything, my stomach seizes up and I barely make it to the toilet before I vomit.

Brew holds my hair as last night's wine makes a second appearance, and he runs his hand down my back. "I'm sorry, Pearl. I know we suspected we were drugged, but I honestly didn't think we'd have it confirmed."

I sit back against the side of the tub after I finally finish retching. Brew hands me a damp washcloth and I wipe my mouth. "That fucker. You know I'm going to kill him, right? Like, pull his spine out through his back and spit on his corpse."

He seems impressed by my imagination. "Okay, well, first things first, we have to get new phones. We can't trust ours. I also sent the video to Graham, because I'm not even sure I can trust my personal email anymore."

I nod. "Okay, so what about Vegas? We can't tell Curtis we're going out there to talk to the police. He'll get suspicious and we can't have that. Whatever he's been working on, he'll burn or trash or whatever to make sure there's no paper trail. Plus, I still have to take Augusta home."

He nods. "Yeah, well, if I can get that detective to meet with us this evening, we can go to Vegas tonight. We'll go as soon as you take her home and we can be back before Monday. Curtis will never know. It's going to suck and we'll probably be jet lagged, but I think we have to do it."

"Okay. Of course." I'm struck with a thought. "What if Florida was a diversion?"

"What do you mean?"

"What if Curtis used Florida to distract us so that he could screen all our emails and see if we got any offers or anything? Didn't you say the other day the guy from the casino said he sent you the video the same day you requested it?"

He nods slowly, seeming to work through some thoughts as well. "Yeah, and other than when Curtis emailed us the script for the promo spot we had to do, I never really checked my email. And I know you didn't check yours."

"Not to mention, why would they sponsor a honeymoon before a reception? Honestly. It really doesn't make any sense, now that I think about it. If they wanted to get the most bang for their buck, advertising-wise, they would've had us promo it a ton leading up to the vacation. They wouldn't have wanted to go straight into it."

He seems unsure. "Maybe. Seems like a big gamble, though, and that place was really nice. It would be much more plausible, knowing Curtis, if he just stuck us in some cheap motel at the beach, not a really fancy resort in the Keys."

I shake my head. "Not if we were supposed to believe it was sponsored. We've gotten really great perks from sponsors before. If a travel agency was sponsoring us, they'd pull out the big guns to guarantee a positive promo. If Curtis really went to all the trouble to clone our phones and have us drugged, I'm not putting something like a fancy resort beyond what he'd do. Especially if he thought he'd be able to cherry pick the best syndication offers for us, so that he got the biggest payday.

"We haven't exactly been quiet about our dissatisfaction with Curtis as our production manager. I've hated him for years. Plus, he knows that we've been a packaged deal pretty much since he put us together and if one of us walked, we'd both walk."

I rise from the bathroom floor and look at my husband. "Call the detective and setup a meeting. We need to get this shit straightened out. As soon as I drop Augusta off at her place, I'll come home and we can go." He nods and pulls out his phone as I start the shower.

A half-hour later, I'm standing in the hotel lobby with two cups of coffee as I wait for Augusta. I check my phone for the third time, and shift my weight from one foot to the other, impatient to get home and head to Vegas to finally get some clarity about our wedding night.

That's the hope, anyway.

As the elevator opens and my best friend spills out, I nearly do a double take at how disheveled she is. Her hair is in a haphazard ponytail, her makeup is smudged all over her face, and her shirt is on backwards. And judging by the myriad of hickeys dotting her throat and how relaxed she looks, she's obviously well-fucked.

I hand over her coffee, so many questions ready to fly from my mouth. She holds up her hand. "Not a word."

Despite how badly I want details of her night, I mime zipping my lips as we troop out to my car. Once she's in the passenger seat, I can't hold it back anymore as I eye her, not even bothering to start the engine. "I have questions."

"Nope."

"Oh, come on. Was it good, at least?" I ask, my tone hopeful. "Because, um, those are some impressive hickeys, my friend. Do I know him? Are you seeing him again?"

She pinches the bridge of her nose and closes her eyes. After a long beat, she blows out a breath. "Yes. It was random. No."

I blink in shock. "Wow. You actually had a one-night stand? You don't do one-night stands."

Her shoulders rise and fall in a nonchalant shrug. "He was hot. I was tipsy and horny. It worked out. He was gone when I got up. We did not exchange numbers."

Still more than a bit shocked, I can only stare at her. Augusta doesn't do one-night stands. Ever. Now she's acting like it's no big deal. Then again, maybe something like this is what she needed, so I keep my tone neutral. "Well. Good for you, I guess. But it was good?"

"Best night of my life."

Okay, maybe I don't need to worry, and my best friend actually did just want to let loose and have fun for the night. Who could blame her? She's young, single, and smoking hot. Good for her.

I start the engine and nod, impressed. "Damn. Alright. Well, hopefully you'll run into him again. Make sure you get his number if there's a repeat performance because I don't think I've ever seen you this...well serviced."

She looks like she wants to smile, but just slides her sunglasses on her face as her head falls back against the headrest. "I'll take it under advisement."

We land in Las Vegas at a little before six local time, and as soon as we get to our rental car, we head to the police station. When we give our names to the desk clerk, we're told to wait in the lobby. I'd forgotten just how hot it is in Vegas and I'm pouring sweat in my dark jeans and silk blouse, wishing I'd opted for a thin sundress instead.

Brew looks cool in his standard jeans and T-shirt, but keeps running his fingers through his hair, the only indication that he's even remotely on edge. I take his hand in mine and I'm about to tell him to chill, when a tall, thin black man with a badge clipped to his belt walks over to us. "Mr. and Mrs. Lincoln?"

When we confirm our identities, he extends his hand and we shake. "I'm Detective Kevin Copeland. I appreciate you all making the trip out from back east on such short notice."

"Of course. Thank you for meeting with us and for taking time out of your Saturday," Brew says with a smile.

He leads us to a small room that I'm sure they use for interrogations and stuff, based on the two-way mirror and the metal loop welded into the top of the table.

As we sit, Brew takes my hand in his and gives it a squeeze. Detective Copeland pulls out a notepad and also has a laptop tucked under his arm that he sets on the table but doesn't open. "Before we watch the video, I wanted to see what you all remember from the night in question." He opens his notepad and sits, ready to take notes. "Mrs. Lincoln, why don't you tell me what you recall?"

"Arguably, it's not much, to be honest. We both remember leaving supper where we'd had a few drinks. We remember going to play craps. After that, it's nearly a complete blank until the next morning. I remember flashes from our wedding night."

Heat creeps up my neck and the detective nods. "You don't

have to tell me details about that, but did anything seem strange that you recall from those flashes?"

"Yes, actually, but it didn't strike me as odd until a few days later. In my flashes, Brewster and I don't seem drunk. We seem giddy and excited and, well, really horny, but not drunk."

He nods, making a note. "And what about you, Mr. Lincoln? What do you remember?"

Brew shrugs. "Even less than Gemma. I remember the restaurant and playing craps for a while, but after that, it's blank, except for one moment from our wedding."

"And do you feel like you were drunk at the wedding?"

Brew seems to think and his eyes widen slightly. "No. I hadn't thought about it, even after Gemma told me we didn't seem drunk in her flashes. But, no, what I remember saying came out clear, not slurred or anything. And I know from our wedding video, we both look sober."

The detective nods. "Yes, it does appear that way. Okay, so I have the video footage from the craps table. And it looks like a man slips something into a couple of shots right before you all take them and leave the table. I want you to look at the man and see if you recognize him."

We both nod and he opens his screen. Before he hits play, I ask, "Would it be possible to watch a few minutes before that? Neither of us remembers anything, so I'd really like to know what all happened, if that's possible."

Copeland looks at me. "You guys are at that table for almost four hours."

Brew asks, "How about just the last hour or so? I know we'd been playing a while and I remember about three hours of it. We were up by about ten grand at that point."

I snap my head to his. "Really?"

He nods. "Yeah. Still, when we woke up, I was worried we'd blown all that and whatever else we had in our accounts."

The detective shrugs. "Okay. Sure." He scrubs the footage back about an hour and hits play. For the first thirty minutes, it's just Brew throwing dice and us cheering with a growing crowd around us, keen on watching us continue to win. There's no sound, but as I watch, and I see me lay my hand over his before he throws the dice, that moment comes back to me, sending goosebumps scattering down my arms.

———

We take a shot of tequila and Brew picks up the dice, ready to place another bet. "Brew, wait." He turns to me as I put my hand on his before he can throw the dice again. We're already up twenty-five grand. "Put it all in."

His eyes go wide. "Pearl, that's twenty-five thousand dollars. You choose this moment in your life to want to do something impulsive? When there's twenty-five grand on the line?"

"Do you trust me?"

Brew's eyes scan my face, his lips pulling up into a sweet smile. "With my life."

"Okay, then go all in." I put my hand on his chest and he blinks in surprise. "You know how you said when I found the right guy, my job wouldn't seem so important?"

He nods slowly, dice still in hand as his eyes continue to hold mine. "Yeah."

"You're the guy, Brew. And the only reason my job is so important to me is because of you. Go all in and if we win, marry me. I don't want to do my job without you. Hell, I don't want to ever do any part of my life without you anymore."

He lets out a shocked laugh. "Gemma. Are you serious?"

I nod. "You're my best friend and I love you, Brew. I just never realized it until now. Marry me."

The dealer pipes up. "What's the holdup?"

Brew doesn't take his eyes off mine, but pushes all our chips up to the pass line.

He searches my face, then grabs the back of my neck with his left hand and pulls my mouth to his for a deep kiss. It's the best kiss of my life. Sweet and tender, with more than a hint of the heat I'm suspecting has always been there, waiting to be discovered. It's enough to make my toes curl. My chest is heaving when he pulls back suddenly. "Yes."

It's my turn to laugh. "Really?"

He nods. "Yeah. Now, blow these dice and let's find an Elvis to get us hitched. I'm not letting you change your mind." He holds his hand up and I blow on the dice. He keeps his eyes on mine as he tosses them onto the table.

The small red cubes thud against the table, but I can only look at Brew. "Lucky number seven. We've got a big winner, folks."

Our heads snap to the dealer, mouths agape.

I put my hand on Brew's arm. "Oh shit, I remember what happened," I say with a laugh.

The detective pauses the video. "Ma'am?"

"Sorry. I don't remember taking anything, but I remember proposing and us winning the money."

Brew laughs. "Really?"

I nod and pull his face to mine for a kiss. The detective clears his throat. "Mind if we continue, Mrs. Lincoln?"

I blush and nod. "Yes, sir. I'm sorry, I'm just so excited to know what happened and what I said." I glance at Brew. "I'll tell you later."

Copeland starts the video again. On the screen, Brew and I are jumping up and down and hugging, then we must be telling the dealer to cash us out. He hands us a receipt and Brew sticks it in his pocket. There's a tray of shots that we'd been working on and sure enough, someone standing right next to me seems to put something into our shots, but you can't tell if it's a powder or liquid. It's also the same guy from Brew's video. We kiss for a moment and then take the shots and I grab Brew's face for one last kiss before we leave the table.

The video feed switches to another part of the casino and Brew and I are standing at a window and it must be when we're splitting our winnings. Once done, he grabs my hand and we start across the lobby and Edward stops us and hands us a room key for our comped room. We seem to excitedly tell him something and he nods and offers us a wide grin as he gestures to another area of the casino and gives us some directions.

Different cameras in the casino pick up our movement and after a few minutes, it's clear that the casino must have a chapel, and that's where we got married. "Well, that was convenient," Brew says with an amused grin.

It seems strange to watch us and not remember any of this, but soon, we sign papers at a desk outside the chapel, pay our fees, and buy our rings. Once we enter the chapel, the detective stops the video.

"The rest is the wedding video. And we have footage from the hallway outside your room, but there wasn't anything strange about it. You guys were just really eager to get to your room, it looks like," Copeland says with a smile.

I nod and huff a laugh. "Yeah, we were. So, what do you think he slipped us?"

The detective frowns. "Without tests, it's impossible to say for sure. If I was to guess, probably GHB. It's a date rape drug, but it doesn't incapacitate like Rohypnol tends to. Usually, when people take GHB, they can experience euphoria and increased libido, but most of the time, memory loss is a huge side effect. It can be tasteless and takes effect really quickly."

I blow out a breath and Brew squeezes my hand before he says, "Detective, at our wedding reception last night, I witnessed our production manager in an altercation with the guy from the video. I filmed it on my phone and I'm happy to share it with you, but he all but admitted to drugging us, as well as cloning our phones and making sure the video of our wedding leaked."

The detective's expression remains neutral. "Why would your production manager go to such lengths?"

Brew shrugs. "Honestly, I'm not sure, other than Gemma and I have a very popular radio talk show. We've been working towards getting syndicated for the past several years, but we've never planned on taking Curtis with us. He's been a decent production manager, and he's good at his job, but he's a slime-ball and we're done putting up with him.

"From the video I have, the bald guy says something to the effect of, 'I'm sorry they didn't get up to the dumb shit you hoped they would'. As if he thought by slipping us the drugs, we'd make fools of ourselves and make it so we could only get syndication offers that he secured.

"And when we were on the honeymoon, he practically forced us to take —"

The detective puts his hand up. "Wait, what?"

Brew sighs and recounts his conversation with Curtis after we'd found out our wedding video had gone viral and him threatening to blackball us if we didn't go along.

"So, your marriage is fake?"

"No," we both say in unison.

"Detective, obviously, we don't have proof, but I think I have some missing emails. We met with an exec from a network in L.A. who was very interested in our show and said he's be in touch. But Gemma and I were both adamant that Curtis would not be a part of the deal. It would just be for us. He was supposed to send me an email, and I never got it. I also was supposed to get an email with the footage from the casino and I never received it. I truly believe our production manager, or his associate from the video, tampered with my emails."

Copeland scratches his jaw and seems to contemplate. "Okay. Well, as it stands, the evidence we have on your production manager is pretty flimsy, even with the video you have, but I will need a copy of that." Brew nods. "But we'll see what we can do. You want my advice, though?"

We both shrug and I say, "Sure."

"Take that fifty grand you guys won and get away from that guy. Just from what you've said, he sounds like an asshole."

CHAPTER TWENTY-SIX

BREWSTER

As Gemma relays the story of her proposal, I can't help the smile of absolute glee that creases my face. "Well, Christ on a cracker, Gem. You're insane. But, God, how I love you."

She nods as we sit at the bar. The same bar at the same hotel we stayed at for the broadcasters' convention last month. "The first time in my life I decide to be completely crazy and I tell you to bid everything. You really did tell me to blow your dice," she says with an eye roll.

"I don't remember the few minutes leading up to that, but I remember, after leaving the restaurant, I was bummed because we'd had that conversation about marriage and stuff and I kept thinking, I hope whoever I end up with is someone like Brew. Maybe my mind and heart were finally like, 'hey dumbass, you realize you could have the real thing, right, not something *like* the real thing.'"

I can't help but laugh. "Kinda like me, comparing all those other women to you. Looks like two methods of reaching the same conclusion."

She sips her wine. "What do you think is going to happen?"

"What, with Curtis and stuff?" She nods and I shrug. "Who knows, Pearl? Honestly, I have no clue. I know I'd love to personally make sure he walks with a limp for the rest of his life, but legally, who can say?"

We'd given the detective both of our old phones and the information about the honeymoon, still unsure if it has any bearing on the now wide-open investigation. Detective Copeland admitted it would probably take a while to see anything come to fruition, if at all, but they had enough evidence to track down the Vin Diesel wannabe and bring him in for questioning, at least. Hopefully, he'll crack and give up Curtis.

She bites her lip. "You know, part of me always wondered if it was the alcohol or whatever that prompted us getting married and that always made me a little sad, because had I known how much I was going to love you, I would've pursued things with you way before then. It made me feel cowardly to think that it would take me being drunk to recognize what I truly wanted and to act on it."

"But you weren't drunk. Yeah, we were buzzed, but completely with all our faculties."

She looks down into her glass, her expression full of guilt. "I know that now. But I just hate that I woke up the morning after our wedding and assumed we'd made a terrible mistake. If we hadn't been drugged, we would've been so ecstatic when we woke up together. I just hate that we didn't get that."

I lift her chin. "Yeah, but we had Florida for that. Remember when we ate the steak and chocolate cake and we decided that's how we were going to spend our anniversaries?" She nods. "And we decided that our first time in Florida was our real first time, right, since we can both actually remember that?"

"Yeah. It was pretty great."

"It was fucking amazing, Gem." She lets out a laugh and presses a kiss to my lips. "Waking up with you every morning since that first morning hasn't stopped being my favorite part of my day. I wouldn't trade it for anything."

"Me neither, Brew. So, what do you want to do?"

"About what?"

Her expression grows stony. "Work. I refuse to work for him any longer. Not after everything he's done."

I hate what I'm about to say, but it must be said. "Gem, if we just up and quit, there's a better than good chance that Curtis will get suspicious. Plus, I need to see if I can get in touch with that guy from L.A.. We'll still need to have access to a studio, and I really don't want to move. If we're not anchored to a station, they may want to relocate us.

"At worst, it would only be until they arrest Curtis. I know the detective said things were flimsy, but I want to believe he only said that so that we wouldn't get our hopes up. They have the bald guy slipping drugs into our drink. I have the video of him extorting money from Curtis and pretty much admitting what he'd done at his request. There's no way Curtis gets away with any of this."

A muscle tics in her jaw. "So, what, we just pretend that everything is normal? We just let Curtis continue to tell us how to do our jobs and we talk to him like we don't know what a dangerous and conniving asshole he is?"

"I don't know, Pearl. I just know that if we up and leave the station, the only ones who lose right now are us. If we leave, we run the risk of having to wait until another station hires us before we can get syndicated. Not that I don't think that can happen, but I don't want to possibly have to move. I love where we live. Lawson and his family are there, your parents and Augusta are there. I know we'll have to move houses eventually, but for now, I like what we have."

She sighs and her shoulders slump. "I just don't know if I can keep my cool around him. He had us drugged, Brew. We could've had some kind of adverse reaction and died. Not to mention all the shit we had to do because he leaked that video of us. He sent it to my parents. And not that I'm not thankful we got to go to Florida; of course I am, I loved it. Still, everything should've been our choice, not foisted upon us. I've been so stressed and exhausted these past few weeks, my hair started falling out. I think I have an ulcer and I'm pretty sure I'm going to need dental work from how much I've been grinding my teeth. I don't know how much longer I can do it."

I'm about to say something reassuring, but as soon as I open my mouth, my phone rings. It's after ten PM, Vegas time, so I have no clue who'd be calling me at this hour and I don't recognize the number.

"Hello?"

"Mr. Lincoln. This is Detective Copeland. I'm very sorry to bother you at this late hour, but I wanted to see if you could come by the station tomorrow. I need you to look at a photo for me. We think we may have ID'd the guy who spiked your drinks."

I can't hide my surprise. "Wow. Okay, sure. We'll be happy to come by. What time would you like us, Detective? We have a flight scheduled for four tomorrow afternoon; is that going to be a problem?"

"No, sir. That's fine. If you can come by around noon, I just need to get your confirmation this is the guy you recognize from your party."

"We'll be there. Thank you for your swift work on this."

"We haven't really done anything yet, Mr. Lincoln; we're just getting started." He disconnects the call and I turn to Gemma.

"What did he say?"

"He said they think they know who drugged us."

Her eyes go wide. "Wow, that was fast."

I shrug. "Maybe he's a known criminal or something and he came up in a facial recognition search or something?"

The next day, Gemma and I find ourselves back in the same interrogation room waiting for Detective Copeland. He enters the room about five minutes after her knee starts bouncing from pent up nerves. I place my hand on her thigh to calm her. "Gem, you act like you're the criminal. Chill. After this, we'll get a drink before we go to the airport. And then when we get home, I promise I'll take off every—. "

I'm cut off by the sound of the door opening and I clamp my mouth shut lest the detective hear about the dirty things I'm planning to do to my wife once we get home. "Mr. and Mrs. Lincoln. Thank you so much for coming back. I know you're eager to return home, so I'll try to get you out of here as soon as possible."

"No problem, Detective. We were honestly shocked to hear from you so quickly."

He takes a seat across from us and I notice he has a manilla folder that he lays on the table. "So, how good a look do you think you got of the guy at your party, Brewster?"

I blow out a breath. "I mean, I never looked at him for longer than a few seconds, but I'm pretty good with faces."

He nods. "Okay. Well, I'm going to show you some pictures and you tell me if any of them are the man. Think you can do that?"

"Sure."

He opens the folder and lays out a line of six photos of bald white men. They're only headshots, so I have no details of height or build or anything, but I scan the photos a few times and keep coming back to the same one, sure it's the guy. I tap the photo. "This one."

Copeland's expression remains neutral. "Okay. That's all we need. You're free to go."

Gemma lets out a small noise of surprise. "That's it?"

"Yes, ma'am."

"Is that the guy?"

"Mrs. Lincoln, I can't tell you that. But if we need anything else from you, we will contact you. If you all want to follow me, I'll be happy to walk you out. I hope you all have a safe flight home, okay?"

I know I'm not the only one feeling as though the bottom has dropped out on us or as if cold water's been dumped on our heads. It's plain on Gemma's face as we climb into our rental car. "What the hell, Brew?"

I shrug, just as confused as she sounds. "I don't know, Pearl. Maybe I got it wrong."

"I don't think so. You're good at remembering faces. If you saw him straight on and that was the guy you picked out, it had to be him. I just wonder why he wouldn't have told us if you were right."

I sigh. "I don't know. Hopefully, we'll find out."

"So, what now?"

"Now, we go get a drink and then head to the airport so I take you home and make you forget about all this."

Gemma gives me a soft, amused smile. "That might take a while."

I take her hand in mine, lift it to my face, and press a kiss to the inside of her wrist. "I'm prepared for it to take all night."

"Well, in that case, I'm happy to let you try."

By the time we make it home, it's after midnight local time and Gemma is dead on her feet, so I put off my attempt to seduce her, as she can barely hold her eyes open. I get her tucked up in bed and when I get our stuff brought into the house, I'm beyond wiped. I strip down and climb into bed with her and curl my body around hers.

Even in her sleep, she rolls toward me, and I pull her closer. Despite the crazy shit going on right now in our lives, I'm still happier than I have any right to be. I have an amazingly beautiful wife who is my best friend. Apart from the drama that Curtis has caused us, I have a career that I love. I can't help but feel that in the last month, my life has changed so drastically, but also, *not*.

All I can think is, *I can't wait to see what happens next.*

CHAPTER TWENTY-SEVEN

GEMMA

Brew and I begrudgingly make it through the next week of work and we beg off Curtis's several invites to lunch. I've never been more happy to be done with a work week in my life.

This morning, I wake up with Brew's lips on the back of my neck, his beard tickling my skin as his mouth moves over my mostly bare shoulder. "That's nice," I say, reaching my hand back for his. I draw it around my waist and he guides it down my hip until he gets to the hem of my nightgown.

"Yeah, it really is." He nips under my ear and my breath catches. "I thought I might make you forget about the week we just had. How about that?"

"That's a tall order. Are you sure you're up for it?"

He grinds himself against my ass and heat blooms low in my belly, feeling him already hard. "You tell me, Pearl."

I huff a small laugh. "Well, it appears you're well-equipped at least."

He chuckles against the side of my neck. "I have all kinds of *equipment* for you, wife."

I reach back and wrap my hand around the back of his neck and into his hair. "Oh, I know all about your *equipment*."

Brew's fingers skim under the waistband of my panties. "Tell me, Gem, how do you want your distraction from this week?" His hand inches southward and his middle finger grazes my clit. I let out a soft huff and shift my hips to allow him better access. "Do you want it slow and easy, or do you want it rough and dirty?"

A soft chuckle escapes my mouth. "It sounds like you're asking if I want you to make love to me or fuck me."

His laugh vibrates against my back and his breath is hot against the skin of my ear, sending goosebumps down my arms. The pad of his middle finger continues to drag lazy circles on my clit and my pulse tics up. "I mean, that's probably the simplest form of what I'm asking. Do you have a preference? I wasn't sure, with the week we've had."

I reach back, dipping my hands into his boxers to grip his cock. "You said you wanted to make me forget, right?"

He blows out a breath as I drag my hand up and down his thick length. "That was the idea."

"Okay, then I don't think slow and easy is going to cut it."

"Thank fuck." He grips my face and covers my mouth with his and I don't even care about morning breath or the way my hair must look or anything remotely superficial. All I want in this moment is my husband.

He rolls me onto my back and tugs my nightgown up until I get the memo that he wants it off, and I sit up a bit for him to yank it over my head. "You know, of all the ways I get to see you, I think this might be my favorite, Gem." His fingers drag down between the valley of my bare breasts and his hand cups a full mound, his thumb grazing the nipple and it puckers and tightens under his touch. "You, just like this. Disheveled and barefaced and only for me."

I reach up and grip his face. "I'm always only for you, Brew."

He gives me a soft smile. "Honestly, you have no idea what the thought of that does to me, Gemma. Fuck, I love you so much and you're so damn beautiful. How did I ever do anything to deserve you? I'll never understand it."

I lift my head and press a kiss to his chest before running my hands down his waist to settle on his hips. "How do you need it, Brew? You're always so giving; do you need it soft and easy today?"

Brew shakes his head, a sweet smile playing across his lips. "No, Pearl, I was just waxing poetic. I'm happy to pound you until you scream."

I can't help the small laugh that escapes me. "Well, okay then. I'm happy to let you pound me until I scream."

His smile turns positively wicked as he tugs my panties down my hips and off my legs and drops them to the floor. I pull his face to mine and there's no mistaking the heat in our kiss. It's not sweet. It's not tender. It's only filled with need and hunger and the promise that I'm definitely going to feel like I've been fucked.

And I love that Brew knows me well enough to know what kind of sex I need. He knows when I need it loving and slow and he knows when I need his filthy mouth and the mark of him left on me for days. Today is definitely a day when I need the latter. Just the thought of all the places I might see his love bites later makes an aching heat build low in my belly.

Brew's mouth moves down my jaw and neck, the heat of his breath making goosebumps rise on my torso and arms. His tongue swirls over the hollow of my throat before moving south toward my sternum. I sink my fingers into his hair and lift my head to bury my nose in his long locks. Still that smell that's so *him*. I never knew I could absolutely crave a scent before until I got to smell him like this. That clean and earthy-woodsy smell that's almost like a fingerprint; unique only to him.

But I do crave it; almost like an addiction. He'll pass by me at work and I'll get a whiff of him and it's all I can do to not drag him into a supply closet for a mid-day quickie.

Even more than his smell, though, I crave his touch. Before we even became an *us*, I always loved his hugs, his reassuring squeezes, his playful nudges. But now that I've had his touch like *this*, even as his fingers skate down my waist and hips to tug me farther down the bed, I crave the feel of his skin on mine.

I've never wanted someone like I want him; which leads me to think that I've never loved anyone the way I love Brew. I mean, I already knew that, because he's *Brew*, but still, I love him so much it nearly hurts.

His mouth continues its journey lower and lower on my stomach and he nips at the soft flesh above my hip until I squeal. He chuckles against my side and his hand slides up my inner thigh. "I'll never get used to this," he says as he presses a kiss into my pubic bone. "Feeling you and tasting you and fuck, even seeing you, Gem." He lifts my leg and hooks my knee over his shoulder.

His fingers part my folds and he slowly licks up my pussy to my clit. I let out a sharp exhale and tighten my grip on his hair. He rises mere centimeters from my pussy and his breath ghosts across my sensitive flesh. "I love how you grab my hair when I eat you, Pearl. Like you want to use me. It's so fucking sexy."

His lips close over my clit and I rock my hips, needing more friction. He brings his thumb in to replace his mouth and his tongue dips lower to my entrance. My head falls back on the pillows as my breathing grows more and more shallow.

Brew continues to work me over, brushing kisses over my inner thigh before sinking his teeth in, hard enough to make me hiss and pop my head up. He quirks a brow at me, even as he kisses the bite. "Sorry, Gem; couldn't resist. You know how I like to leave my mark."

He brings his mouth back to my pussy and flicks his tongue over my clit before sucking hard, and I gasp. His fingers thrust and crook as he slides them in and out and my toes curl as he hits my g-spot. "Fuck, Brew. Don't stop." And he doesn't, not until my body nearly quakes with a powerful orgasm and I let out a deep moan.

I blink rapidly, trying to dislodge the haze from my brain as Brew rises on his knees to shed his boxers. I watch as he drags a hand down his beard and I can't help the pleasure it gives me to know that his face is covered by *me*.

He tugs my hips lower on the bed and settles between my thighs. "I think you requested a hard fuck; is that right, Pearl?" I nod and pull his face to mine, tasting myself on his kiss and as he slams into me, I let out a low moan. He drags his mouth to my ear as he slowly pulls out almost to the tip. "I love that sound you make when I first slide into you, Gem." His hips punch forward and I grip my fingers into his hair. "It's like I'm coming home."

He keeps a deep and deliberate pace that has my heart crashing against my ribs, his thrusts brutal but measured and my body begins to nearly hum with pleasure. "You are my home, Gemma. Fuck, I love you."

I feel the sweat that has popped on his forehead when he trails his mouth down my neck and chest and I lift my head to brush a kiss across his brow.

His lips close over my nipple and his tongue flicks over the hardened peak and I gasp and arch my back. I rock my hips and the change in angle is just what I need to trigger my release. A hoarse cry falls from my lips as I dig my nails into Brew's scalp as I let go.

"But that sound when you come, it's fucking music, Pearl.

Jesus. Fuck." His hips buck a few final times and a guttural grunt works its way up his throat as his head falls to my chest. He braces on his arms to keep his full weight from crushing me and nudges my chin with his nose until I tilt my head back. He brushes a soft kiss across my lips and shifts his body until he's lying beside me.

I roll to face him and brush his hair off his forehead, tucking it behind his ear. "Music?" I ask with an amused smile, my breathing still labored.

Brew lets out a soft laugh. "Totally music."

I grip his face and press a kiss to his lips as he pulls me toward him.

While I'm making a late breakfast of waffles and bacon, there's a knock at the front door. I glance out the window to see a black sedan in the driveway, but don't recognize the vehicle, so I turn off the stove and unplug the waffle iron before wiping my hands on a kitchen towel and walking to answer the door.

When I open it, there's an Asian man in his late fifties in a suit with very short, gray hair and a white woman in her early thirties, also in a suit with short, blond hair in a severe bob. Their body language screams *official business*. I don't open the screen door. "Can I help you?"

The man gives me a small nod. "Yes, ma'am, are you Gemma Lincoln?"

I frown in confusion. "Yes, what can I do for you?"

"And your husband is Brewster Lincoln?"

I'm getting a nagging sense of dread with these two people standing on my porch. "Yes."

The man pulls out a small leather wallet and flips it open. My eyes immediately focus on the FBI symbol and my heart lurches. "Ma'am, I'm Agent Franks with the FBI." He gestures to his partner. "And this is Agent Brennan. We wondered if you might have a few minutes to speak with us? We apologize if we've caught you at a bad time, but it's imperative that we speak with you and your husband."

It takes me nearly a full minute to form words. "Can I ask what this is regarding?"

Agent Franks looks around. "If we can come in, we'd be happy to explain. We promise not to take up too much of your time."

Unsure what else to do, I open the screen door and gesture for them to enter. They both wipe their shoes on the entry rug and look around the kitchen and living room. I motion toward the living room. "You can have a seat if you'd like."

They nod and step toward the sofa. Agent Brennan looks at me as she sits. "Is your husband at home today as well?"

"Yes, ma'am. He's in the shower. I'll go get him. Can I get y'all coffee or water to drink?"

They both decline and I rush toward the bedroom to our ensuite bathroom. I open the door and Brew is just stepping out of the shower. When he sees my face, his brows draw together in concern. "What's wrong, Gem?"

I open my mouth to speak and for some reason, no words come out. Brew closes the distance between us, not even bothering to dry off, and takes my face in his hands. "What is it? What's happened, Pearl? You look freaked out."

"There are two FBI agents here. They want to talk to us."

He blinks rapidly in shock. "What?"

I nod. "Yeah. They're sitting on our couch. They wouldn't tell me what they're here for, they just want to talk to us. Do you think it has anything to do with Curtis?"

Now Brew is the one who looks as though he's struggling

for words. "Shit. Who knows? Alright. I'll be out in five minutes, okay?"

He gives me a quick kiss and I nod, leaving him to finish drying off. I try to take some calming breaths, since I know full well Brew and I have nothing to be nervous about, but there's just something so ominous about a visit from the FBI.

I half expect the agents to be up looking at our photos or examining the books on our shelves, but they're still where I left them on the sofa. I take a seat on the loveseat perpendicular to the couch and wish I was wearing more than my faded cotton jogging shorts and one of Brew's old college T-shirts. My hair is still wet from my earlier shower and up in a messy bun. "Brewster will be out in just a moment. You're sure I can't get you anything to drink?"

They both smile and Agent Brennan says, "No, thank you, ma'am. You have a lovely home. Have you lived here long?"

"Brewster's lived here about five years, but I moved in after we got married last month." I feel my palms starting to sweat and I rub them on my thighs. She nods.

A moment later, I nearly breathe a sigh of relief when Brew's footsteps echo down the hall. He comes into the room wearing a pair of jeans and a station T-shirt, his wet hair down and loose. He walks over to the agents and they both stand and shake his hand. After introductions are made, he comes to sit next to me and takes my hand in his, giving it a reassuring squeeze.

"So, agents, what can we do for you today?" Brew asks, looking between Franks and Brennan.

Agent Franks takes out a notepad. "You visited Las Vegas last month, is that right?"

We both nod, but it's Brew that supplies, "Yes, sir. Gemma and I attended a broadcasters' convention. We've gone for the past five years."

Franks jots a note in his pad. "And you got married, is that correct?"

"Yes, sir. Although, if you know that, you probably also know we don't remember most of that night."

Brennan leans forward and props her elbows on her knees. "Yes, we have the report from Detective Copeland, as well as the video footage from the casino. You suspect you were drugged, correct?"

"Honestly, it's more than suspicion. An associate of our production manager's all but admitted to that. I'm assuming this has something to do with him?"

"Your production manager is Curtis Levitt, correct?"

"Yes."

She pulls out her phone and taps the screen before swiping a few times. She turns the screen until Brew and I can see the image. "And you believe that this is the man who was with your production manager the night of the wedding reception that your production manager orchestrated, correct?"

Sure enough, it's the guy that Brew picked out of the lineup in Vegas. My husband nods. "Yes, that's him. Can I ask, do you know who he is?"

Franks nods. "Yes, sir. We need to ask both of you, have you noticed any changes in your production manager over the last few years? Change in attitude, behavior, spending habits, anything like that?"

I nearly snort. "He's pretty much been the same slimeball he's been the whole time we've worked for him. We've been trying to get away from him for years."

He nods. "Okay, so as far as you know, he's maintained the same lifestyle for several years?"

We both nod and Brew pipes up, "Can y'all just tell us why you're really here? Whatever help you need to take Curtis or his henchman down, we'll be happy to help. Gemma and I have had a pretty shitty last few weeks thanks to Curtis, not to mention all the stuff we've put up with working for him for ten years, so just lay it out for us, please."

Brennan and Franks seem to have some sort of unspoken conversation through eye contact and Brennan says, "The man you identified as the one you saw with your production manager is Alexi Galkin. He's an enforcer for the Popov crime family."

Brew lets out a surprised bark of laughter. "*Crime family?* As in, mob?"

Franks nods. "Yes, sir. It would seem that your production manager is in debt to them. A lot of debt. Our theory is that he got in over his head and thought with your popularity, he'd be able to cash in. Which, it appears he has, quite a bit, but we assume he thought if he had you all drugged, you'd do more crazy things than just get married and he'd be able to leverage whatever publicity you received from your shenanigans against syndication offers."

I say, "So, let me see if I have this straight. Curtis is in debt to the mob and he thought we could get him enough quick cash by drugging us and hoping that we'd make fools of ourselves. Then, whatever viral footage he got from that, he could use to get syndication deals for *us*, so that he'd make higher commissions? You realize how absurd this all sounds, right?"

Brennan nods and gives me a sympathetic smile. "Yes, ma'am. Although, in our experience, desperate men will do really stupid things to get themselves out of a bind. We've subpoenaed the financial records of the radio station, as well as Curtis Levitt's personal financials. We also have the cloned phones you provided to the Vegas PD.

"It would appear that the honeymoon you guys went on in Florida was paid for by him, routed through a shell company setup to look like a travel agency. It also appears that while

Curtis was negotiating the sponsorships for your wedding party, he was skimming off some of the advertising money for himself; we're assuming to pay his debt to Popov."

Brew nods. "And not that it probably matters, but do you know how many emails we may have missed from our phones being cloned? Or do you even have a way to know that? Also, I have to ask, are we looking at any kind of trouble for accepting things, like the honeymoon or our wedding jewelry or anything relating to the party?"

I hadn't thought about anything like that, and panic immediately swells in my chest.

Franks sees the stricken expression on my face and shakes his head. "No. We know you all had no part in any of this. Most of the things having to do with the items sponsored for your party are completely legitimate. Curtis just took some money off the top of the advertising dollars the sponsors paid to the station, as far as we know. And we can try to find out if any missing emails can be retrieved. The main reason we came by today is to let you know that we have Alexi Galkin in federal custody. But you may be called to testify about what you saw the night of the party, as well as anything you remember from the night at the casino."

Relieved, I can't help but ask, "And what about Curtis?"

"He's also going to be taken into custody. We're hoping that Galkin will want to cut a deal and turn on Levitt to save his own ass."

I nod. "Can we be there when he's picked up and can you do it at the station? Please, I beg you."

Brew snorts a laugh and tries to cover it with a cough. The agents' jaws tic and it's clear they're trying not to smile. "We'll see what we can do. But would you both be willing to testify?"

We both nod. "Of course. Anything we can do to help."

The agents stand and Brew and I get to our feet as well.

"Well, we won't take up any more of your time today. We appreciate you both speaking with us. We'll let you get back to your Saturday. Congratulations on your wedding."

As they're leaving, they both shake our hands and Franks goes out the door. Just before she heads out, Brennan turns to us. "I just have to say, I love your show. I listen to it all the time and I've thought for years that y'all would make a cute couple; you just have such great chemistry. I'm so happy for you two."

"Thank you, Agent. And thank you for everything y'all are doing to take down Curtis and his associate," I say with a smile. Once she leaves, I shut the door and lean against it, letting out a long, slow breath.

Brew shakes his head and rakes his fingers through his damp hair. "Well, I'll be damned, Gem. The fucking *mob?* Are you kidding me? Curtis is such a dumbass."

CHAPTER TWENTY-EIGHT

BREWSTER

The following Friday, Gemma and I are sitting in the conference room for a monthly staff meeting and we're leaning against a far wall next to a side door. Gemma is examining her nails as Curtis drones on about the projections for the next quarter and I glance over my shoulder through a crack in the blinds. I see a familiar black sedan and I nudge Gemma when a certain couple of three-letter agency officials climb from their car. I lean over to her. "Looks like Christmas came early, Pearl."

She follows my gaze, and her eyes widen.

"Brewster, Gemma, I understand that y'all only have eyes for one another now and we're all thrilled for you, but if you can keep the goo-goo eyes to yourselves until you get home, that'd be great," Curtis says with a near snarl.

Gemma just squares her shoulders and folds her arms, levelling Curtis with a death glare. He returns to his presentation. "As I was saying, we're on track to exceed our —."

"Curtis Levitt?" Agent Brennan steps into the room and she has on a dark windbreaker with "FBI" on the chest and I'm sure across the back. Her badge hangs from a chain around her neck and she has her hand on her holstered weapon.

Curtis's fight-or-flight instincts must choose today to exercise flight, because he doesn't even respond, just takes off in a run. Most of the other staff members are too shocked to even react, and he gets by all of them. He makes for the side door near where Gemma and I are standing and she gets in front of him, draws back her fist, and nails him right in the nose.

My mouth falls open as he drops to the floor with a groan. He covers his face with his hands. "What the hell, Gemma?"

Gemma scoffs and pulls her foot back to kick him, and Agent Brennan steps up. "I'll take it from here, Gemma. Thanks for the assist," she says with a wink.

I pull my wife out of the way as Brennan escorts Curtis out the door he was just trying to escape through. We hear her reading him his rights and I open the blinds to let the rest of the staff see them stuff him into the back of a car.

Gemma shakes out her hand and flexes it. I take it in my own and bring it my lips. "Hurts like a bitch, doesn't it?"

"You were right; totally overrated. But also, totally worth it in this case," she replies with a laugh and wraps her arms around my waist.

Rosie comes up to us as everyone chatters amongst themselves. "Why didn't y'all look surprised to see Curtis get picked up?"

We both just shrug. "With Curtis, nothing much surprises us anymore."

I notice Agent Franks on the other side of the conference room and he's directing other agents to possibly gather statements. Once he makes eye contact with me, he makes his way over to us. "Public enough for you, Mrs. Lincoln?" he asks Gemma with a smile.

She returns his grin. "Oh, yeah. Thank you for that."

He nods and turns to me as he pulls something out of his pocket. "So, I had our techs comb through your emails to see if there were any missing. Turns out there were several. I had them put them on this drive for you all. Hope this helps." He extends the drive to me and I take it from him.

"Thank you so much, Agent Franks. Honestly, we weren't sure when this would all go down, so we appreciate your speed."

"Our pleasure. I'm sure we'll see y'all again as the trial gets closer, but if you have questions, don't hesitate to call the field office, alright?"

"Will do. Thanks."

He heads out the same side door and Rosie steps up to us again, hands on hips. "Y'all totally knew. Oh, my gosh. Wow, that was like something out of a TV show. You're supposed to be on air in fifteen minutes. Do you want me to just play a 'Best Of' show? I would get it if you didn't feel like working today with all the drama."

Gemma and I both laugh and she pats Rosie on the arm. "We'll be fine. We promise. You know Brew and I thrive on crazy shit. I'm oddly energized."

I press a kiss to the side of her head. "Pearl, I think that might have more to do with you getting to punch Curtis in the face."

She considers. "Probably, but we're still going to work."

Our assistant producer nods. "Alright. Sounds good to me. Topic lists the same?"

Gemma and I exchange glances. "For today, but starting Monday, we come up with our own topics."

"Okay. I'll get the ads queued up. Twelve minutes."

My wife looks up at me. "Why do I feel lighter for some reason?"

I give her a smile. "Probably because we're free from Curtis."

She nods. "Fucking finally."

After we wrap up the show, Gemma and I settle back into the conference room to access the flash drive and see how many emails we've missed since we were in Vegas. As I click on the folder, I say a silent prayer that there are additional syndication offers aside from the ones Curtis showed us.

I scan through the list and sure enough, there's an email from the station manager out of Dallas, as well as ones from L.A. and New York. I point them out to Gemma and her eyes go wide. "What do you think, Pearl?"

She lets out a bark of surprised laughter. "Duh, call them. It's still plenty early in L.A. and Dallas."

I nod and blow out a breath as I dial the station manager in L.A..

"Reynolds."

"Yes, Mr. Reynolds, this is Brewster Lincoln from WXOR out of Knoxville. I'm sorry to bother you on a Friday afternoon, but I was hoping you'd have just a few minutes to talk."

"Brewster, hey. I was wondering when I'd hear from you. Sure, I've got a few minutes."

"Great. Thank you so much. I also have Gemma on the phone as well."

"Your new wife, is that right?"

I huff a laugh. "So, you've heard about that?"

"Oh, yeah. Crazy party you guys had, too. I figured that was the reason I hadn't heard from you guys before now."

"Well, that wasn't the only reason, but I'm glad we could finally connect. We wanted to continue the discussion we started in Vegas. I know when we spoke then, your station was interested in possibly brokering a deal for ten hours' worth of content weekly?"

"That was the original plan, yes. But I don't think that's going to work for us anymore."

Gemma and I share a nervous glance. "Oh?" I don't supply a new figure in the hopes that he will.

"Yeah, I've been speaking with my boss and we want access to your entire show every week."

Gemma's mouth falls open and I attempt to remain calm. "I see. All twenty hours?"

"Yeah, that's right. Although, I must say, the shows you've been producing for the last few weeks have been a bit tedious. I understand you guys were trying to capitalize on your wedding and everything, but it was starting to seem like you were trying to beat a dead horse."

Gemma and I both laugh. She pipes up, "Believe us, we know. You can trust that our content going forward will be much more fresh and much closer to our own personalities."

"I'm glad to hear that. Listen, I'm getting ready to head into a meeting. I'll have my assistant send over a contract for you to have your production manager and lawyers examine. I think you'll find the fees to your liking."

"Thank you, Mr. Reynolds. We'll look those over. Have a great weekend." I disconnect the call and grab Gemma's face for a deep kiss.

When we break apart, she has a surprised smile on her face. "Well, that was nice."

"We did it, Gem."

She nods. "Yeah, hopefully, we did. And, hey, even if we didn't, we're still free from Curtis. I just hope whoever they hire as the new production manager will be better."

"I think I can assure you of that." Gemma and I both snap our heads in the direction of the voice.

I'm shocked to see Herman Easter, the owner and CEO of Easter Media, a large company that owns our radio station, as well as several others in this market. I can only count on one hand the number of times I've ever seen him, but I've never actually met him before. Gem and I both jump to our feet. "Mr. Easter," Gemma says with a smile. "We didn't realize you'd be making a trip to the station today."

He nods and closes the distance between us and extends his hand to Gemma and then me. "I've been meaning to come by and congratulate you two for a couple weeks now. I'm sorry I missed your wedding reception. One of my own children was actually getting married that weekend as well."

I wave off his apology. "Of course, we completely understand."

"I won't keep you all, I'm sure you'd like to start your weekend, but I wanted to let you know that I'm very sorry for everything Curtis put you all through. I've been in contact with the FBI and the Las Vegas police and have promised them they'll have E.M.'s full support in whatever way they require. And I wanted to personally assure you two as well that you're both very important to this company. We hope that just because of what Curtis did, you won't be leaving us or anything like that."

Gemma shakes her head. "No, sir. We love it here. Curtis was the only issue we've ever had. We wouldn't be above a bit more creative control, if we're honest, but no, we love working for Easter."

As much as Gemma says that I stand up for us and our show, watching my wife tell the head of the entire company what we want is downright sexy.

Mr. Easter nods. "We can definitely do that. I'm not above

letting you both have full creative control over your content. You guys know what you're doing. And Gemma, I know you won't let Brewster get too crazy, just like I know Brewster won't let you be too safe. I'll be conducting interviews for a new production manager for your show, but I wanted to see if you all would sit in on the interviews as well, so I can get a feel for your take on them."

I nod. "Yes, sir, we'd be happy to do that."

"Perfect. Alright. Well, I'll let you get back to it. I'm sure you've got time to call Dallas if you hurry," he says with a wink.

We shake his hand again just before he turns to leave. Gemma shakes her head. "Could this day really get any better?"

I nod. "Oh, yeah. After we call Dallas, we go pick up some Big Ed's pizza. Then I take you home to watch some *Hell's Kitchen* to get you all randy and let you take me to bed."

She offers me an amused smile. "Now how can I say no to that?"

"I don't think you can, wife. Pretty sure that ring on your finger says that obligatory pizza, reality TV, and dirty sex are part of the package."

She laughs. "Well then, better make that phone call."

EPILOGUE
GEMMA — EIGHTEEN MONTHS LATER

"Disgraced former WXOR production manager of the popular radio talk show *Lincoln and Hopkins* was sentenced yesterday in the trial linking him to organized crime. Some of you may recall that just over eighteen months ago, he was charged with having two of his radio personalities, Brewster Lincoln and Gemma Hopkins, drugged while they were on a business trip in Las Vegas, as well as embezzling money from Easter Media's talk radio station, WXOR. He was sentenced to ten years in prison with the possibility of parole after seven years."

The television cuts off and I see my husband standing on the other side of the living room with the remote in his hand.

"Brew, what are you doing?" I ask in a whisper.

He comes over to give me a kiss on the side of my head while I nurse our six-week-old son, Collier, at six AM. "Just trying to be a supportive husband. Weren't you just up a couple of hours ago? I thought he'd started sleeping through the night?"

I nod and let out a yawn. "Yeah, but he must be going through a growth spurt. But, for real, go back to bed. You have to work later and it won't do for you to be a zombie on the show. I won't have it fall to shit just because I had a baby."

He dismisses my protest with a chuckle. "I'm not going to let you be dead tired if I'm not willing to be, too. All these years we've supported each other, Pearl, I'm not about to stop now. And besides, he won't be this little for long. I don't want to miss any of it."

"You're such a romantic, husband."

He squats down to brush a dark hair from Collier's forehead. "I think I just really love my family, wife."

I give him a sweet smile. "Your family really loves you, too. Did you see all that report?"

He nods. "Yeah, I caught it last night on the way home. You were already passed out, or I would've told you. I'm just glad all that's behind us."

"Me, too. Hey, I meant to tell you, I caught the show yesterday. Normally, I'm passed out during that time while Collier naps, but tell Rosie she's doing a great job."

He grins. "She's not you by a long shot, but she holds her own. And Tallie's doing a great job filling in for Rosie, so you made a good call there. Not gonna lie though, I'll be glad when it's you back across that table from me."

I roll my eyes. "You'll survive six more weeks. Although, I think if Mom had her way, I would've gone back to work on day two or something. She can't wait to start babysitting." I notice the baby has nursed himself back to sleep so I shift him so I can get off the couch.

"Here, I'll take him." Brew holds out his hands and I place our son into his arms and pull my nightgown up and stand. I move the hair off his shoulders so it doesn't get in Collier's face.

"Pretty soon, he's gonna be grabbing for all this glorious hair, you know."

"Just like his mama," Brew says with a slow smile.

"You're not wrong." I stretch and walk over to the kitchen to put on a pot of coffee and he follows me, gently bouncing the baby to avoid him waking. He leans against the counter as I fill up the carafe and pour the water into the reservoir.

"Jen wants to know if we're planning on going to Vegas for the conference next year. I know it's still six months off, but she's trying to figure out the budget for next quarter, so she wanted to see if she needed to account for that."

I consider as I scoop grounds. "We probably need to, since we didn't go this year, right? Since I was so sick?"

"I didn't know if you'd want to leave the baby. I mean, I know it's just for a weekend, but still."

"Maybe we should. It's our anniversary. And I didn't get my steak, wine, and chocolate cake this year, so I'm expecting it big time next year."

Brew chuckles. "Sure, we can do that. Hopefully, what happens in Vegas this time will stay there."

I nod. "Although, the fact that it didn't stay in Vegas the last time turned out pretty great. You know, except for the drugging and the memory loss part."

He leans over and gives me a kiss. "Very true. But it was still a pretty great weekend. The week after that was pretty good, too. Maybe if we win big money again, we could visit that resort again. Might be kinda nice to get you naked in a cabana for old time's sake."

I nod. "Yeah, that was something alright. I'm glad I decided to be crazy for once in my life. Best gamble I ever took; wouldn't trade it for anything." I grip his jaw and rub my thumb over his cheek. "You look fantastic holding a baby, you know."

"I really enjoy *making* babies with you."

I roll my eyes. "You also like *not* making babies with me. Which is all you're going to be doing for a very long time."

"I'd very much enjoy *not* making a baby with you very soon."

"Keep it in your pants. Although, yes. I go back to the doctor next week, so after that, I'm all yours again."

His expression grows serious. "No rush, Pearl, you know that."

I sigh. "Yeah, I know. But a girl has needs. I'm very much looking forward to having a date night and us spending some much needed time together. I've already talked to Mom. In a couple of weeks, she's going to take the baby overnight and I'm going to wine and dine my husband."

Brew looks impressed. "Wine and dine? Well, don't I feel special?"

I chuckle. "Okay, well, Big Ed's, beer, and a football game, then probably an early bedtime, but it'll still be nice since we won't have to get up with the baby."

He pulls me to his side and presses a kiss to the top of my head. "Big Ed's and beer? Even better. Count me in."

ACKNOWLEDGMENTS

For all the words I've ever written, you will never see me struggle more than when I have to articulate my own emotions. Honesty, "thank you" never seems like an adequate enough phrase to express gratitude. But sadly, it's about all we have.

I don't know that I could ever begin anything like this without first thanking my amazing husband, Derek, for being the reason I know what epic love feels like. You'll never know how much your daily encouragement means to me. Thank you for loving the mess that is me.

To my sons, who proudly tell their friends and teachers that their mom is a writer. I love you more than life itself, but please don't ever read my books!

Megs (Megan Holt), you are not only one of the greatest friends I've ever had, but you're also an amazing editor. Your notes and critique made Gemma and Brewster shine even more. You are an incredible human and I love you big. I owe you ALL the Blade and Bow.

For my amazing ARC readers, whose feedback keeps me going. You are the unsung heroes of the book community and without your tireless work, I wouldn't be where I am today.

ALSO BY RACHAEL OGLE

Until Duet

Until August and onto Forever (Until Books 1 & 2)

Summer Lovin' Series

Fake it to Forever (Summer Lovin' Books 1 & 2)

Knox County Series

My Ada Mae (Knox County Book 1)

Not Your Girl (Knox County Book 2)

Change My Life (Knox County Book 3)

Crash Into Me (Knox County Book 4)

ABOUT THE AUTHOR

For as long as she can remember, Rachael has been a voracious reader. At the age of eleven, she discovered her grandmother's stash of clench-cover romance novels and she was forever changed. A lover of many, many fictional men and one very non-fictional one, she strives to write real and emotional characters who always get their happily ever after. Rachael lives in East Tennessee with her husband and two sons on their family farm. When she's not tackling her endless TBR, she can be found drinking all the coffee in existence.